Amy Cross is the author of more than 300 horror, paranormal, fantasy and thriller novels.

OTHER TITLES
BY AMY CROSS INCLUDE

1689
American Coven
Angel
Anna's Sister
Annie's Room
Asylum
B&B
Bad News
The Curse of the Langfords
Daisy
The Devil, the Witch and the Whore
Devil's Briar
Eli's Town
Escape From Hotel Necro
The Farm
Grave Girl
The Haunting of Blackwych Grange
The Haunting of Nelson Street
The House Where She Died
I Married a Serial Killer
Little Miss Dead
Mary
One Star
Perfect Little Monsters & Other Stories
Stephen
The Soul Auction
Trill
Ward Z
Wax
You Should Have Seen Her

THE ANCHORESS

AMY CROSS

This edition
first published by Blackwych Books Ltd
United Kingdom, 2025

Copyright © 2025 Blackwych Books Ltd

All rights reserved. This book is a work of fiction.
Names, characters, places, incidents and businesses are
the product of the author's imagination or are
used fictitiously. Any resemblance to actual persons,
living or dead, or to actual events or locations,
is entirely coincidental.

Also available in e-book format.

www.amycross.com
www.blackwychbooks.com

CONTENTS

PROLOGUE
page 15

CHAPTER ONE
page 25

CHAPTER TWO
page 37

CHAPTER THREE
page 47

CHAPTER FOUR
page 57

CHAPTER FIVE
page 65

CHAPTER SIX
page 75

CHAPTER SEVEN
page 83

CHAPTER EIGHT
page 91

CHAPTER NINE
page 101

CHAPTER TEN
page 109

CHAPTER ELEVEN
page 119

CHAPTER TWELVE
page 129

CHAPTER THIRTEEN
page 139

CHAPTER FOURTEEN
page 149

CHAPTER FIFTEEN
page 159

CHAPTER SIXTEEN
page 167

CHAPTER SEVENTEEN
page 177

CHAPTER EIGHTEEN
page 185

CHAPTER NINETEEN
page 195

CHAPTER TWENTY
page 203

CHAPTER TWENTY-ONE
page 213

CHAPTER TWENTY-TWO
page 221

CHAPTER TWENTY-THREE
page 231

CHAPTER TWENTY-FOUR
page 241

CHAPTER TWENTY-FIVE
page 249

CHAPTER TWENTY-SIX
page 259

CHAPTER TWENTY-SEVEN
page 269

CHAPTER TWENTY-EIGHT
page 279

CHAPTER TWENTY-NINE
page 287

CHAPTER THIRTY
page 295

CHAPTER THIRTY-ONE
page 303

CHAPTER THIRTY-TWO
page 311

CHAPTER THIRTY-THREE
page 321

CHAPTER THIRTY-FOUR
page 329

CHAPTER THIRTY-FIVE
page 339

CHAPTER THIRTY-SIX
page 349

CHAPTER THIRTY-SEVEN
page 357

CHAPTER THIRTY-EIGHT
page 365

CHAPTER THIRTY-NINE
page 373

CHAPTER FORTY
page 381

CHAPTER FORTY-ONE
page 389

CHAPTER FORTY-TWO
page 403

CHAPTER FORTY-THREE
page 415

CHAPTER FORTY-FOUR
page 423

CHAPTER FORTY-FIVE
page 431

CHAPTER FORTY-SIX
page 441

CHAPTER FORTY-SEVEN
page 451

CHAPTER FORTY-EIGHT
page 463

EPILOGUE
page 473

THE ANCHORESS

PROLOGUE

"WAIT FOR ME! TILLY, stop! Wait!"

Struggling to climb over the low stone wall, Barbara Dewhurst realised after a moment that her dress had snagged on something. She stopped and looked down; sure enough the fabric was caught on a sharp piece of stone, and she felt a shock of fear as she saw that a small rip had already begun to stretch down to the hem.

"No!" she gasped, carefully unhooking the damaged piece of fabric before rolling over the top of the wall and dropping down onto the other side. "Mam'll kill me!"

For a moment the rip in her dress was more

important than anything else in the whole world. She pulled it up and examined the damage more closely, and she instantly knew there was no way she was going to be able to hide it forever. She might be able to delay the moment when her mother noticed, however, but she was already wondering how she was going to explain precisely what had happened. Her mother tended to get very angry whenever clothes were damaged, and Barbara knew that her father would likely be called through to punish her with his slipper.

"I'm gonna be in so much trouble," she stammered, on the verge of panic now. "Tilly, me mam's gonna be furious!"

Tears were gathering in her eyes. She wanted to think of some excuse, to blame somebody else, but deep down she knew she couldn't lie. Not to her own mother.

Turning, she looked across the field and saw that Tilly was far away now, almost at the church itself.

"Hey, wait for me!" she yelled, hurrying after her friend again. "Tilly, what are you doing? Don't get too close! You promised we wouldn't get too close!"

***

By the time she reached the gravestones, Barbara began to slow her pace. Tilly had disappeared from sight a few minutes earlier, slipping around the side of the church; Barbara, meanwhile, was much more hesitant and finally stopped between two stones as she saw the church's ominously dark wooden door ahead.

She was already much closer than she'd intended to get.

A moment later she looked up at the spire. Something about St. Jude's just seemed so imposing, and she felt almost as if the air itself was trying to hold her back. Tilly had promised – really *promised*, on her nana's life – that they were only going to take a look at the place, yet now she'd bounded on ahead and Barbara was kicking herself for having been tricked. She wanted to turn around and run home, but she knew that would only mean facing her mother even sooner and having to explain the damage to her dress.

She was – she understood in that moment – already in so much trouble.

"Barbara!" Tilly shouted suddenly from somewhere around the other side of the church.

"Hurry!"

"I don't want to!" Barbara yelled back at her. "You said we wouldn't come this close!"

"I said we wouldn't go inside!"

"No," Barbara called out, "that's not true. You said we wouldn't come as close as the graveyard and you know it!"

She waited for a reply, but she could already tell that the situation was spiralling out of control. Tilly was always the more daring of the two, always the one who wanted to have an adventure, while Barbara had a tendency to try to hang back. Eventually, however, it was *always* Tilly who got her way, while Barbara *always* ended up tagging along and invariably getting into far more trouble. Tilly's parents were very relaxed, they hardly ever shouted, whereas Barbara was always getting told off for the tiniest of infractions.

Already she could tell that the pattern was repeating, but she told herself that perhaps nothing actually bad would happen this time. After all, how could her parents get angry about something they didn't know?

Supposing that she had no choice, she set off between the gravestones while taking care to avoid getting too close to the church itself. She felt as if the air was already becoming colder, and she couldn't help glancing at the gloomy stained glass windows and wondering what it was like inside the old, abandoned church; she thought of the rows of empty pews and the untouched altar, and she felt a shiver run through her body as she realised that some of the stories might even be true. After all, everyone in the village knew that nobody was supposed to go anywhere near St. Jude's. In fact, some people even went out of their way to avoid seeing the place.

Even the nearest road tended to be less travelled.

Reaching the corner, she looked along the side of the church. At first she couldn't see Tilly but after a few seconds she realised that she could perhaps *hear* her. Something was scrabbling against stone, and after several more seconds a brief gasp rang out.

"Tilly?" she called out. "What -"

"Up here!"

Sighing, Barbara made her way through the long grass while taking care to avoid stinging nettles. She passed several small tombs surrounded by metal railings, and then as she looked up she saw to her horror that Tilly had climbed onto a shed-like building and was tentatively inching toward one of the church's windows.

"What are you doing?" she called up to her.

"Having fun," Tilly replied smugly. "Have you ever heard of that?"

"Come down!"

"Why?"

"Because you're not supposed to be up there!" Barbara hissed, inadvertently stamping her foot in a fit of sheer frustration. "No-one is! No-one's supposed to be here at all!"

"Exactly," Tilly continued, reaching up and touching the bottom of the window as if she meant to haul herself up even higher. "Think about it. If no-one comes here, then there's no-one around to see that *we* came here. It's perfect."

"I want to go home."

"Then go home."

"I can't leave you here."

"Yes, you can," Tilly replied. "You can run home and tell on me, if you really like. You can tell your mammy and daddy what we did, and you probably won't even get into too much trouble if they think you've confessed everything. Then someone will come out here and tell *me* off, and I'll probably be the most hated person in the whole village and probably other villages nearby as well. They might even put me in the old stocks on the village green. And you'll be little Miss Perfect because you'll have tattled on me."

"I'm not doing that," Barbara said wearily. "I just don't like it here, that's all."

"Why not?"

"I don't know."

"You must know," Tilly continued, edging further along the roof of the shed before turning to grin down at her. "Is it because of the stories?"

"I don't know about any stories," Barbara lied, but her eyes – momentarily unable to even look at her friend – betrayed the truth.

"*Everyone* knows about the stories," Tilly told her with a grin. "Do you believe them? Do you think there's really a ghost here?"

"I don't know."

"Because I do," Tilly continued, clearly enjoying the ability to wind her friend up. "Joseph Digby's sister knows someone who saw it, and Joseph Digby can't lie. Well, he can, but he doesn't. Everyone knows that."

"That's not true," Barbara replied sulkily. "You're making things up again."

"I'm not," Tilly said, turning and craning her

neck as she tried again to look through a gap at the very bottom of the window. Finding that she was a little too short, she began to stand on tiptoes. "Joseph Digby's sister's friend came out here all by herself one time and she found a way to get inside."

"You can't get inside without a key," Barbara told her.

"Use your imagination," Tilly replied, straining even more to see into the church. "I don't know how she did it, but she got in and she looked all around. She said it was really creepy inside and that she immediately knew she wasn't alone."

"You're lying."

"I'm not, and neither was Joseph Digby's sister's friend. She said she started to hear footsteps and then she saw a scary old woman. She said she ran away so fast, she fell over. She said the old woman chased after her and that she almost didn't get away in time. She even felt the old woman's hand grabbing at her ankle with its long bony fingers. After that, she told everyone she didn't want to come anywhere near the church ever again. And she hasn't."

"I don't believe you," Barbara replied.

"She also told Joseph Digby about the tiny hole in this window," Tilly continued, craning her neck a little more. "It works! Barbara, I can just about see inside!"

"You can't."

"I can! I can see lots of empty seats!"

"You're just guessing," Barbara complained. "Anyone could guess that. *Obviously* there are empty seats in there, because the door's locked and no-one's allowed to go inside."

"It's really spooky," Tilly called down to her. "Oh Barbara, you simply *must* come up and look. If you don't, then on Monday morning I'll tell everyone at school that you're the most dreadfully cowardly little thing."

"You won't do that," Barbara said through gritted teeth.

"Just see that I do!"

As much as she hated the idea of complying with her friend's demands, Barbara was already starting to realise that once again her best bet was probably to just go along with the whole thing. She felt a weary familiarity with the situation as she looked at the side of the little shed and saw that climbing up wouldn't be too difficult; indeed, the entire rigmarole seemed preferable in that instant to the alternative; going against Tilly's wishes would only serve to invite trouble, so with a distinct air of reluctance she made her way around to the side of the shed and assessed the best route. Finally she stepped up onto an overturned crate and grabbed hold of the guttering, and then she began to haul herself up.

"There's somebody in there!" Tilly gasped suddenly.

Stopping halfway up to the shed's roof, Barbara waited for some fuller explanation.

"I'm not lying!" Tilly shouted, pre-empting the obvious charges to come. "There's somebody inside the church! It's a woman, I think! It must be the same old woman that Joseph's sister's friend saw!"

"Now you're just making things up to try to scare me," Barbara replied cautiously.

"I swear I'm not!" Tilly insisted. "She's standing down by the empty rows, she has her back to me but – oh Barbara! She's turning around!"

"You're lying," Barbara said again, although she felt a growing sense of fear in her chest, a sense that she couldn't quite ignore even though she knew it was all a load of piffle. "Stop being such a fool, Tilly, and -"

Suddenly Tilly screamed. Startled, Barbara looked up just in time to see her friend stumbling back across the roof, and then she watched helplessly as Tilly tumbled down and slammed hard against the grass and the gravel path.

"Tilly!" she shouted, jumping down and racing along the path, then dropping to her knees so that she could start rolling her friend over. "Are you okay?"

At first Tilly resisted, as if she didn't want to roll onto her back at all. Finally she complied, however, only to look up at Barbara with eyes that were now swimming with blood. The eyeballs themselves appeared almost to be segmenting as Barbara watched, as if the various constituent parts were coming away to become individual plates swimming in a rising tide of blood.

"I saw her!" the girl gasped as the first bloodied tears began to run from the corners of her eyes, and as a deeper – darker – blood erupted from beneath the lids. "Barbara, run! Don't look at her! Barbara, help me! We have to get away before she comes for us!"

CHAPTER ONE

January 1940...

ON THAT COLD WINTER'S morning, as they traipsed along the foggy mountain road, the two travellers almost missed the church completely.

Stopping next to a low stone wall, one of the men peered into the white expanse. As the fog parted a little, the spire of St. Jude's briefly became a little clearer, causing the man to immediately call out and point. The other man, who by this stage had progressed a little further along the road, stopped and looked in the same direction. For a few seconds the fog thickened and the church vanished, only to then re-emerge as a chill wind blew through the valley.

The first man shouted something before stepping off the road and climbing over the wall. The second man did the same – a little more easily – and then together they set off together through the graveyard, making for the church that had already disappeared once again into the foggy Welsh weather.

***

Footsteps traipsed closer to the church, making their way between the gravestones and tombs, and finally Father Stanley Neville stopped and looked up at the granite facade of St. Jude's. For a few seconds his lined and weathered face could only stare, even as a second set of footsteps made their way up behind him and the younger figure of Father Harry Stone caught up.

"Is this it?" Harry asked.

Father Neville turned to him.

"I mean," Harry continued, "*obviously* this is it. I'm sorry, Father, I don't quite know why I said that."

After hesitating for a moment, and keeping

to himself whatever thoughts sprung to mind, Father Neville stepped past the younger man and followed the path that led to the large, arched wooden door.

Harry Stone, meanwhile, took a moment to reassure himself that he hadn't said anything *that* stupid before following his superior.

The keys rattled as Father Neville took them from his pocket. He tried first one, then another, before finally the third proved to be the correct choice. Even so, the lock was stiff after so many years of neglect and the older priest found himself having to really push in an effort to get it to turn.

"Might I try?" Harry suggested.

He waited, but Father Neville was clearly determined to get the door open without help.

"Have you tried taking it out and then... putting it back in again?" Harry suggested.

At this, Father Neville hesitated for a moment before turning to him.

"Just a thought," Harry replied, immediately understanding that his ideas were neither welcome nor tolerated. "I'm sorry, Father Neville."

Reaching out, he touched the top of a nearby gravestone.

"The moss is damp," he observed, hoping to change the subject. "No doubt because of the fog.

The air's damp too. I suppose that'll be the fog as well."

As his superior continued to work on the lock, Harry turned and looked out across the graveyard. A young man in only his fifth year in the priesthood, Harry had certainly never seen a church like St. Jude's before. Situated around five miles beyond the small Welsh village of Laidlow, St. Jude's had once been a thriving parish church but change had come to the valleys and the two other nearby villages had ended up abandoned. In turn, St. Jude's had eventually been closed in the winter of 1914 – and vague promises that it would eventually be reopened had gradually petered out until the place had been left empty and untouched.

For a little over twenty-five years now, St. Jude's had simply been locked up and forgotten. The fog was so thick that Harry could barely make out more than a few of the nearest gravestones, although he'd seen several photographs and he understood that around two hundred graves were in fact dotted all around the church. He couldn't help but think about the place having been left alone for so long, and part of him felt that no church should ever suffer such a fate. Why, could not even one priest have been found to unlock the place at least once a month?

He had asked his superiors about that very possibility, but he had received no real answers.

Hearing Father Neville muttering to himself now as the lock refused to yield, Harry was on the verge of making another suggestion when he spotted a stone tomb nearby with a black metal railing running all around the edges. Stepping over, he touched the railing and found that it was sturdy enough, and a moment later he saw a similar grave just a few feet further away. He turned and looked at the church, and he immediately noticed some more metal above the doorway.

"There certainly looks to be plenty here," he called out to Father Neville, hoping to inspire some confidence in their hitherto rather dour expedition. "I rather think that our trip won't be a wasted one after all."

He waited for an answer, although Father Neville was clearly focused entirely on the task of getting the door open, to the extent of even using his shoulder to push. Harry, meanwhile, quickly realised that he himself had made no deep observations and that Father Neville had no doubt already noticed the considerable amounts of metal that appeared to have been left all around.

"Stop saying obvious things," Harry whispered to himself. "It's completely unnecessary."

In that moment, he realised that he could actually see clouds of fog drifting through the graveyard and passing between himself and Father Neville. He wanted to make some remark upon that fact, although he managed to refrain; he already worried that the older priest found him a trifle irritating and he really didn't want to add to that impression. Besides -

"Blast it!" Father Neville gasped, suddenly bumping against the door and pulling his hand away. "Wretched thing!"

"Is something the matter?" Harry asked, hurrying over and immediately seeing some blood on the older man's hand. "What happened?"

"This wretched door will not yield!" Father Neville hissed, before taking a deep breath. "I am sorry, Father Stone. My language there was not appropriate at all."

Taking a handkerchief from his pocket, Father Neville wiped the blood away, revealing an inch-long cut that had apparently been caused by a protruding piece of metal jutting out from one end of the lock. He turned his hand a little and saw the bone beneath; he winced, but instead of panicking he merely curled the loose flap of skin back into place and pressed down hard again with the handkerchief.

Harry wanted very much to offer to take over, but he supposed that he should instead wait for instructions. After all, he was very much the junior member of the party and he already worried that he'd made too many unhelpful suggestions.

"Well?" Father Neville barked. "Have you lost the use of your hands, man? See what you can do."

Stepping past him, Harry took a moment to examine the key, which certainly seemed to fit very comfortably in the lock. He tried to give it a turn and immediately felt something blocking the revolution, but he was on the verge of shivering now and he wanted to at least get into the relative shelter of the church for a few minutes before starting the long walk back to the village.

As he heard Father Neville sucking blood from the cut to his finger, Harry carefully dropped down onto his knees and examined the lock more carefully. He had always been of a mind that any problem could be resolved with sufficient application of intelligence, and he was trying to imagine what kind of impediment could possibly exist within the lock. He tried the key again and felt the same stubborn obstacle, and then he noticed that the lock itself seemed to have slipped slightly, as if it was out of its proper place in the broader configuration of the wooden door.

Taking hold of the lock, he applied a little pressure and found that indeed it was possible to raise the entire thing slightly. Once that was done, he turned the key; he felt the blockage again, but it seemed minor this time and he supposed that he might apply some additional pressure. This he did, and after just a couple more seconds the key finally turned and the lock gave out a satisfying click.

"Did you do it?" Father Neville asked.

"I think so," Harry replied, standing up and turning the handle, and finding to his relief that the door – although heavy – could now be pushed inward. "Yes, I do seem to have -"

"Get out of the way," Father Neville said, pushing past him and trying to open the door, only for the trailing edge to catch a little on the rough stone floor. He gave it another shove and managed to open it enough, and finally he slipped through into the gloom on the other side.

"It was quite easy, really," Harry said, although he could tell that the older man wasn't interested and – besides – he quickly reminded himself that under no circumstances should he feel any pride. "I'm sure you had already loosened it."

"It was nothing," he added, before turning sideways so that he too could slip through the gap and enter the church. "I am quite sure that anyone would have been able to work it out, given enough time. But tell me, Father, how is your hand? Have you managed to stop the bleeding?"

CHAPTER TWO

AS SOON AS HE was inside the church, Harry noticed that – contrary to his hope – the interior was somehow colder than the exterior. How that could be possible, he did not know, although he managed to keep the observation to himself. On the journey up from London, he'd learned that Father Neville seemed entirely uninterested in any attempt to make small talk.

At least, he noted subsequently, the air was more dry.

Ahead, Father Neville had already begun to make his way along the aisle that ran between rows of neat, empty pews. The church itself, although somewhat bare, was of a classical design with an altar at the far end of the nave and two transepts, one on either side of the crossing. Large stained glass windows lined the walls high up, although the fog outside meant that Harry was not able to really make out the images too well since there was insufficient sunlight. Having long held an interest in such designs, however, he made a mental note to perhaps study the windows at greater length if he got the chance.

Not that he really expected to get such a chance, since as far as he understood the visit to St. Jude's was intended to be rather brief.

He waited for Father Neville to say something, but instead the older man merely made his way toward the altar. As far as Harry was concerned, Father Neville was entirely in charge of their little expedition and there was no need to interfere.

"You are to go to an empty church of your choosing," Father Sloane had explained a week earlier in London, "and make an inventory of any metal, lead or other material that might be useful to the war effort. If there is sufficient, we shall then arrange at a later date for such items to be removed from the church so that they can be used by the relevant industries."

At the time, Harry had been somewhat shocked by the idea of removing anything from a church, although after conversations with others he'd come to understand that every effort would be required in the push to overcome Germany's forces. Up and down the country, buildings of every description were being stripped of unnecessary metal and other items that could be taken away and used in wartime production, and Harry supposed that churches should not be absolved of the same task. Especially, as Father Sloane had observed, if those churches were no longer in active use.

Father Neville had then, rather quickly, identified St. Jude's as the perfect location for their first journey.

Why, then, did Harry still feel a smidgen of doubt about the whole endeavour? Why could he not get over the idea that this turn of events still carried just a whiff of sacrilege? Older and wiser minds had ordered the action, however, and he had simply told himself that it was not his place to question his superiors; it was his place to obey orders.

Realising that the sound of Father Neville's footsteps had come to a halt, he saw the older man standing now in front of the altar. He waited, wondering whether he should advance, and then finally he too began to walk along the aisle. As much as he didn't want to intrude, he was also keenly aware of the need to seem resourceful. The last thing he wanted was to gain a reputation for just standing around like an idiot, even if he often felt as if half his life was spent waiting for other people to tell him what to do.

There was a fine line, he felt, between patience and inaction.

"This is a fine church," Father Neville said finally, turning to him. "Do you not agree, Father Stone?"

"Oh, yes," Harry replied. "Without question. It is of the cruciform style modelled after the Norman designs, is it not?"

"You know your history."

"I try."

"The tower," Father Neville went on, "and the nave are from the twelfth century, no less. Originally it would have been aisle-less, and then over the following centuries the north chapel and chancel would have been extensively redeveloped and most likely rebuilt. The chapel features a gospel-step that has been built into the altar dais and the altar stones themselves have been put back to their proper use, having for a time served as tombstones. I could regale you with further history of this fine building, but to do so would perhaps distract from our mission."

"Indeed," Harry replied. "Our mission."

"I should like you to get on with the job of determining what can and cannot be removed and transported for the war effort."

"Indeed," Harry said again, before hesitating. "I must ask, though, just how much is to be taken? Is the church to be entirely stripped?"

"Every scrap of metal can be used. It will melted down first, if necessary."

"I understand that," Harry continued, before taking a step forward. "It's just that I feel uneasy about the idea of leaving our churches as little more than empty shells. Must so much of these holy spaces be carted away and turned into... well, into guns and other weapons? Bullets and so forth?"

"I share your dismay at the state of the world," Father Neville replied, "but we must trust that the Lord will see us through our darkest hour. There shall come a time when we are able to rebuild churches such as St. Jude's, but for now we must do our best. You and I are both exempted from active service, for one reason or another, but we can at least help in this manner."

"Of course," Harry said, supposing that he should ask no further questions.

"Please busy yourself with the task at hand," Father Neville continued, before turning and looking toward the apse. "I shall join you shortly, but first there is one other matter to which I must attend."

***

"A metal railing," Harry whispered as he scribbled some more notes down. "Approximately six feet long. Iron of some sort, I suspect."

He had to turn to the notebook's next page in order to complete the entry. As much as he disliked the idea of dividing such a holy space up into lists of items to be carried away, he kept reminding himself that ultimately the war effort was more important than any earthly concepts of material value. Besides, was it not the building itself that was holy? He tried to focus on the idea that mere metal could always be replaced and that the most important thing was to keep the actual church standing.

At the back of his mind, he was even wondering whether – once the war was over – he might campaign to have St. Jude's reopened for the people of the local area.

"Another railing," he murmured, stepping to the other side of the transept. "Ten feet long and quite thick. Yes, quite thick indeed."

Reaching out, he gave the railing a tug and found that it was most firmly attached to the wall. The church was by no means falling apart, and this steadfast strength made him even sadder at the thought of the place being ransacked so that its metal could be used to make guns.

Guns, of all things. Weapons of such terrible destruction.

"Lord," he added under his breath, "I am not doubting my superiors, not for one moment, but this war..."

His voice trailed off for a moment as he tried to imagine the horrors taking place at that very moment on the continent.

"Are we merely a species that must have war all the time?" he asked softly. "Is that what must come to define us? Is there any hope for -"

Before he could finish, he heard the faintest sound of whispering coming from somewhere nearby, accompanied after a few seconds by a series of gentle bumps. Confused, he listened for a moment longer before setting his notebook down and making his way toward the chancel, and sure enough he saw that Father Neville was muttering away to himself while gently tapping at various spots on the wall at the entrance to the sacristy. For a few seconds the sight was so unusual that Harry really wasn't quite sure what to say, and he quickly realised that Father Neville had no idea that he was being observed.

Finally, not really knowing how else to proceed, Harry carefully cleared his throat.

"Hmm?" Father Neville said, turning to him. "What are you doing there? Have you completed your inventory of the church already?"

"That I have not," Harry said, "but I heard a knocking sound and wondered what might be causing it. I didn't know that you were going to be..."

His voice faded as he tried to make sense of everything he'd just seen.

"Well, I'm not quite sure what your purpose was," he added, "although I would never try to second guess you. I'm sure that you have your reasons."

"See to it that you stick to the task you have been given," Father Neville said, clearly a little annoyed that he'd been questioned. "You'll be busy enough with that. Never mind what I'm up to, I have my work that needs doing and I can accomplish it without assistance. I should like to do it without interruption, too."

"Of course," Harry replied, taking a step back. "I'm sorry, Father. I shall stop being so curious and shall return to my task."

He did just that, although after a minute or two he realised that he could hear Father Neville still tapping at the wall near the sacristy door. This time, however, he told himself that his superior's actions were none of his business, and that he must simply focus on the task at hand.

CHAPTER THREE

"A METAL CANDLESTICK," HARRY whispered, holding up that very same item and turning it around in his hand. "But this cannot possibly be included in the list. Nobody in their right mind would seek to take such a thing from this holy place."

He paused before looking across the transept.

"Father Neville?" he called out. "I have another question. Might I trouble you for just a moment?"

He waited, but as the seconds passed he began to realise that he'd heard no inkling of Father Neville's presence for quite some time now. Indeed, since the tapping sound had abated he'd heard not so much as a footstep, which seemed strange – unless Father Neville had surreptitiously slipped outside. He certainly didn't want to start worrying unnecessarily, yet in that moment he couldn't help but feel that he and Father Neville were not entirely alone in the building. The sensation, although entirely inexplicable, was rather strong.

"Father Neville?" he said, stepping past the end of the transept and looking toward the altar. "Father Neville, are you there?"

Still hearing no response, he again stood in silence for a moment, convinced that soon he would be answered by a set of footsteps or perhaps by the clearing of a throat. When no sounds emerged, however, he made his way toward the altar and looked all around, yet now he could not deny the fact that he seemed to have been left entirely and completely alone. Still, however, the sense of company remained.

"Father Neville?" he said for a third time, loathe to raise his voice in such a holy place yet keen to determine that he had not in fact been abandoned. "I'm sorry to disturb you, but might I ask you something?"

He looked down at the candlestick he was still holding in his right hand.

"It's about some of the items here in the

church. I was wondering whether -"

Before he could finish he heard a brief scratching sound coming from nearby. Turning, he saw the door leading to the sacristy; the sound had already stopped, but after a moment he made his way over to that very same door and looked through, utterly confident that Father Neville would be somewhere in the next room.

When the next room proved to be entirely empty, however, he frowned and found himself wondering once more where his superior had gone.

And then, just as he was about to leave the sacristy, he heard the scratching sound again. Turning to look at one particular wall, he felt as if something was perhaps trying to catch his attention. He stepped closer and the sound persisted. Reaching out, he put a hand on the wall and felt the cold stone, but he really couldn't quite work out where the sound could be coming from. Leaning closer, he turned his head and pressed an ear against the stone. A fraction of a second later, however, he was startled by the sound of footsteps somewhere out in the main part of the church.

Stepping over to the doorway, he saw Father Neville hurrying around from the other transept. In that same moment, the scratching sound came to an abrupt halt.

"What are you doing there?" Father Neville barked.

"I merely came to -"

"Get back to work! You're not done, are you?"

"No, but -"

"Then get back to work!" Father Neville snapped angrily. "I don't need you under my feet the whole time. How many times must I give you these very simple instructions? Get back to work and don't stop until you've documented every scrap of metal in this entire church!"

***

If anything, the fog was stronger by the time Harry pulled the wooden door open and looked outside. He saw thick
clouds of the stuff drifting past, almost obscuring the gravestones entirely, and he couldn't help but wonder whether the rest of the world had simply vanished. Certainly he found, when he looked around, that he could see only nine or ten feet in any given direction.

"There you are," Father Neville said, marching along the aisle and quickly joining him in the doorway. "Did you finally complete the task that was assigned to you?"

"I most certainly did," Harry replied, holding up his notebook. "There is a lot of metal here, more than I might have anticipated. If it is all to be removed and transported away, I daresay there is much that can be done with it. Of course, some is bolted in place and would require quite some effort to break free."

Snatching the notebook, Father Neville began to flick through the pages.

"No," the older man muttered after just a few seconds. "No, this isn't any good at all. Young man, it's clear that you've entered only the most cursory information here. Had I know that you were wasting your time all afternoon, I should have intervened sooner. What good are these descriptions? Metal? Any fool can write down that something is made of metal, but what *type* of metal? That is the question!"

"Well, I'm not sure," Harry admitted, rather taken aback by the thought that he'd performed poorly. "Most of it was black and some -"

"I should have known better than to trust you," Father Neville said with a sigh, before shoving the notebook back into his hands. "We shall have to do this all over again tomorrow."

"Tomorrow?" Harry replied, horrified by

that idea. "But I thought -"

"We shall have to travel the day after," Father Neville said with another theatrical sigh. "We can't go back to the bishop and tell him merely that there is metal here. Tomorrow I want you to do this all again, and come up with much more detailed descriptions. Sketch what you see if necessary."

"I fear that this is beyond my area of expertise," Harry admitted. "Father, as much as I hate to suggest such a thing, would it perhaps be better if we worked together? I am quite sure that your wisdom would be more suited to the task, and I would be happy to function as your assistant."

"You want to abandon your responsibilities, do you?"

"Absolutely not, I just -"

"We shall come back tomorrow," Father Neville insisted, in a tone that suggested he was under no circumstances to be crossed, "and this time I shall instruct you properly. Evidently you need to be guided like some kind of... child."

"But -"

"Do not argue with me!" Father Neville snapped angrily. "For the love of all that is holy, why do you insist on answering back?"

"I did not mean any offence," Harry replied, shocked by the older man's reaction. He wanted to apologise over and over, but he managed to hold himself back at the last second. "Of course, you are absolutely correct," he continued. "If I have failed in any way, then I shall certainty correct it. Tomorrow I shall produce the most detailed inventory possible and I assure you that you will never again have cause to be unsatisfied with my work."

"We shall see," Father Neville sneered, before checking his watch. "For now, I want you to return to our lodgings and prepare for tomorrow. Go through your so-called inventory and determine how you can make it better."

"Are you ready to leave?" Harry asked.

Father Neville opened his mouth to reply, before turning and looking back into the church. He hesitated for a few more seconds, and when he turned to Harry again there was no anger left in his expression; instead he seemed almost fearful, and he seemed to take a moment to pull himself together.

"No," he said finally. "I must stay. I have... work to which I must attend."

"Then might I remain and assist with -"

"No, you must return to our lodgings," Father Neville said, cutting him off. "Let there be no argument on this matter. You will return and prepare for tomorrow's work. I shall follow accordingly, once I have finished with some other matters here."

"If -"

"Do not question or cross me," the older man added, speaking a little more firmly this time as if he meant to emphasize his own authority. "I shall follow in due course, but you need not worry about me. Father Stone, I am more than capable of looking after myself. Now please, leave before night begins to fall."

"Do you intend to stay here after dark?"

"I intend to stay here for as long as necessary," Father Neville said, and he seemed almost to be struggling to keep the fear from his voice. "No more and no less. But I must be alone, and you must trust that I know what I am doing. Now go."

With that he stepped back and pushed the door shut, leaving a rather stunned Father Harry Stone standing alone on the step.

"Of course," he murmured, realising that he couldn't possibly argue as he turned and began to make his way across the graveyard, hoping that he wouldn't get too lost as he searched for the road.

A few minutes later he was on that very same road and had begun the long walk back to the village. Each time he glanced over his shoulder he saw that the church was receding further and further into the fog. After another minute or two the place was gone entirely, and Harry couldn't help but wonder just how long Father Neville was planning to spend alone in there, and why he felt the need to linger at all.

He knew, however, that it was not his place to question his superior. His job was to prepare for the next day, and to ensure that his second attempt at the inventory would be far more successful than the first. So as he made his way alone along the foggy road and trusted that it would eventually deliver him to the village, he told himself that he had to do as he was told and cause as little trouble as possible.

CHAPTER FOUR

"JOHN!" A VOICE SHOUTED above the already raucous hubbub of the Red Lion public house. "Put another one in here when you get the chance! A man could die of thirst over here!"

As he stood at the bar, Harry began to wonder whether he was ever going to be able to get anyone's attention. Was there some trick, some secret knack, that as a priest he naturally did not know? Everyone else seemed to have resorted to shouting, but Harry certainly had no intention of doing any such thing.

When he and Father Neville had arrived earlier in the day and checked into their rooms, the place had been almost entirely empty. Now that evening was drawing in and darkness had settled outside, however, the men of the village – those who hadn't already been called away to fight – had flooded through the front door and now filled the saloon bar as they set the world to rights.

And if rationing was supposed to limit the amount of beer available to the men of Britain, Harry couldn't help but notice that the effects hadn't yet filtered through to the denizens of the Red Lion.

"Excuse me," he said as the landlord – a large, red-faced gentleman named John – carried some empty glasses past. "Might I trouble you for -"

"It won't be like this much longer," John said firmly to an older man who was leaning against the far end of the bar. "Mark my words, Alf, there's plenty around who don't get how bad things are going to get. Why, it might get so desperate that the likes of you and I end up being called over to fight."

"I'd've gone already if they'd've taken me," the older man said, sending a blast of foul-smelling breath straight against Harry's face – accompanied by some specks of saliva. "There's nothing wrong with my leg that can't be sorted with a good brace, and I'd march anyone else to shame. They could tie me to a chair and leave me to shoot any German who came within twenty feet."

"I don't doubt that for a second," John said, taking one of the empty glasses and starting to fill it from a pump directly in front of the spot where Harry was standing. "Let's hope it doesn't get to that point, though."

"If it's not too much trouble," Harry said, "I was hoping that -"

"This thing's already spreading wider than I would have liked," John continued, clearly speaking not to the priest but still to the man at the end of the bar. "When Old Mother Russia wakes up, we're gonna have to change our tune sharpish. Sometimes I think those in charge of things haven't read their history books. I know there's them that complain about Mr. Chamberlain, but if you ask me he did the right thing. We weren't ready for war back then so he bought us time, that's what it was all about. Not *enough* time, but then there was never going to be enough, was there? That man doesn't get the credit he deserves."

"Mr. Churchill's snapping at his heels," the other man opined as a loud cheer – on some completely different topic – rang out at the far end of the room. "If you ask me, there'll be change before too long."

"I do hate to interrupt," Harry said, feeling his stomach starting to rumble now, "but I was hoping to order a plate of -"

"I'm not sure about that Churchill bloke," John said firmly, carrying the pint of beer back to his associate. "There's something about him that makes me wonder. I don't know what it is, but I'm not convinced that he's the man we need at the moment. He's too much of an attention-seeker, if you ask me. He's trying to use world events to get himself into a position of power, and then what? Does he really think he can stand up to Adolf? We need a younger man!"

Sighing, Harry realised that – for whatever reason – he was never going to get through to anyone. He was desperately hungry and only wanted a simple plate of bread and cheese. As he glanced at the clock on the far wall and saw that the time was almost eight o'clock, he couldn't help but wonder whether his fate was to go to bed hungry, although he quickly reminded himself that this might indeed encourage him to better appreciate the challenges faced by many around the world. As much as he was desperate for a little food, he knew that there were others in the world who were in a far worse position.

Finally giving up, he resolved to simply retire to his room. As he turned to go to the stairs, however, he was surprised to find a strikingly beautiful young woman with dark hair standing directly behind him.

"Father," she said with a smile, "you seem to be having trouble getting my uncle's attention. How about you sit down and I'll see what we can rustle up?"

***

"You are far too kind," Harry said a few minutes later, once the woman – who had introduced herself as Barbara, the niece of the landlord – had found him a quieter table in the corner and had then produced a fine-looking plate of bread, cheese and chutney. "There is clearly too much here."

"Nonsense," she replied, setting a knife and fork next to the plate. "You need your strength. I'm sorry about Uncle John, he can become quite blinkered when he's having one of his long talks. And with the way the world is these days, I'm afraid he never runs out of anything to talk *about*."

"Indeed," Harry said, still touched by the woman's kindness. "Thank you again."

"And what of your companion?" she continued. "I'm sorry, I didn't catch either your name or his, but is he upstairs in the room? Should I take something up to him as well?"

"Father Neville has not returned yet," Harry replied, glancing at the clock on the wall again and seeing that only ten minutes had passed since he'd last checked the time. "To be honest, I'm not entirely sure when we are to expect him."

"Out taking a look around the village, is he?" she asked with a smile that brought shadows to the dimples on either side of her mouth.

"Not quite. He is still out at the church we came to examine."

"Church? What church?"

At this news her smile faded and she immediately turned and looked over at the window. With darkness having fallen outside, she saw only the lights of the pub's interior reflected in the glass, but she was clearly thinking of the night air outside.

"Father Neville and I were sent from London to conduct some work at St. Jude's," Harry explained. "It's a small abandoned church about -"

"Yes, I know where it is," she said, cutting him off as she continued to stare at the window. After a few seconds she turned to him again. "I also heard that you'd been sent here to go looking around, but it never crossed my mind that St. Jude's would be the object of your attention. After all, there are other churches in the area."

"It's part of the war effort, I'm afraid," Harry went on. "There's a rather surprising amount of metal and other resources that can potentially be removed and sent to the factories. Mansions and public buildings up and down the country are being eyed up for their resources. Father Neville and I have been sent to take a look at St. Jude's and determine whether there's sufficient metal there to merit a proper operation to strip the place down. I confess that I am unsure how I feel about the task, but Father Neville is quite insistent that we are doing the right thing."

"I'm sure," she said cautiously, although

now she looked a little pale. "There are gutters and such things, but wouldn't it just be better to -"

She stopped herself at the last second, as if on some deeper level she had resolved that perhaps she shouldn't give voice to her thoughts.

"It's not my place to ask," she added finally. "I'm sorry, Father, I should leave you to your meal. The last thing you want is to have me wittering on."

"Not at all," he replied, before looking toward the empty chair on the other side of the table. "In fact, if you would like to join me, I could -"

"I don't think so, Father," she said, taking a step back as more loud voices yelled at the bar. "I've got work to do."

Her earlier composure was gone and, instead, she seemed rather nervous.

"Uncle John will want me to get back behind the bar, and besides, I can't go sitting around at tables with men I don't know. Even if they *are* priests." She turned to squeeze her way back across the crowded room. "I'm sure your friend will be fine out there. A man doesn't get to be a priest – and a high-falutin' one at that – without possessing some sense."

"Indeed," Harry said again, amused by the woman's tone.

Although he knew he should simply focus on his meal before retiring to his room, Harry couldn't help but watch as Barbara slipped past some particularly rowdy and loud men. She seemed like a very capable young woman, someone who could certainly hold her own against the regulars of the Red Lion. Harry knew that with many men away in the war, women were having to step up and take on responsibilities that would ordinarily be beyond them, and he had to admire Barbara's determination to thrive in the busy public house. He watched until she had entirely disappeared from view, and then he looked down at his meal.

"Lord," he said as drunken voices yelled and hollered all across the room, "bless us for the food we eat today, and bless the hands that prepared and served the food. Bless the men and women toiling in the fields..."

CHAPTER FIVE

A SOLITARY CANDLE BURNED in the window as Harry sat several hours later in the cramped room upstairs in the pub. Voices could still be heard shouting downstairs, although a steady stream of drinkers had begun to leave the building and Harry had hope that finally – at a little after eleven o'clock – the noise might be about to die down.

For his part, since making his way up following his meal, Harry had spent a couple of hours jotting down notes about his experiences since leaving London. He always liked to write down his thoughts in this manner, and he was taking his time since he liked to really think deeply about all the people he'd encountered and all the places he'd seen. He also liked to make small sketches to remind himself of such things. Already he'd produced simple pencil drawings of the train station and the bus, and of St. Jude's and the exterior of the pub, and now – although he worried that he perhaps should refrain – he found himself carefully sketching out an image of Barbara.

Finally he stopped and, in a moment of self-reflection, he began to worry that perhaps he should stick to images of buildings rather than people. He carefully tore the page out of the book before reaching over and burning it over the candle. At the same time, he told himself that he would pray for forgiveness in the morning and ask the Lord to give him a little extra strength.

As the paper burned, he looked out the window and saw no lights beyond the village. After a few seconds he noticed several twisted, clearly quite old nails that had been left on the sill. Reaching out, he picked up one of the nails and turned it around, wondering where it had come from and what journey could have delivered it to such an unremarkable spot in an upstairs room of a small country public house.

Suddenly someone knocked at the door. After taking a moment to make sure that the sketch was no longer discernible, he set the nail down, then he turned and looked toward the door.

"Come in," he said, although in truth he wasn't sure who could possibly be calling upon him so late.

"Mr. Stone," Barbara's voice replied, "or... Father Stone, rather. I'm sorry. I don't mean to trouble you, but... I wanted to check that your colleague made it back safely."

Getting to his feet, Harry made his way across the room and opened the door to find the young woman standing out in the corridor.

"*Did* he make it back safely?" she continued, before looking over at the two undisturbed single beds.

"Father Neville is not here," Harry told her, trying to hide the sense of concern in his own voice. "He didn't actually tell me when I might expect him. I suppose it's possible that he decided it's now too late for him to return."

She opened her mouth to reply, but at the last second she held back.

"Is something troubling you?" Harry asked.

"No," she said cautiously, before turning and looking back along the corridor. "Yes. I can't lie, Father. I am rather worried about your colleague."

"I'm sure that he can look after himself."

"But he's not out there all alone, is he?" she continued, turning to him again. "He can't be. Not at... that place."

"I agree that he must be a little cold," Harry replied, "but he should be able to protect himself from the elements, at least."

"Protect himself how?"

"I suppose he will shut the door and find a warm spot in which to wait out the night."

"Shut the -"

Staring at him, she seemed scarcely able to believe what she was hearing.

"Shut the door?" she said finally. "Father Stone, you don't mean to tell me that Father Neville is... *inside* the church, do you?"

"Of course he is," he explained. "As I mentioned earlier, he and I have been entrusted with the task of determining whether there is much metal there – and other items too, actually – that might be used in the war effort."

"I thought you meant on the outside only," she continued, and now she was clearly very shocked by this news. "It never occurred to me that you meant he was actually inside the church." She hesitated, before turning and hurrying away along the corridor. "Someone must go and fetch him at once! He can't be allowed to stay there for even a moment longer!"

***

Once he'd made his way down the stairs and through the bar area – where a few inebriated locals were still finishing up the slops of their last drinks – Harry pushed the pub's front door open. Finally he saw Barbara standing ahead in the cold night air, next to a bicycle that had been left leaning against the wall.

"I thought I might never catch up to you," he said, letting the door swing shut. "You moved fast. Might I ask... what is the matter?"

He waited, but she said nothing and instead seemed content to merely stare out into the darkness.

Stepping closer to her, Harry looked at her face and saw the fear in her eyes. He wanted to break the tension with some witty or insightful comment, but as the seconds passed he began to realise that she seemed genuinely shocked. Besides, he'd never really considered himself to be a witty or insightful person.

"Father Neville," he said finally, "is a man who can very much be trusted to look after himself. If he decided to remain at the church overnight – which indeed seems to be the case – then I have no doubt that he will be perfectly alright."

Again he waited for an answer, but now he realised that there appeared to be the first stirrings of tears in Barbara's eyes.

"Is something the matter?" he continued.

"I don't quite know what I was thinking," she replied, turning to look at the bike. "I certainly can't go charging out there, and I know none of the others would take my fears seriously. I suppose I just felt as if I had to do *something*, even if..."

Her voice trailed off and she was clearly lost in thought.

"I want to believe that it will be alright," she continued, "but... no, I *must* believe that it will be alright. What foolishness would it be to go back into the pub and try to raise the alarm? There's not a man here who would venture anywhere near that place at night. Or during the day, for that matter. And I doubt Uncle John would let me borrow his van, not this late."

She took a deep breath, as if she was attempting to regain control over her emotions.

"I must remember that I can tend to overreact," she added. "That's what everyone always tells me, anyway. I pray that I am only doing that now."

"You seemed to take fright quite easily just now," Harry replied. "Is there some reason why Father Neville should not stay at St. Jude's overnight?"

"Ssh!" she hissed before she could help herself. "I'm sorry, but please... don't even say its name."

"The name of St. Jude's? Why -"

"Ssh!"

"I'm sorry," he continued. "Is there some reason why you're acting this way? That place is just an abandoned church. Obviously its current state is terribly sad and is to be regretted, but I see no reason to worry about Father Neville's safety. Or is there something I do not know?"

"What do you understand about the history of that place?" she asked.

"I know that its doors were closed a little over twenty years ago," he replied, "due to a lack of enough worshippers, and I know that it has stood empty and abandoned ever since. I know that it is a simple enough church, of a style that I myself much prefer, and that -"

"How?" she snapped.

"How what?"

"How do you know that?"

"Well, I saw it myself today," he told her. "When Father Neville and I went inside, I -"

"*You* went inside?" she gasped, conspicuously taking a step back.

"I confess that I did," he admitted, and he was starting to wonder just why she was reacting in such a strange manner. "Should I not have? I was with Father Neville the whole time, it was he who carried the key – which I believe he obtained from Father Sloane's office. We were looking for metal and anything else that could be used to... well, I have explained all of that already. My point is that we were merely taking notes in the place. I am sure that some of the locals don't like the idea of us stripping the metal from such a holy site, but the war -"

"It's not that," she said, cutting him off. "It's not that at all."

"Then what concerns you?"

She opened her mouth yet again to reply, but Harry could tell now that she was being very careful with what she said – or, just as much, with what she did *not* say.

"Nothing," she said finally, although a twitch on one side of her face betrayed some greater concern. "Ignore me, please. My fears are those of a weak and foolish child who has no understanding of the way the world works, and I should not try to foist my superstitions upon you. It is most likely that your Father Neville will return safe and sound, and I can only hope that you will forget that I said anything at all."

"If something is troubling you -"

"No, nothing is troubling me," she replied, before turning and hurrying back into the building. "Nothing at all. Please, pretend that I did not disturb you. And whatever you do, do not tell anyone about this conversation. I can't have that whole awful mess brought up again. This might be just what I need, to put it all to bed."

"What awful mess?" he called after her, but she had already gone inside and he knew that there was no point chasing after her. The young woman was clearly quite agitated and he could only hope that she would manage to pull herself together soon.

Turning to look out at the darkness, he thought of St. Jude's standing far away in the cold night air. The fog had eased but the night had become much colder, and he wasn't quite sure how Father Neville could possibly be keeping warm in that bare stone church. Indeed, at the back of his mind he was already a little worried by his superior's apparent decision to stay out there, yet he knew that it wasn't his place to fret too much. As ever, he had to trust that Father Neville knew exactly what to do in any given situation.

CHAPTER SIX

WIND BLEW THROUGH TINY gaps in the church's roof, howling as it twisted through the cold air. Far below, at the end of the aisle directly in front of the apse, a solitary candle struggled to keep burning.

"Where are you?" Father Neville whispered, standing near the door to the sacristy and once again running his hands across the stone wall. "I know you must be close."

Every step he took, no matter how small or shuffling, sounded louder than ever in the otherwise silent space. Every breath that slipped from his mouth was visible in the chilly air. Every touch of his hand against the wall could be heard all around the church.

"Come off it," he said finally, taking a step

back as he regarded the stone wall and tried to come up with a better plan. "There's no way you could possibly be -"

Suddenly he turned and looked over his shoulder. Nobody in that moment – not even a man with the most perfect hearing of all – could possibly have detected any kind of noise, yet Father Neville's attention had been piqued by something that had seemed to flicker into existence at the very edge of his senses.

He looked past the altar and tried to work out what had alerted him, and already he could feel his heart racing.

"Is that you?" he called out, finally daring to raise his voice above a whisper. He had tried everything else, he reasoned, so why not attempt to communicate more directly?

He waited, but all he heard was the wind still raging outside.

"Why do you hide from me?" he continued. "Don't you know that I am here to help you? Don't you sense the nobility in my heart? I could have let others come here in my stead, yet I insisted on coming myself because I know that I am the only person who can possibly understand you. I'm not like all the rest!"

He swallowed, but the entire church remained stubbornly silent.

"I'm certainly not like that detestable fool

Wardell. He's dead now, by the way. Did you know that?"

Looking all around, he told himself for the thousandth – perhaps even the millionth – time that there must be some clue. Some discolouration of the stones, perhaps, or a perfect crack or... just something, anything, had to offer a hint as to where he should look next. The frustrating part was the sense that he must be missing something, that he had perhaps looked directly at this clue so many times without seeing it for what it really was. And for what it really meant.

"You *are* here," he said out loud. "There can be no question about that. But you are hidden so well, aren't you? You probably think that I shall give up and simply leave. How wrong you are. I came here to find you, and find you I shall, for I..."

He hesitated, wondering whether he should give up this last scrap of information.

"For I have seen you before," he added. "Do you not realise that? Do you not recognize me? Well, why would you? I was but a boy back then and I saw you only very briefly. Yet I have never forgotten, not since that day, and I have always known that eventually I would come back and find your final resting place. I know you have much still to teach me. I just wish that I could remember exactly *what* I learned all those years ago. That would make it so much easier."

Again he waited for a response, but he knew full well that there would be nothing.

"I am going nowhere," he said finally. "You are here and I shall find you before the night is through. Indeed, I refuse to leave until I do."

***

Several hours later, with the wind having died down a little, Father Neville stood in one of the transepts and ran his hand across yet another wall. He was still searching for even the slightest hint of a crack or an opening, and he'd been working in silence for so long now that his throat was becoming a little dry.

Leaning closer to the wall, he began to examine a hairline crack that ran down from one of the windows. He knew this couldn't be a direct clue, of course, but he had taken to going over even the tiniest hints in case they might come together to offer some suggestion about the overall structure of the building. He refused to believe that there was not at least one clue waiting for him somewhere.

A moment later, out of nowhere, a single bumping sound briefly rang through the church.

He did not immediately turn around, did not utter a shocked gasp, did not even obviously react. This time he stayed calm. He kept a fingertip against the crack and he kept his eyes on the wall, and he told himself that under no circumstances must he disturb whatever force had caused that noise to occur. Any presence was clearly so delicate and so tentative, and so easy to scare away.

So he waited, convinced that this might be the start of something. And he refused to let himself turn around.

After a few more minutes, doubts began to creep into the edge of his mind. The wind was weaker now but it might yet have been striking the church in unusual ways, in ways that might have produced strange sounds. He had heard creaking noises earlier and the constant gentle shuddering of the door, yet he had managed to filter those interruptions from his consciousness. This latest bump, meanwhile, seemed like something else – even if he knew all too well that his senses might be playing tricks on him.

And then, just as he was contemplating the possibility that he was mistaken, he heard the same sound again except...

Except now it was a little closer.

The urge to turn around was becoming stronger, and harder to ignore, yet he knew that he could not risk interfering. He felt increasingly certain that some presence was making itself known, that something was waking up in the church. He tilted his left arm slightly until he was able to see his watch, and he noted that the time was a little after two o'clock in the morning. For a moment he wondered how Father Stone had reacted to his absence, but he quickly reminded himself that the young priest was – mostly – an obedient and well-mannered individual. Most importantly, the bloody fool hadn't rushed back out to the church to 'help'.

This task, meanwhile, was one that he knew he had to complete alone.

He allowed several more minutes to pass, and he couldn't help but ask himself why the presence seemed so unwilling to reveal itself. Then again, he supposed that it might instead have remained entirely silent, and he focused on the fact that the two bumps had been cause for optimism. Indeed, if -

Suddenly he heard a third bump, this time coming from just a few feet away, as if something had brushed against one of the pews.

His body shuddered and the first few muscles tensed in preparation for turning around, but he told himself yet again that he had to be disciplined. The plan was clearly working and he worried that any attempt at forcing communication would only terminate the contact. In his mind's eye, he saw the woman's fearful eyes once more and he thought of the many decades that had passed since that day. Had his entire life been dedicated to the need to eventually return to St. Jude's? In some ways no but, in certain other ways, absolutely.

"You're so close to understanding it all," he remembered her rasping voice saying many years earlier. "You're the first one I've found who might yet see through to the reality! Let me teach you the true word! It will take time but I can open your eyes and your mind to truth that comes to us from the void of nothingness. I only ask -"

Ask what?

For his faith? For his patience? For his presence?

Standing in the church now, he understood that this moment was the culmination of so much prayer and preparation and thought, and he was absolutely certain that he wasn't going to waste all that work now by reacting too quickly.

He heard no fourth bump, yet after a couple more minutes he began to notice instead the faintest creaking sound. The light from the candle was fading now, flickering as it began to burn down. As much as he wanted to remain entirely still until he was contacted, he knew that he needed some light. Finally, while keeping his back very much turned to the spot from which the sounds had come, he turned and walked slowly over to the candle.

Leaning down, he took another candle from his pocket and set it on the plate, before taking care to light it carefully. His hands, he noticed, were shaking violently – and he could not keep them still.

The pool of light immediately grew once he'd lit the candle, and as he stood up and looked to one side he saw not only his own shadow but also a second, less distinct shape.

His mouth opened as he debated whether or not to speak now, but he still worried that any words might scare her away. Was it not better, he wondered, to let her make the first move? After all, he had waited this long – so did another few minutes matter? She, in turn, had come this far; he felt certain that at any moment she would finally respond properly to his presence.

To his return.

A moment later, as if to reinforce this sense, he began to hear the first faint rasping groan. A shiver ran through his body as he realised that all his previous conjectures had turned out to be correct. Until that moment he'd still worried that he might be wrong, that his senses might be deceiving him. Now, however, he understood that after all those decades he had made contact again. And as the groaning sound continued, he allowed himself to very slowly turn around so that he could finally see her eyes.

CHAPTER SEVEN

AS HE SAT UP in his bed in the small guest room, Father Harry Stone realised that the sounds of early morning village life were very different to the sounds of London. As light streamed through the window, he heard no shouting voices, no beeping horns or other signs of busy humanity. Instead he heard only the faintest rumble of a solitary motor vehicle passing the building, followed a moment later by the hint of two men having a conversation almost entirely out of earshot.

Looking over at the other bed, he saw to his dismay that Father Neville still wasn't back from the church. The entire night had passed without his return.

Climbing out of bed, he wandered over to the table and began to search through his bag for the small toiletry bag he'd packed. Once that had been acquired, he slipped into his dressing gown and opened the door, before making his way onto the landing and walking to the small communal bathroom at the far end. He had to duck down slightly to pass through the cramped doorway, and then he headed over to the sink and set about his ablutions.

Outside, beneath the bathroom's small open window, two men were discussing the weather. As he washed his face, Harry absent-mindedly listened to their conversation and wondered just when Father Neville would make his return. At what point should he instead merely go out to the church? Resolving to make a decision after breakfast, he began to dry his face. By now the two men outside the window had changed their topic and were each querying when the other thought it might be worth preparing for the next growing season.

***

"As you can probably tell from the smell," John said, cleaning some glasses behind the bar downstairs, "my niece is already preparing your breakfast. I trust that bacon and eggs will be sufficient?"

"More than sufficient, thank you," Harry replied, supposing that he should be grateful even though he was not accustomed to such an extravagant meal to start the day. As he entered the room, he was unable to miss the smell of stale beer. "I would have been happy with mere bread and a little water. Back at the -"

"Will you wanting a pint to wash that down with?" the older man asked.

"Oh no, I -"

"Course you will," John added, taking a glass and immediately starting to fill it from the pump. "I don't understand them who don't take something strong with their breakfast. This stuff sets you up for the day and no mistake."

"I really think..."

As those words left his lips, Harry realised that he couldn't possibly be so rude as to turn down the landlord's kind offer. Having only tasted beer on a few occasions, and then very little, he watched with some dismay as the man filled the glass up to the brim, and he told himself that he was simply going to have to pretend to enjoy the drink. Part of him worried that Father Neville might walk in at any moment and find him imbibing beer, but he supposed that he would be able to explain himself easily enough.

"It's good stuff," John said, setting the glass on the bar and sliding it toward him. "It'll put hairs on your chest, if there ain't any there already."

"Oh, not many," Harry admitted.

John raised an eyebrow.

"You are most kind," Harry continued, realising that he hadn't been supposed to offer so much detail. Opting to pick the glass up, he realised now that he was being observed and that the landlord most likely thought him unaccustomed to such things.

Resolving to prove a point, Harry took a long sip from the glass. As much as he found the taste to be rather disagreeable, he managed to drink fully a quarter of the pint without so much as a hiccup, and then he wiped his top lip as he set the glass down. Truthfully he was a little surprised that he'd done so well.

"Refreshing," he suggested with a smile, convinced that he'd hidden his discomfort with aplomb. "Rather hoppy."

As he spoke those words, he feared that he might have exposed himself as a terrible amateur. After all, were not all beers hoppy? As a man with little experience in such areas, he worried that he was speaking utter nonsense.

"Hmm," John said dubiously, before turning and heading through to the back room just as Barbara emerged from the kitchen with a plate of eggs and bacon.

Watching as she headed over to a table by the window, Harry wondered how exactly he might break the ice with his hostess on this chilly morning. She had seemed very much out of sorts during the night and he wanted to think of something to make her feel better, but after just a few seconds he realised that she seemed not to be in the mood to talk. Indeed, she set the plate down and then conspicuously avoided meeting his gaze as she turned and headed back toward the bar.

"Nice morning," he suggested.

He waited for a reply, but she simply proceeded toward the door that led through to the kitchen.

"Absolutely," he added, before turning to go over and begin his meal.

"How can you just stand there like that?"

Stopping at the table, he turned to see that Barbara was watching him from the doorway. He looked around, genuinely wondering whether she was talking to him or to some unseen figure who might be better placed to answer the question, and then he once again met her rather intense gaze.

"He didn't come back last night, did he?" she continued.

"If you're referring to Father Neville," he replied, fully aware that this was precisely who she meant, "then no, he did not. I imagine that he came to the conclusion that there was no point wasting a few hours on the journey to the village only very swiftly have to turn around again."

"Is that what you really believe?"

"I see no reason to think otherwise."

She stared at him, and in that moment he felt as if he was woefully ill-prepared for whatever conversation she was trying to start. He could tell that she was still concerned about Father Neville being out at the church all night, but while he felt that her worry was a sign of good character, he couldn't quite understand why she seemed to be *so* set against the idea. In fact, the more he observed her, the more he began to think that he was picking up on the faintest hint of fear in her expression.

"What do you mean to do?" she asked.

"*Do?*"

"Are you going out there this morning?"

"I see no other satisfactory course of action," he told her. "Father Neville and I still have work to complete and I'm quite sure he's waiting for me. There is a lot of metal and suchlike at the church, and perhaps other items that we have not yet identified. As much as it pains me to admit the fact, there is a great deal at St. Jude's that will no doubt aid the war effort considerably."

He took a moment to check his watch.

"The time is a little after eight o'clock," he added. "If I set out shortly after breakfast, I should be able to reach St. Jude's by eleven at the absolute latest. I imagine we shall be there for most of the day but we shall be requiring a meal this evening once we return, if that will not be a problem. And perhaps some bread that I can take with me, just to provide us both with a little sustenance while we work?"

Barbara sighed, before turning to the window and muttering something under her breath, something that Harry couldn't quite make out.

"Father Neville must be hungry," he added.

He waited, but still she stared out toward the road.

"I appreciate your concern," he continued, "and I'm sure that Father Neville does too, but you must understand that we are hardier than we seem. Father Neville will have prepared for a night at the church and while he might have been a little chilly, he will no doubt have warmed himself with prayer and hard work. Believe me, I have known that gentleman for quite some time and I have observed him to be the most diligent individual I think I have ever encountered. He will not complain about the cold, not at all."

Again he waited for her to reply, but she was still watching the window. Indeed, the expression on her face was so fixed and so intense that Harry began to wonder whether she'd heard a single word that he'd just said.

"Barbara!" John called out suddenly from somewhere at the rear of the building. "Where are you? The yard needs sweeping!"

"I'd better go," she said, barely glancing at

Harry at all before turning and hurrying through into the kitchen, already untying her apron in the process.

"Perhaps we can resume our discussion later," Harry replied, although he knew that most likely she hadn't heard him at all. "I would be most eager to do so."

Once he was sure that he was alone, he pulled a chair out and took a seat. The two eggs on the plate certainly looked appetising, and he supposed that he could quite happily eat the bacon. Picking up the knife and fork, he set to work cutting up some bread that had been left on the plate's side, although a moment later he heard footsteps entering the room. As he slipped the first mouthful of food between his lips, he saw a thick, hairy arm placing the glass of beer in front of him.

"Don't forget this," John said with a hint of mirth, as if he was quite enjoying the task of torturing his guest. "Get it down you. Trust me, you'll feel all the better for it later."

CHAPTER EIGHT

BY THE TIME HARRY stepped outside half an hour later, with eggs and bacon and bread and a full pint of beer in his belly, the village had woken up a little more. Several older men were making their way past in rough, dirty clothing, no doubt heading off for a day working in the fields, while women had emerged to sweep the pavements outside a nearby row of cottages.

"Morning, Father," a man said as he wandered past. "Nice to see a man of the cloth in our midst for a change."

"Indeed," Harry said, smiling pleasantly as he turned to watch the man disappearing around a corner and heading into a country lane. "And good day to you, Sir."

For a moment he wondered whether he

should do something before setting off for the church. What this 'something' might entail, he wasn't quite sure, but as he glanced around at the various villagers he worried that they were singularly lacking in ecclesiastical support. They certainly seemed to be getting on with things, yet he couldn't help fretting that he should be able to offer them some more tangible encouragement. Finally, resolving to ask Father Neville whether there might be anything they could do before departing the village, he turned and began to follow the road that he knew would take him out of the village and away toward St. Jude's.

Nearby, the two men from earlier – who had been busily discussing the weather beneath the pub's bathroom window – had at least moved a little way around toward the open ground at the front. They were still deep in their continued conversation, however, which from their body language alone seemed to be of the utmost importance. Something about the calm placidity of country life seemed so appealing, to the extent that Harry began to think that he would like – eventually – to serve such a community.

After just a couple of paces, however, he stopped as he saw a familiar figure coming from the other direction.

"Father Neville?" he whispered, and indeed it was that same individual who was now walking past the sweeping women and making his way – a little unsteadily, perhaps – toward the front of the public house.

Harry watched as his colleague approached, but after a few more seconds he saw that Father Neville's course was taking him directly to the pub's front door itself, as if he hadn't even noticed that he was being observed.

"Father Neville!" he called out.

Stopping, the older priest turned and looked directly at him.

"Father Neville," Harry said for a third time, unable to stifle a faint smile. "What a surprise! I was about to set out on the walk to meet you at St. Jude's."

He waited for a reply, yet after a couple of seconds he realised that Father Neville looked unusually pale, almost as if he was in a state of shock. Something else seemed different about him, too, something that Harry couldn't quite put his finger on. And then, before he could ask anything, he watched as Father Neville turned and staggered – yes, staggered was the right word – to the pub's front door and pulled it open.

Looking up, Harry saw a figure watching from one of the building's upstairs windows. He made eye contact with Barbara briefly, and he saw the concern in her eyes, before she stepped back and disappeared into the gloom of whichever room she was in.

***

"Father Neville," Harry said once he'd made his way back into the pub and saw Father Neville standing next to the table by the window, "I must apologize. I have rather organised my morning around the assumption that I would be making my way out to join you at the church. Is that..."

His voice trailed off as he realised that the older man seemed to be almost frozen in place.

"Is that no longer the plan?" he added.

He waited, but the silence of the room seemed to mirror some stony silence that had now taken full possession of Father Neville himself. Indeed, standing next to the table that still held a dirty plate and dirty cutlery from Harry's breakfast – not to mention the empty beer glass – Father Neville appeared to be a man entirely bereft of momentum, as if he had stalled entirely. Indeed, for a moment the scene looked less like a scene from real life and more like some gloomy, under-lit photograph.

For his part, Harry wanted desperately to ask exactly what was happening and whether anything might be the matter, yet he also worried that it was not his place to pepper his superior with questions. It was precisely that sort of behaviour, he had learned, that tended to irritate Father Neville.

"Would... would you like something to eat?" he asked finally, preferring to stick to easier topics as he surreptitiously took the empty pint glass away and headed over to the bar. "Landlord?" he called out. "Sir? Father Neville has arrived and he must surely be hungry. Might it be possible to acquire something for him to eat?"

Heavy footsteps clomped through from the back room and a moment later John stopped in the doorway. He looked over at Father Neville, and for a moment he seemed shocked by the sight of the older priest.

"Didn't think he was coming back just yet," he said darkly.

"Neither did I," Harry said, keeping his voice low, "but he has just made the long walk in from St. Jude's and I am quite sure that he had no sustenance with him during the night. He must be starving."

"Aye, he must be."

"But no beer for him," he added. "Truly, that would... not go down well."

He could tell that John was rather offended by this insistence, but the larger man merely rolled his eyes and headed through to the kitchen. Within seconds he could be heard shouting for Barbara and instructing her to make another plate of eggs and bacon. For a moment Harry could only listen to the man's rather abrupt tone, and he couldn't shake the feeling that nobody should talk to a young woman in such an abrasive manner. After a few seconds, however, he realised that he could hear a whispered voice coming from the other side of the room.

Turning, he saw that Father Neville was still standing next to the breakfast table, but that now he appeared to be talking to himself under his breath.

"Well," Harry said brightly, trying to lighten the mood a little, "I hope you were not too uncomfortable during your night at the church. I must admit that as I settled down to sleep in my warm and comfortable bed upstairs, I said a little prayer in the hope that you would at least not be too cold. I trust that you passed the night well?"

He waited for a response, but slowly he began to realise that Father Neville appeared to be in a world of his own. As much as he wanted to come up with something else to say, with some comforting words, Harry was starting to notice that the older priest in fact seemed remarkably changed, as if he was barely the same man as before.

"Father Neville?" he said cautiously. "I know you do not usually like such questions, but I must... are you quite alright?"

Again he waited, and again he felt the first stirrings of doubt starting to crawl through his chest. He knew he could not simply ask the same question again, however, so finally he turned and looked through toward the kitchen.

"I say!" he called out. "Hello there? I was wondering, might it be possible to get a glass of water for my colleague here? I just realised that as well as food, he was also deprived of water all night!"

"Hang on, hang on!" the landlord shouted. "Give me a moment, will you?"

Supposing that he should do just that, Harry hesitated for a few seconds and tried to work out exactly how he should proceed. He wanted to ask some more questions, to perhaps understand a little better exactly what might have transpired out at the church during the night, yet he felt as if any question he might ask would only be met by a wall of silence. At the same time, he realised that he could still hear Father Neville whispering. Finally he turned and saw that the priest had shifted slightly, that he was now looking down at the table with his back turned to the room.

"I'll wait, then," Harry said uncertainly.

Outside in the yard in front of the pub, the two men from earlier were still engaged in their conversation, which seemed destined to go on all day. One of the men briefly glanced into the pub before turning back to his companion.

"I suppose we shall plan our activities once breakfast has been completed," Harry continued. "I must say that while it is certainly still cold, the weather appears a little more conducive to some time spent walking. Indeed I am rather looking forward to our journey out to the church. The lack of so much fog should certainly be a good thing."

As he waited for Father Neville to reply, he saw that one of the men outside had glanced into the pub again – and that this fellow appeared to be focusing now on some sight that had caught his attention. The other man, meanwhile, also turned to look, and after a few seconds they both stared at the Father Neville.

"Breakfast won't be long now," Harry said, unable to ignore a niggling sense that something might be really wrong – but also determined to ignore that very same sense. "Just a matter of minutes, I'd judge from the aroma. And the young lady Barbara is an excellent cook. I'm sure you won't be disappointed."

"What was it?" John muttered disapprovingly as he stomped through from the kitchen. "If you ask me, if man wasn't supposed to drink beer, then water would never have been invented."

Outside, the two men were still staring at Father Neville. After a moment one of them – as if wanting to see a little better – stepped forward and cupped his hands around his eyes, all the better for looking through the window and seeing inside. No sooner had he done so, however, than he pulled back and let out a shriek of horror that even penetrated the pub's gloomy interior.

"Father Neville?" Harry continued, before stepping up behind him as he realised that the two men were rushing to the front door. "Is something the matter? What -"

In that moment, as he stepped around the table and finally saw the older man from the front, he realised that Father Neville had been using the breakfast knife to slowly and methodically gouge into his own left wrist. A fraction of a second later blood began to spray from the wrist and then – before Harry could even think to react – the man reached over and began to excavate his other wrist as well. Finally, after reciting one more line of the Lord's Prayer – and as the two men from outside raced yelling and shouting through the door – Father Neville dragged the knife's ragged blade clear down onto the palm of his right hand.

Blood sprayed against the window, the men from outside yelled for somebody to do something and Barbara – who was in the process of carrying a plate of food in from the kitchen – dropped everything and screamed as Harry felt blood splattering across his own shocked features.

AMY CROSS

CHAPTER NINE

"ONE MOMENT, PLEASE," THE voice on the other end of the telephone line said calmly. "Hold while I check to see whether -"

"I don't think you heard me properly," Harry stammered, unable to hold back any longer. His mind was racing with a million thoughts and he was scarcely able to explain himself, yet he knew that he absolutely had to try to make somebody understand. "This is an emergency. I must speak to Father Sloane at once!"

"One moment, please," the voice replied, sounding just a little more irritated than before. "Hold while I check whether or not Father Sloane is available."

"Tell him that it's Father Stone," Harry hissed. "He might not know who that is. Tell him that I'm with Father Neville. He'll definitely know who you mean then. And tell him... tell him that Father Neville is..."

His voice trailed off for a few seconds as he thought back to the awful sight of so much blood spraying from the older man's wrists. In many ways, he found that the more he tried to block that image from his mind, the more it seemed determined to force its way to the very forefront of his thoughts, as if all the blood was determined to torture him and make him scream. He'd wiped as much blood as possible from his own person, yet when he looked down at his left hand he saw that some was still caked around his fingernails.

"One moment, please," the voice on the other end of the line said again. "Hold while I check whether or not Father Sloane is available."

"Hurry," was all Harry could say now as he realised that he had come up against another wall of the church's interminable bureaucracy.

Standing all alone in the pub's back room, with the cold black telephone receiver against one side of his face, he felt as if he might scream at any moment. He'd rushed through a few minutes earlier after begging permission to use the telephone, and he'd told himself that Father Sloane would surely know exactly what to do. Unable to quite remain still, he paced back and forth, advancing as far in each possible direction as the length of cord between the receiver and the telephone would permit him to go, and he felt as if an enormous amount of pent-up nervous energy was about to be released at any moment.

Hearing a door opening, he spun round and saw that Barbara was leaning through.

"Anything?" he asked.

"Doctor Connor is still with him," she explained, but the fear in her eyes said so much more. "I don't know, I think he'll have to be moved to a hospital, but Doctor Connor says it's not safe to do so. He seems... he seems to think that he should remain here under *our* care. Is that a good idea?"

"I don't know!" Harry exclaimed. "How should I know the first thing about medical treatment?"

"I'll go and ask him again," she replied, although she still lingered in the doorway for a moment. "Have you had any luck getting hold of your superiors?"

"I'm trying now," he told her, "but -"

Hearing a clicking sound on the line, he turned away from her.

"Yes?" he blurted out.

"Father Sloane is away for the day," the voice said calmly. "If you would like to leave a message and a number at which you can be contacted, I'm sure he'll get in touch at his earliest possible convenience. There's really nothing else I can do for you."

Shocked by this news and realising that he was going to have to take charge himself, Harry felt for a few seconds as if he might never speak ever again.

"Father Stone?" the man on the other end of the line continued. "Are you still there? Father Stone, can you give me a number at which you and Father Neville can be contacted? Father Stone?"

***

"He has lost a great deal of blood," Doctor Harold Connor said a short while later as he and Harry stood in a corridor upstairs in the pub, "but not enough to be immediately life-threatening. It is extremely good fortune that I happened to be just two doors down at the time the alarm was raised, tending to poor Mrs. Murphy. Her bunions might well have saved your Father Neville's life."

"So he'll live?"

"I don't want to make any predictions about Father Neville's immediate future," the doctor continued, clearly choosing his words with a great deal of care. "He's resting at the moment. I gave him a mild sedative to ease that process, although I didn't want to give too much since I can't be sure how it will affect him in his current condition. The important thing now is that he gets some rest for a day or two until we can arrange to have him taken to a hospital."

"He can't go today?"

"I'm afraid not."

"Why?"

"For one thing, the journey would be too arduous and might be too much for him. For another, the nearest hospital is quite some distance away and I happen to know that they're terribly over-stretched at this point in time. The best thing for Father Neville is for him to receive attentive care, and it seems to me that such care can be provided here. The landlord's niece has already promised to do all that she can. As for the rest... well, I rather think that is your department."

"Mine?" Harry replied. "What do you mean? What can I possibly do for him?"

"Well..."

The doctor looked him up and down for a moment.

"You *might* think of praying," he suggested cautiously.

"Of course," Harry said, nodding frantically. "I just can't get over how much blood there was. It must have been the most shocking thing I have ever witnessed in all my life. And to see that knife there in his hands -"

"I wouldn't focus on such matters if I were you," Doctor Connor said, interrupting him before he could launch into a full account of everything that had happened. "In my experience, the details are often quite harrowing and it's better to think of the bigger picture. Father Neville is alive and he is resting, and that is what matters the most."

He paused for a moment, watching Harry carefully.

"Were you and he here alone?"

"We were sent to assess St. Jude's," Harry explained. "There's metal out there that might be useful for the war effort."

"Ah," Doctor Connor replied, nodding sagely. "Vandalism in a worthy cause. I'm not quite sure what I think about that."

"It is not vandalism," Harry said firmly, although he wasn't quite sure that he believed those words. "It's... we have to do what we can. All of us. A house of the Lord is no exception. Apparently."

"Well, it's none of my business," Doctor Connor replied, turning and walking over to his bag on the table. "I've left some medication for Father Neville, along with the necessary instructions, and I shall check on him again in a few days when I pass through the village again. Until then, I can be reached on the number that John already has, although lately I'm stretched rather thin so I might not get here as quickly as I'd like. This war seemed to have turned everybody into a hypochondriac."

Reaching down, he tapped his left leg just

above the knee.

"I'm not exactly fighting fit, if you catch my drift. Otherwise I suppose I'd have been enlisted by now." He stared at Harry for a few seconds. "I suppose you've got your reasons for not being out there?"

"I do, yes," Harry said, not wanting to go into detail. "Thank you for everything you have done here, Doctor Connor. It's quite clear to me that without you, Father Neville..."

Not wanting to finish that sentence, he preferred to let an uncomfortable silence fill the room for a moment.

"When I return in a few days from now," the doctor said as he closed his bag and carried it to the top of the stairs, "we shall know one way or another how Father Neville is doing. He's not out of the woods yet, far from it, but we must always be optimistic. Even when times seem tough. That's what I tell my children whenever they ask me about this beastly war. Of course, if it goes on for too long, then they'll grow old enough to fight. I hope it's all over by that point."

"As do we all," Harry replied.

"I wouldn't go placing any bets on that fancy, though," the doctor said, already starting to make his way down the stairs. "If you ask me, we're all at the very beginning of a long fight. We might have emerged victorious two decades ago, but that was a different type of war. This one's going to take even more out of us. Even if we win, the cost might be so high that there's very little of us left at all."

" A sobering thought indeed," Harry said, feeling more than a little unsettled by the doctor's words. "As with all matters, we must pray that the Lord guides us through the darkness and leads us back out into the light."

CHAPTER TEN

AS HE SAT IN a cool bath, in the communal bathroom at the far end of the pub's upstairs corridor, Harry tried once again to scrub the last of Father Neville's blood away from the edges of his fingernails.

Although he'd been engaged in this process for some ten minutes now, he hadn't managed to achieve much. The larger flakes of blood had come away, but some stubborn dark stains were refusing to budge and he was starting to fear that he might have the other man's blood on his body for the rest of time. Even now, muttering to himself, he found that a terribly thin red line could still just about be seen around the top of the cuticle, where it had splattered after -

For a moment he froze and thought back to

that awful sight.

"Father Neville?" he'd said, stepping up behind him as he realised that the two men from outside were rushing to the front door. "Is something the matter? What -"

In that moment he'd seen the breakfast knife gouging into the man's wrists. Everything after that had seemed to take place in slow motion, as if the entire world had begun to come to a grinding halt. He'd heard voices shouting, calling for cloths and water and all sorts of other items, but for a few crucial seconds he'd frozen as if struck dumb and insensible by the sight of so much blood. At a time when action had been needed, his response had been the complete opposite and he'd been of no use to anyone. Others had rushed all around him, doing everything in their power to help even as Father Neville had collapsed, but Harry himself had – for several vital seconds – been unable to offer any assistance whatsoever.

Yes, he'd eventually shaken himself out of this useless state and had done what little he could, but he had no doubt that – had it been left to him alone – Father Neville would undoubtedly have died.

Now, still sitting in the bath, he stared at the man's blood on his own fingernails. Why had he not been able to do more? Why had he stood there like a fool? Why had he not known how to help? Why -

Suddenly the bathroom door's handle turned.

Startled, Harry looked over his shoulder just as the door began to open. He barely had time to even open his mouth before he saw Barbara. She immediately let out a gasp and turned away, hurrying back out onto the landing and pulling the door shut so hard and so fast that it rattled in its frame.

"I'm sorry!" she shouted from the door's other side. "Father Stone, forgive me! I was so certain that nobody else was up here!"

"It's quite alright," he replied, although his heart was racing. "Please, don't trouble yourself. I should have locked it, I -"

Looking at the door now, he saw no sign of any key or bolt. Still, he felt sure that he should have found some way to make his presence better known, and he also realised after a few more seconds that he had spent far too long soaking in the tepid water. Getting to his feet as water flowed off his naked body, he reached out for the towel he'd brought through from his room and began to dry himself.

"It's perfectly alright," he continued. "I'm sorry if I gave you a fright."

He waited for a response. Although he heard nothing, he felt sure that Barbara was still out there. After a moment he stepped out of the bath and onto the mat. Still dripping water everywhere, he tried to dry himself as swiftly as humanly possible.

"I shall be out in just a moment," he told her. "Please, just give me two minutes and the bathroom will be all yours. I have lingered in here for far too long. Give me one moment and... and I shall be done with this room for the rest of the day."

***

Once he was dressed, Harry made his way cautiously along the empty landing until he reached the door to the room in which he and Father Neville were staying. He saw the two empty single beds, and then – hearing a rustling sound – he turned to see that Father Neville was in a bed in another room, with Barbara sitting next to him.

"It's all yours," he stammered.

She turned to look at him.

"The bathroom, I mean," he continued, while hoping that he wasn't blushing. "I'm done in there now. I'm sorry I took so long, there's absolutely no excuse but... it's all yours now."

He waited for a reply, but he quickly realised that she was sobbing gently as she continued to sit next to Father Neville's bed. As much as he wanted to go into his own room, Harry knew that he couldn't in good conscience leave a woman in such a state, so he instead stepped into the doorway of the gloomy room and tried to think of some way he might be of use.

The curtains had been drawn, no doubt to let Father Neville rest more comfortably away from the sunlight's glare, and Barbara had placed a simple wooden chair next to the end of the bed. She was clearly trying to hide her sobs, even going so far as to turn away and look toward the window, but even Harry – whose experience with women was almost entirely limited to the company of his mother and one grandmother – was able to tell that she was upset.

"It will all be alright," he said, although he immediately realised that these particular words weren't of much use. "I mean... we must pray, and hopefully those prayers will be answered."

Again he waited for her to say something. Part of him really didn't want to disturb her, yet at the same time he felt equally compelled to try to make her feel at least a little better. Father Neville himself, he felt sure, would know precisely what to say in order to soothe the soul of anyone in distress; Harry, on the other hand, was unable to shake a profound sense of his own inadequacy.

"You should never have gone there," Barbara said suddenly, speaking through clenched teeth.

"I beg your -"

"What were you thinking?" she asked,

turning and glaring at him with tear-filled eyes. "Both of you. What was going through your minds?"

"We... were sent to check for metal and -"

"But not there!" she snapped angrily, before letting out a sigh as she attempted to get her emotions back under control. "Why *there* of all places? Are there not plenty of other churches you could have tried first?"

"I... don't know," Harry admitted. "I had no role to play in the decision-making process. I was simply told to accompany Father Neville here, so I did as I was instructed."

"And you had no idea, no inkling, that it might be a terrible mistake?"

"No," he admitted plaintively. "I still don't."

"You *still* don't?"

"I don't know what is supposed to be wrong with that place!" he replied, allowing his exasperation to show through just a little. "It is a plain little church. It was abandoned long ago. The key stuck in the door. Aside from that, I know almost nothing about it."

He waited for a reply, but she simply sighed before – leaning forward – she put her hands over her face.

"Is there more to know?" he asked innocently.

He glanced at Father Neville, who was still

sleeping in the bed with his bandaged wrists and hands resting on his chest.

"Is there more to know?" Barbara replied, parroting his question while adding a note of utter incredulity of her own – and perhaps a trace of bitterness as well. "Is there more to know? Of course there's more to know. How could you not be aware of what has gone on at that place?"

"I asked Father Neville why St. Jude's had been abandoned," he told her, and he could hear the tentative nervousness in his own voice. "He gave me no precise answer, other than that it was generally not being used by what remains of the local community."

"And why do you think nobody wanted to go there?"

"I'm afraid that I don't have the faintest idea," he admitted, and now he worried that with each utterance from his lips he was making himself seem more and more simple-minded. "I am from London, and before that I was born and raised in Sussex. I do not know this part of the world at all."

"So nobody in London recognized the name of St. Jude's when it came up?"

"Not that I am aware of, but... why would they?"

"Oh, you fools," she said, shaking her head as if she could scarcely believe what she was hearing. "Let me guess. Someone who's never even been near the place probably decided that – even if the stories were true – enough time had passed. That's it, isn't it? Isn't that always the way? Outsiders think they know better and they come charging in, or they send a couple of useful idiots, and they ignore all the warnings."

Harry hesitated for a moment, trying to digest the phrase 'useful idiots' before replying.

"You make it sound so serious," he said finally. "St. Jude's, I mean. What could possibly have happened there to make you talk like this? What could possibly have happened to make Father Neville react in such a manner?"

Looking at the priest again, he saw the thick bandages on the man's wrists. In truth, he still had no idea why Father Neville had acted in such a way, and he was a little scared to ask too many questions. He had to admit, however, that Father Neville – usually such a straightforward and clear-headed man – *had* seemed to act with a little more abrasion once they'd reached the church. Indeed, now that he thought back on the matter, he couldn't help but feel that the older man hadn't quite been himself once the pair of them had made their journey out there. Even during their travel from London, he'd been unusually quiet.

"No-one should go anywhere near St. Jude's," Barbara said bitterly, shaking her head again. "I thought no-one would, not after -"

She stopped herself just in time.

"After what?" Harry asked.

"After last time," she continued, staring at Father Neville's sleeping face for a moment before turning to Harry with fresh tears in her eyes. "After what happened all those years ago when I went there with my friend Tilly."

AMY CROSS

CHAPTER ELEVEN

Twenty years earlier...

"HURRY!" ANDREW SCURRON as he raced along the street, carrying young Tilly in his arms. "Call a doctor! We need help!"

"I'm sorry!" Barbara sobbed, with tears streaming down her face as she followed – almost tripping with every other step. "It's not my fault! I didn't know!"

Already the cries and shouts had roused half the village. Afternoon light was turning to evening as Andrew carried Tilly toward her family's cottage, where the girl's father David and mother Elizabeth were already hurrying out from their front door. As a crowd began to gather outside the village pub, Elizabeth let out a shocked scream and fainted, while David began to slowly lift their daughter out of Andrew's arms.

"I was cycling past when I heard their cries," Andrew explained, turning to look at the others as all the colour drained from his face. "The cries were coming from the church. I went to investigate and... and that's when I found them."

"I'm sorry," Barbara whimpered, watching as David stared down in shock at Tilly's face. "I didn't want to go. She made me. She -"

"What happened?" her own father snapped, grabbing her arm from behind and forcing her to turn to him. "My girl, what have you done?"

"It's not my -"

Before she could get another word out, her father slapped her hard across the face. Had he not been holding her arm, she would surely have fallen back and landed hard against the ground, but instead he forced her to remain standing.

"What have you done?" Bob roared again.

"They've been out there," one of the other men said, stepping closer. "I heard it just now from Andrew Scurron's own mouth. He was cycling past the church and he heard them. He heard your Barbara screaming and he went to see what was wrong, and he found them both around the side of the place."

"Is this true?" Bob asked, looking down at Barbara. He waited a few seconds for her to answer, and then he yanked her arm again. "Tell me! Is it true?"

"I'm sorry," she cried, trying to twist free. Her face was red and puffy now, partly from the tears and partly from her father's strike. "It was all Tilly's idea! I kept saying that I didn't want to go there but she made me!"

"What has happened to her?" Bob continued, looking over at the row of cottages just in time to see that David was carrying Tilly inside, while several women were attending to Elizabeth and trying to get her up off the ground. "Is she still alive?"

"She breathes," another woman said, white as a sheet and on the verge of tears as she turned to him, "although some might yet wish otherwise. I saw her, I saw what had become of her eyes and... it was too awful to contemplate. I certainly can't put it into words."

"What did you do?" Bob shouted, looking down at Barbara once more. "How many times have I told you never to go out to that place? How many times have I told you to never even go close enough to see it? And what do I find now? You've ignored me and let your friend pay the ultimate price!"

"I didn't mean to," Barbara sobbed breathlessly, barely able to get the words out as her knees buckled and she began to hang by the arm from her father's grasp. "It was her idea! Why won't you believe me? I begged and begged for her to stop but she wouldn't! She just kept going on and on, until she climbed up so she could try to look through the window. And then -"

"Enough of these pathetic excuses!" Bob roared, turning and starting to drag her toward their own home, not even slowing as her knees scraped against the ground and she let out a series of pained cries. "Ellen, where are you? Has anyone seen my wife Ellen? Tell her to fetch my belt! It's time this girl learned a lesson about listening to her parents! And this time it's going to be a lesson she never forgets!"

***

"What... what has happened to her?" David Whitten asked, standing in the kitchen and watching as Prudence Grimshaw stepped around the table and continued to examine young Tilly. "Can it be fixed?"

He waited for an answer, but Prudence was too busy leaning down so that she could examine Tilly's eyes. Usually a woman of quick action, on this occasion Prudence seemed almost too scared to get started, as if the mess was too much for her to contemplate.

"Tell me that it can be fixed," David continued, before glancing into the front room and seeing that some other women were attempting to bring his wife around following her fainting fit.

"I have never seen anything like it," Prudence whispered, taking the nearby candle and holding it closer to Tilly's face. "I never even dreamed that it might be possible."

Although she gave no other sign of being awake, Tilly's eyes were open – or what remained of her eyes, at least. In both cases, the retinas had detached and the irises, which had originally been a kind of bluey-green colour, had somehow ripped and torn as if the integrity of the orbs was breaking down. The eyes themselves were swimming in blood, as if some catastrophic event had squeezed them until they were on the verge of bursting. A kind of clear, slightly bloodied liquid was running from the corners of both eyes and the irises appeared to be bleeding, almost leaking as if they were on the verge of peeling away. Every constituent part of each eyeball appeared to have separated from its neighbour, as if the fundamental anatomy of each orb had broken down in sheer fright.

After a few seconds, a larger pool of blood began to soak up from beneath the ruptured cornea, forming a perfect red ball that shimmered briefly before losing its form and dribbling slowly down. In the process, part of the eye's lens seemed to go with it, although in truth there was barely any way now to really determine what part of the two eyes was what.

"It is as if they have almost burst open from the inside," Prudence continued, "yet the girl is not screaming. She is breathing but she is in some kind of trance. Perhaps the pain has driven her conscious mind away..."

"What can you do for her?" David asked. "Can you save her sight?"

"I do not know."

"How can this have happened?" he went on, sounding more and more agitated with each word that left his lips. "I don't understand any of it! An injury to one eye, perhaps, but both?"

"I do not know," Prudence said again. "You must remember that I'm only a district nurse, I usually just -"

Suddenly Tilly blinked, or at least she tried to: her eyelid closed some of the way, only to catch on parts of the ruptured eyeball, sliding thick pools of blood away. As the eyelids tried once more to close, fresh blood began to cake in the lashes, until finally Prudence could stand no more; reaching down, she took hold of both pairs of eyelids and did her best to hold them open so that no more damage could be caused.

"There," she said. "Just wait a moment while we try to determine what we might do next. Just -"

Before she could get another word out, she spotted an unusual shape in both eyes. Leaning a little closer, she narrowed her own eyes in an attempt to work out exactly what she was seeing. Each passing second seemed to bring fresh damage, or another slightly viscous oozing of blood to the surface, but the eyeballs themselves also appeared to be shifting their shapes within the sockets. Peering ever closer, however, Prudence tilted her head first to one side and then to the other as she still felt she could see the faintest shape somehow burned into the rupturing blood, almost as if...

"I see a woman," she whispered softly.

"What did you just say?" David asked.

"I see a woman's face," she murmured, as if she could scarcely believe this news herself. "In each eye. It's the same image almost, it's as if something *she* saw is burned into her eyes and is causing this to happen."

"How is that possible?"

"It is not," she said firmly, "yet I see it now with my own two eyes. It is as if -"

In that moment Tilly's left eye split down the middle and blood burst from the wound with a faint popping sound, and a few seconds later the same thing happened to the other eye. At the same time the girl's legs began to twitch, as did her whole body a couple of seconds after that, and finally her lips started to move as if she was trying to say something. Slowly a low murmur began to emerge from the back of her throat, quickly becoming a kind of pained whine, and she began to try to turn her head first one way and then the other.

"What is happening to her now?" her father asked.

"I think perhaps she was in shock before," Prudence exclaimed, unable to hide a sense of panic. "Has anyone sent for a doctor yet? Someone must send for a doctor at once! No matter how long it takes for help to arrive, please, someone has to -"

Suddenly Tilly sat bolt upright, screaming as she did so and letting the remains of her burst eyeballs dribble down her cheeks. Shaking violently, she leaned forward and tried to crawl off the table, only for Prudence to put an arm around her from behind and try to hold her back.

"It's the eyes!" she shouted at David. "Your daughter's eyes... we can't wait for a doctor, we have to get what's left of them out right now before that image spreads to the rest of her!"

"What are you talking about?" he gasped.

"I need a knife," Prudence snarled, wrapping her arm tighter across Tilly's chest to hold her in place as the girl's screams became louder and louder. "The sharper the better, but any knife is better than none! Bring me a knife and a bowl of water! We have to get them out before this evil contaminates her entire body!"

"No," David said, shaking his head as if he couldn't believe what he was hearing. "You can't be serious!"

"Do you want your child to die?" Prudence shouted angrily. "Fetch me a knife before it's too late!"

Reaching down, she dipped a fingertip into the girl's left eye. Tilly merely continued to shake, so the woman slipped her fingertip a little deeper into the socket and stirred it around, before lifting it up and watching as the gooey blood dribbled back down and splattered against the flesh. At the same time, Tilly struggled with such force now that the table's wooden legs had begun to bang repeatedly on the kitchen's stone floor.

AMY CROSS

CHAPTER TWELVE

SEVERAL WEEKS LATER, AS she continued to sweep the yard behind her parents' cottage, Barbara felt another twinge of pain in her back. She stopped for a moment – still holding the broom in case she was spotted slacking – and a few seconds later she felt a wet sensation dribbling down from between her shoulders.

Reaching round, she tucked a hand beneath her shirt and then brought it back out. The bead of blood on her fingertip immediately told her that one of her wounds must have opened again, although at least there was no pus. Her father had beaten her several times since that awful day when she'd gone out to St. Jude's and sometimes she worried that he might never stop. The beatings were particularly bad whenever he was drunk. Then again, she knew that she deserved all her punishment and more besides, and nothing he did to her could ever be worse than the guilt and anguish that filled her soul every single night.

Some men were calling out to one another in a nearby lane, but Barbara forced herself to get back to work. Already she was making a mental note about her other chores, and she knew that she was going to be busy until long after sundown.

And then, as she turned to sweep the farthest corner, she saw a pair of bare feet standing at the open gate. She froze, already convinced that she recognized these scratched toes, and when she looked up she felt a shudder run through her bones as she saw that Tilly was standing directly in front of her.

Ever since their trip to the church, Barbara had been avoiding Tilly as much as possible. She'd heard whispered rumours about her friend's injuries, but now she found herself face to face with the awful truth: while her eyes had in the end not been cut out by the frantic and superstitious Prudence Grimshaw, they had also not been saved. What remained of her eyeballs sat packed tight in their sockets, but the pupils had been torn and deformed and nobody could possibly be expected to see through such things.

Although she felt awful for even admitting such a thing to herself, Barbara was sickened by the sight of her friend's face and had to resist the urge to turn and run away.

"Barbara?" Tilly said cautiously. "Is that you? Are you there?"

Realising that Tilly still couldn't see a thing, Barbara immediately wondered whether she could simply sneak away and pretend that she had been absent all along. She took a step back while trying to calculate whether this course of action would make her an even worse person.

"I know it's you," Tilly continued. "I can hear you breathing. And I know this is the yard behind your parents' cottage. I counted the gates with my hand as I came along the lane."

"It's me," Barbara admitted finally. "I was going to come and see you soon, I promise. It's just that I've been so very busy and I heard that you needed lots of rest, so..."

Her voice trailed off as she realised that all her excuses were so painfully thin and obvious. Tilly was no fool and she most certainly understood the true reason for Barbara's reluctance to visit.

"I don't know what to say," Barbara added finally. "Every time I thought to come and see you, I tried to work out what I would say to you first, but I just couldn't think of anything. At least, I couldn't think of anything you might want to hear. I'm so dreadfully sorry about what happened, Tilly. I told you that we shouldn't go near that church but I should have been more insistent. I should have found a way to hold you back."

She waited for an answer, and she half expected Tilly to scream at her furiously, but instead a kind of sticky silence spread out between them. As much as she still wanted to run away, Barbara felt as if the silence was attached to her now and that its other end was attached to Tilly, and that it was now holding them together.

"Do your parents know that you're out here?" she asked. "I can walk you home, if you like."

She hesitated, before stepping forward and leaning the broom against the wall. She knew that her father would be furious if he caught her slacking, but she told herself that she would just have to try to explain. Reaching out, she tentatively took hold of Tilly's hand and flinched as she felt the girl's cold, clammy skin.

"Come along," she said, trying to sound friendly as she gently encouraged her friend to turn so that they could make their way back along the lane. "It's cold. You shouldn't be out here in just your nightgown. Let me get you home so that you can rest again. At least let me do this for you."

**

By the time she'd managed to lead Tilly all the way

to the next row of cottages, Barbara had succumbed to silence. An initial nervous urge to somehow keep the conversation going had given way to the acceptance that perhaps a dignified silence was the best approach after all. Already she could see Barbara's parents' cottage up ahead and she just wanted to deliver her home and then get back to her own chores.

A few people had noticed the two girls as they made their slow progress through the village, and Barbara had no doubt that this walk would reignite the gossip that had only recently begun to die down.

"Not far now," she said finally, glancing briefly at Tilly again. "You'll be glad to rest, won't you? And you're not wearing any shoes. Aren't your feet so terribly cold?"

She received no reply – and she tried to convince herself that this was a good thing. She had no desire to get into a conversation about everything that had happened out at the church, indeed she'd tried to think of it as little as possible, and she felt guilty about the fact that she was already desperately keen to simply drop Tilly off and run home. After a few more paces, however, Tilly suddenly stopped and Barbara – not immediately noticing and instead taking a few more steps – almost let go of her hand.

"We're nearly there, Tilly," she said, turning

to her. "Don't worry, I'm leading the way."

"I don't want to go there," Tilly whispered.

"What do you mean?"

Although she waited for a reply, Barbara was once again worried that nothing would be forthcoming. As much as she'd tried to convince herself that Tilly had merely wandered to find her on some whim, now she was starting to worry that her friend might have something more important on her mind.

"Did you see her?" Tilly asked.

"Who?" Barbara replied, even though she knew the answer full well.

"The woman at the church," Tilly continued. "The anchoress."

"No," Barbara said, and a shiver ran through the marrow of her bones. "I didn't see anything."

"I did. I saw her so very clearly."

"Well, that's because -"

"And I see her still."

"I'm sorry?"

"I see her still," Tilly continued as the late morning sunlight glinted in the moist cuts that criss-crossed the remains of her eyeballs. "I see her right now."

"I thought... I thought you could see nothing at all."

"I see *her*," Tilly replied, seemingly staring straight ahead.

After a moment she blinked, although her fleshy lids struggled to get over a few of the rough ridges on the fronts of her eyeballs.

"The doctor says I need an operation," she explained, "but I know that won't help. I tell Mam that there's no need to fuss and that it won't change anything, but she and Daddy are convinced that I must be taken to Cardiff so that a surgeon there can fix me. They say there's no hope of restoring my sight, but they think at least they can avoid any more infections."

"We're nearly at your home," Barbara said, hoping to avoid getting drawn into a long discussion about something that made her feel so terribly awkward. "Perhaps fifty more paces at most, so why -"

"And they won't stop me seeing her," Tilly added. "No-one can do that. It's as if the sight of her was burned into my eyes and nothing can get rid of her now."

"I'm sure it'll get better with time," Barbara said, more out of hope than any firm belief. "I really think that you should get home and -"

"I even see her at night," Tilly said. "When I close my eyes and try to go to sleep, she's there. And when I dream... no matter what I dream *of*, she's right there in front of it all. Do you think there's *any* chance that I can make her go away? I keep trying to think of a way but I can't imagine anything working at all."

"You could try praying," Barbara suggested, "and -"

In that moment Tilly turned and looked directly at her. Although Barbara quickly reminded herself that the girl couldn't see her at all, she still felt uncomfortable as she thought of Tilly 'seeing' some ghostly figure from the church wherever she stared, and after a few seconds she had no choice other than to step sideways out of the way.

"Tilly?" a voice called out, and Barbara felt a rush of relief as she turned and saw the girl's mother rushing toward them both. "Tilly, what are you doing out here? Get back inside at once!"

"I want you to help me," Tilly said softly, trying once more to look directly at Barbara. "Will you come and find me some time? I need help and... and I think you're the only one."

Grabbing Tilly's hand, Elizabeth Whitten cast a furious glare in Barbara's direction before dragging her daughter away. Admonishing the girl for having strayed from the family home, Elizabeth seemed determined to hide her away from public view as if she was some dreadfully shameful secret. Already some more neighbours had emerged from nearby cottages to witness the scene, but after a few more seconds Barbara realised that many of them were now turning to look at her instead.

Feeling horribly embarrassed, she began to

hurry back to the yard, keen to get back to work before her father noticed she was missing. After all, her back was still bleeding and she was utterly terrified by the thought of another beating from his belt – even if she knew that more punishment was inevitable.

AMY CROSS

CHAPTER THIRTEEN

"AND THIS," JOHN SAID a few years later as he held up the hose, "is what we use to swill out the front garden each morning. Why do we have to swill out the garden, you ask? Well, Barbara, I'll tell you. It's because of men like Alistair Emery and Bernie McCullen who can't leave the pub at night without vomiting their last pints all over the bloody place."

With that he turned the tap on and aimed the hose, taking a moment to wash away the pinkish yellow vomit that had been left to fester overnight.

"Now that you're working for me," John continued, "and living here at the pub, I'm afraid this will be one of your duties. My advice is not to delay it but to do it right away, first thing. The smell's not so bad, not once you get used to it, and the job's over in a matter of seconds."

As if to emphasize that point, he turned the tap off and hung the end of the hose back up, as the last of the foul liquid mess dribbled away into the flowerbed.

"See?" he added. "Voila! Plus I get complaints if it's left too long each morning, so it's as well to get it done. And I don't think it's *too* bad for the flowers."

He glanced around for a moment.

"Just don't tell your aunt," he added with a whisper.

Before she could reply and promise her uncle that she would be out at sunrise each morning, if not before, Barbara spotted a figure walking past. Flinching at the sight of her own father, she briefly made eye contact with him before he turned and marched away.

"Things still aren't good between the two of you, then?" John asked.

She turned to him.

"He's a stubborn git," he continued, "and I say that as his brother."

"I thought that moving out of home and coming to live with you might improve things with my parents," she admitted, "but if anything, it has all become worse now. At least when I lived with them, they were forced to occasionally make small talk with me. Now that I'm out of the home, it's as if they have decided they're free of me." She paused, struggling to hold back tears. "I shouldn't complain, though," she added. "I know they've both hated me ever since that awful day when Tilly and I went out to the church."

"They don't hate you," John replied.

"But they do," she insisted. "You know it's true. They detest me, just as half the village detests me. In truth, I'm not even sure that they're wrong. I'd move away if I could, but I have no money and nowhere to go. Uncle John, what if my presence causes people to stop coming to your pub? I can't bear the thought that I might bring trouble to your doorstep."

"You've already shown yourself to be an asset to us here at the Red Lion," he told her. "Bea and I were just talking last night about how happy we are to have you with us. And as for your parents, if they can't see beyond the ends of their own noses and make things good with you, that's their problem." He put a hand on her shoulder. "You're a good lass, Barbara Dewhurst, and I won't have anyone saying otherwise. Honestly, do you think I'd have taken you on if I thought any other way?"

"I hope not," she said softly.

"Come inside and I'll show you how to pour a pint," he continued, turning and making his way back into the pub. "If you can do that right, you'll soon be the most popular girl in the whole village."

She allowed herself the faintest flicker of a morsel of a smile, although deep down Barbara still felt uncommonly awkward. A moment later this sense of discomfort was only heightened a thousandfold as she spotted movement in the distance: a figure, with her face mostly hidden by a large white hat, was being led out from one of the cottages, and Barbara instantly knew that this was Tilly being taken somewhere by her parents. Having not seen her former friend for several years now, Barbara felt as if her heart might soon break, but a moment later she heard her uncle calling for her again from inside the building.

"Coming!" she said, lingering for a couple more seconds before finally turning and heading inside.

***

"I had to go out along the back road last Tuesday week," Michael Morley said as he sat on his usual stool in the pub, with his dog Jasper sleeping soundly on the next stool along. "I didn't want to, but I had no reasonable alternative. And of course going that way meant I saw... you know... that place."

"Aye," Gerald McCreedy said from his spot a little further along. "You wouldn't get me heading out that way. I wouldn't even want to set eyes on that church."

He fell silent for a moment before turning to watch as Barbara continued to dry glasses and stack them on a shelf.

"There's some round here that've learned their lessons, at least," he added.

Barbara glanced briefly at him but, preferring to not take the bait, she quickly forced herself to focus once more on the task at hand. She was quickly learning that although people liked to needle her from time to time when she was behind the bar, for the most part they seemed to respect her more if she simply got on with things. Her uncle had told her that eventually the gossip would settle down and she was simply hoping that he was correct.

"I don't think," Michael said after a moment, "that anyone has actually set foot on that land since the incident with the Whitten girl all those years back. How long ago was it, anyway? Ten years?"

"Must be," Gerald said darkly. "I still see her occasionally. Her parents take her out, I think it's just to -"

"Eleven years," Barbara said suddenly.

Both men turned to see that while she hadn't looked at them again, she was drying the glasses with a little more determination than before.

"It'll be eleven years ago next month," she added through gritted teeth. "Since Tilly and I went out there, I mean. That's what you're talking about, isn't it?"

"Aye, eleven years sounds about right," Gerald muttered, peering at her intently for a moment. "Eleven years is a long time for a place to be left untouched, but in this case, I'd say it's not nearly long enough. Even after a thousand and eleven years, you wouldn't catch me going near it."

"It's a church," Barbara said, turning to put the empty tray away before hauling another – this one filled with glasses – onto the counter. "Why do people always refer to it simply as a *place* or a *building*? We all know that it's a church, so why not say so? And for that matter, why will no-one say its name?"

"I think we'd all rather forget that it's there," Michael told her.

"You can still say the name St. Jude's," she suggested as she set a glass on the side. "For that matter, you can still refer to the reason no-one wants to go out there."

"P'raps," Gerald said, "but -"

"We all know it's the anchoress and -"

As soon as those words left her lips, Barbara turned and the glass fell from the counter, smashing against the floor. She froze, looking down at the broken shards, and then she turned to her two customers.

"I brushed it," she said uncertainly. "You

must have seen, both of you. I brushed it with my arm. I... I think I did, at least."

"I'm not sure about that," Michael said cautiously, leaning back slightly. "It looked to me more like -"

"Are you really *so* superstitious?" she asked, no longer able to hide a sense of genuine irritation. Grabbing a dustpan and brush, she knelt down and began to sweep up the mess. "To think, two grown men actually believe that merely *mentioning* the existence of St. Jude's and the *possible* existence of the anchoress could be enough to bring a glass crashing down. What exactly do you think happened just now? Did the anchoress reach out across the miles and smite the glass herself?"

Michael looked over at Gerald, and Gerald in turn looked at Michael.

Getting to her feet, Barbara saw the rather gormless confusion in the eyes of both men.

"You *do* think that, don't you?" she continued, sounding increasingly exasperated now. "The whole village thinks the same way, I'm sure. It's one thing to fear something, but it's quite another to act so irrationally."

"Is everything alright through here?" John asked, ducking through the doorway and stepping behind the bar.

"It's fine," Barbara lied as she tipped the broken glass into a nearby bin. "Just some superstitious nonsense that needs putting to bed. But perhaps they're right. Perhaps we shouldn't mention that place by name again."

"Barbara," John continued, eyeing both Gerald and Michael with a hint of concern, "would you mind going into the back room and seeing if Bea needs some help? She's got a lot of chopping to do before tomorrow and although she spurned my offers, she might be more amenable if you try to assist."

"Don't you want me to finish drying these glasses?" she asked.

"I can do that myself," he told her. "Go on, help Bea for a while. I think she'll be glad of it."

"I'm sorry," she muttered as she turned and hurried away. "I shouldn't have risen to it."

John waited until she'd left the bar before heading to the glasses and starting to dry them. He glanced several times at both Gerald and Michael as if he wanted to say something, while they in turn seemed happy to study their pint glasses, the contents of which had seemingly become as fascinating to look at as they were enjoyable to drink. Jasper the dog, meanwhile, was still sleeping happily on his own stool.

"There are a few things," John said finally, "that I've asked you fellows and the other regulars not to discuss when my niece is around. Can I trust you to remember that request?"

"You can," Gerald said, although he sounded as if he was holding his tongue a little. "We were just making conversation, that's all. No harm intended."

"I'm sure you fellows won't have trouble thinking of other things to talk about," John murmured as he dried another glass. "There are plenty of other topics. No need to starting talking about that... *place*."

CHAPTER FOURTEEN

THE RATTLING WINDOWS SHOOK Barbara awake. On her side in the small bed, in her cramped room at the back of the pub, she tried to remember the dream that had been filling her mind; the details had already faded, however, and after a moment she supposed that there was no real need to keep trying.

Rolling onto her back, she listened to the wind for a few seconds. She had no idea of the time, but there was no sign of the sun rising outside and she told herself that she could afford to close her eyes and at least try to get back to sleep. She did exactly that, and for several minutes she was able to listlessly doze until she heard a rustling sound and her eyes flicked open again.

After a few seconds she heard the noise for a second – third? fourth? - time. Although she tried to convince herself that it was nothing, finally she propped herself up on her elbows and looked across the room. At first she saw nothing amiss, but as her eyes adjusted to the darkness and the shapes of various items of furniture began to emerge from the gloom, she noticed a shape that appeared to have manifested itself at the very foot of the bed. She couldn't be certain, but this shape seemed rather out of place so finally she reached over and switched on the lamp.

As soon as she saw Tilly sitting at the foot of the bed, she let out a gasp and pulled back against the headboard.

Not reacting at all, Tilly merely sat half facing the window.

Barbara, meanwhile, could only stare at her for a moment as she felt her heart racing. Several years had passed since she'd last had any interaction with Tilly at all, and whereas they had both been just young girls when they were friends, now they were old enough to be considered adults. Not knowing what to say, Barbara looked at the door and saw that it was shut, and then she turned to Tilly again and wondered just how and why she had found her way into the pub in the middle of the night.

The windows shook again as the wind briefly picked up outside.

"Tilly?" Barbara said finally, realising that

one of them had to break the silence. "What are you doing here? Are... are you lost?"

"I still see her," Tilly said darkly.

"Who do you mean?" Barbara replied, although once again she already suspected the answer.

"She hasn't gone away," Tilly continued. "In fact, I fear I see the anchoress more clearly now than ever before. More clearly even than on that day so many years ago."

"I'm really sorry to hear that," Barbara said, sitting up a little more, "but I must ask, why are you here tonight?"

"Everyone tells me that the image will fade in time," Tilly said softly. "Often they tell me to stop being foolish, as if they think I'm imagining it. I know that's what my parents believe. Whenever I dare to mention the anchoress at all, they try to change the subject immediately. Do you know what it's like not to be able to talk about something so important?"

"I really can't imagine," Barbara said. "Listen, if you let me get dressed, I'll be happy to walk you home."

"You're just like the rest of them."

"No, I'm not," Barbara protested, "I just... it's the middle of the night, Tilly, and I'm sure you're tired."

"The anchoress -"

"I don't want to know about the anchoress!" Barbara snapped before she could help herself. "Just stop, okay? Enough! I don't want to hear another word about her!"

Close to tears now, she climbed out of bed and put her hands over her face for a moment, before lowering them just as Tilly turned to her.

Before she could get another word out, Barbara saw Tilly's scarred eyes. There had been no improvements over the years, although the remains of the eyeballs appeared to be glistening a little more than before. Any planned operation clearly hadn't taken place. Both eyeballs twitched briefly, as if they were trying to move. The irises could still just about be made out, at least in part, and after a moment a kind of clear liquid began to dribble from the left eyeball, running slowly down Tilly's cheek like some kind of malformed tear. And something was...

Yes, something was moving in one of the eyeballs, and a moment later a pale brown maggot emerged. Barbara's first thought was that she must remove the creature, but then – as quickly as it had appeared – the maggot burrowed its way out of sight again.

"I imagine things sometimes, too," Tilly whispered. "Feelings. Sensations. Sometimes... the backs of my eyes... of what's left of them, anyway... sometimes they tickle."

Barbara, meanwhile, very much wanted to say something reassuring but could think of no words that might be appropriate.

"I meant to come and see you," she managed finally, even though she knew once more that any apology or excuse would sound so very woeful. "Honestly I did, but I have been so busy here since I moved to the pub and... and I wasn't sure whether or not you would really want to see me at all."

"So many times," Tilly replied, "I thought of going back to that place."

"To the church, you mean?"

"In some ways, I think I have never fully left."

"That's not true at all," Barbara replied, wondering now whether she should wake her uncle and ask for his help.

"Perhaps if it had been easier to find my way," Tilly continued, "I would have returned. I don't exactly know what I would have done when I got there, but I wonder whether the anchoress has been waiting for me."

"You don't even know that the anchoress is real," Barbara told her.

"Oh, but I do," Tilly said calmly, "for it is her image that I see always. Even when I sleep." With her eyes aimed more or less in Barbara's direction, she tilted her head slightly. "Even now."

"I must get you home," Barbara replied, stepping past her and hurrying to the chest of drawers on the far side of the room. "Let me get dressed and then I'll take you, okay? It's really no trouble at all, I shall be only too glad to help you."

She began to slip out of her nightdress, although her nerves were becoming apparent and she fumbled several times. Almost in a state of panic, she struggled to remove the nightdress and then she struggled even more to find a skirt to wear.

"Forgive me," she muttered, glancing over at Tilly again. "I must wake up fully before -"

Stopping suddenly, she saw that Tilly was holding out her left hand, revealing two rusty and slightly bent old nails – thick and black and at least six inches long each – in her palm.

"I must wake up fully," Barbara continued cautiously, trying to make sense of this latest development as she reached for a bra and began to put it on, "before I can think properly."

She waited for Tilly to reply, before opening the chest of drawers and taking out a pair of tights.

"You really shouldn't go sneaking up on people in the middle of the night," she said, turning her back to Tilly for a moment as she began to slip her legs into the tights. Looking into the mirror, she saw the fear and desperation in her own eyes and told herself to get this awkward situation over with as swiftly as possible. "You can't expect them to be ready to receive you."

"I understand now," Tilly replied wearily. "I understand that there is no other way to get rid of the image that haunts me so."

"Time will heal it," Barbara said, almost falling over as she pulled the tights up. Next she grabbed the skirt and began to put that on as well. "It always does. At least, that's what wiser people than I always say, and I suppose they must be right. I hope so, anyway."

"I can only hope to shatter her," Tilly continued, "so that she might finally let me rest. Do you think that shattering her might work?"

"These things are sent to test us," Barbara added, although she was aware that many of these observations were nothing more than simple pleasantries she had heard being parroted over the years by her aunt's friends – or, worse, by drunks downstairs in the pub. "The most important thing is to keep your head held high and remember that it's always, uh, darkest before the storm. No, wait, that's wrong isn't it?"

She took a blouse and tried to get into it, but she found to her frustration that her arms were somehow catching in the sleeves.

"Dear me," she muttered, "whatever is wrong with this thing? It's darkest before the dawn, isn't it? That's the correct saying. I'm so stupid sometimes."

She twisted her arms, convinced that she could force them down the sleeves, yet if anything they were becoming more stuck then ever. No matter what she tried, she was unable to make the recalcitrant blouse yield, until finally she resolved to push hard. This she did – and a loud tearing sound immediately erupted from the material as one of the sleeves tore away from the shoulder.

"No!" she said with a sigh. "This was one of my best ones, too. It's never going to be the same after I mend it!"

"Time to try," Tilly said, still sitting on the bed. "I hope this works. If it doesn't, I fear I shall be cursed to see the image of the anchoress of St. Jude's forever. Even in my coffin."

"That simply isn't possible," Barbara said with a sigh. Her arms were still caught in the torn blouse as she turned to look at her old friend. "You mustn't think like that, because... wait, what did you just say about a coffin?"

In that moment she froze as she saw that Tilly had her head tilted back and was holding the sharp tip of one of the nails against her damaged left eyeball. In her other hand she was holding a hammer, and she immediately began to tap the nail, driving it down into the eyeball and then tapping again until the tip began to scrape against the back of the socket.

Too horrified to react – and trying to

convince herself that what she saw couldn't possibly be real – Barbara could only watch as Tilly tapped the nail again. This time the bone at the back of the socket could be heard cracking, yet Tilly tapped a couple more times before placing the other nail against her right eye. She began to hammer this nail in too, quickly shattering the socket and driving the nail deeper before stopping as she let out a gasp. A bubble of blood-filled pus erupted from one side of the socket, sending two maggots dribbling down onto the girl's cheek.

"It hasn't worked!" she sobbed suddenly as her face contorted into a vision of anger and terror. "I still see her! What must I do to make her go away? How can I ever make her leave me alone?"

Pulling back, Barbara bumped against the side of the dresser. Feeling her knees starting to weaken, she slid down until she was on the floor and she could only watch in horror as Tilly began to hammer the nails deeper and deeper into her eye sockets – perhaps even into her brain.

"I can still see her!" the girl screamed. "Why can I still see her? She won't shatter! Someone make her go away!"

CHAPTER FIFTEEN

SEVERAL HOURS LATER, SITTING downstairs in the pub, Barbara watched as three men slowly carried Tilly's covered body out through the front door. A few people had gathered outside in the cold night air, drawn by the sound of raised voices, and Tilly's mother could be heard sobbing somewhere in the darkness.

"Drink this," her aunt Bea said, putting a hand on Barbara's shoulder while setting a glass of whiskey in front of her.

"No, I'm -"

"Drink it," Bea said firmly. "It'll make you feel better."

"I -"

"Drink it, girl. Trust me."

As much as she really didn't want the

whiskey – and didn't even like the taste – Barbara was in no mood to argue. Besides, she knew that her aunt was a wise woman, so she took the glass and downed the whiskey in one go, choosing to think of it as medicine rather than alcohol. A shudder passed through her bones as the force of the drink hit her, but as she set the glass down she had to admit that she already felt a little more centred.

"You'll be better off sleeping in the spare room tonight," Bea said softly.

Barbara looked up at her.

"I'll clean up in the morning," Bea continued, clearly choosing her words with care.

"No, I shall clean up," Barbara said, getting to her feet. "I can do it right now."

"No," Bea said firmly.

"But -"

"I said no," Bea added, and now she too was close to tears. "There's not a lot of mess in there, but there's a little. It'll be better for you to go in there in the morning and find it all fresh again."

"Why did she do it?" Barbara asked. "She said she could see her. She must have meant the anchoress of St. Jude's, but that's not possible. She was blind, so how could she still see anything at all?"

"Don't trouble yourself over it," Bea continued. "You'll never get the answers you seek, you'll only drive yourself loopy. Tilly was a troubled girl and -"

"You did this!" a woman's voice screeched, and Barbara turned to see that Elizabeth Whitten had stormed into the pub despite the efforts of several men to hold her back. "It's your fault that my daughter's dead!"

"No," Barbara sobbed, stepping toward her. "Mrs. Whitten, please, I did everything in my power to help Tilly tonight but -"

"You went with her all those years ago!" Elizabeth screamed, and now it was taking the combined efforts of three men to keep her restrained. "My Tilly was a good girl, she never would have gone out to that place if it hadn't been for you! Now she's dead and you're sitting there laughing!"

"I'm not laughing," Barbara said, shaking her head as tears streamed down her face. "You have to believe me, I tried everything to stop Tilly going to the church but she wanted to look inside. I tried to stop her so many times but she was so curious. I don't know what she saw when she looked through that window, but whatever it was, I don't think she ever *stopped* seeing it."

"You're a liar!" Elizabeth snarled, pulling one hand free and pointing at Barbara. "Everyone knows that you were a bad influence on my Tilly, and now look what you've done! She's dead because of you!"

"Come on, Lizzie," a man said, manhandling her out through the front door and back into the night air. "This isn't the time or the place. Let's get you home."

"I tried to help her," Barbara whimpered again, as both Bea and John made their way over and put their hands on her shoulder. "If I could switch places with her, don't you think I would? I never wanted any of this to happen. It's not my fault that Tilly wanted to go to St. Jude's that day!"

***

By the time the crowd had left and everything had settled, Barbara found herself sitting alone in the pub with just the light of a single candle for company. Her aunt and uncle had gone back upstairs to try to get some sleep and she'd promised to follow them, but deep down she knew that she wouldn't be able to rest.

Indeed, in that moment she wondered whether she would be able to sleep ever again.

Finally, at a little before six o'clock in the morning, she got up from her seat and made her way slowly toward the front door. The tears had stopped a while earlier and she felt completely empty, as if she could barely think straight. As she opened the door and stepped out into the cold morning air, she barely even shivered and she certainly wasn't entirely sure where she was going. All she knew was that she had to get out of the pub and try to find peace somewhere.

"Everyone knows that you were a bad influence on my Tilly!" she heard Elizabeth Whitten shouting at her, and now the words were echoing in her thoughts. "She's dead because of you!"

Stepping out across the yard, she stopped at the edge of the road and looked toward the moonlit fields. She couldn't see the church, but she knew it was out there and she couldn't help but imagine it standing all alone and untouched in the night. So many people in the village chose to ignore St. Jude's and preferred to pretend that it wasn't there at all, yet ever since that awful day with Tilly this hadn't been an option for Barbara. She was always painfully aware of the church's presence, as if she could feel it constantly pulling slightly on her soul. Now that sensation was stronger than ever.

"I tried to help her," she remembered herself saying earlier. "If I could switch places with her, don't you think I would?"

Those final words echoed round and round in her thoughts.

"If I could switch places with her, don't you think I would?"

"Perhaps it's not too late," she whispered as a sense of immense guilt once again began to build in her chest. "I might be able to... to reason with the thing in the church. I might be able to get the anchoress to change things."

She knew the idea was desperate, yet deep down some part of her was determined to try. Stepping across the yard, she fetched her bike and climbed onto the saddle. Although she had only the faintest outline of a plan, she told herself that she could figure the rest out on the way. She was going to cycle to the church and break down the door if necessary, and then she was going to find some way to contact the ghostly figure and beg for Tilly's life. While her friend was already dead, she was still hoping that perhaps some way could be found for their fates to be swapped.

A moment later, hearing the pub's front door creaking open, she turned to see her uncle in the doorway.

"Barbara?" he said cautiously. "I couldn't sleep and I heard a noise. What are you doing?"

"I'm going to save her," she replied as fresh tears found their way to her eyes.

"What do you mean?" he asked, stepping outside and making his way over to join her.

"I'm going to save Tilly," she sobbed, although she was already aware that her plan was filled with nothing but desperation.

"Tilly's dead," he reminded her.

"But I might still be able to do something," she continued, even as she heard the sense of hopelessness in her own voice. "Uncle John, please, I have to at least try. The anchoress might -"

"Don't speak like this," he said, cutting her off. "Barbara, I'm serious. There's nothing you can do for Tilly, not now. Her soul is with the Lord and I'm sure she'll be shown mercy. But if you go out there, you'll only be throwing yourself into the clutches of that... that thing. You won't be helping Tilly at all, but you might well be consigning yourself to the same misery that claimed her. Do you really think that's what she'd want?"

"I have to do something," she cried, and now she was starting to break down. "It's not fair! This shouldn't have happened to her!"

"We can agree on that," he said, hugging her tight as she stepped away from the bike. "My girl, I won't let you throw your life away like this. The whole sorry tale of Tilly's death just proves that we were right all along to abandon that church and to pretend that it doesn't exist. If you really want to honour Tilly's memory, you must do it by helping the whole community to avoid the same mistakes that she made. That's not the easy way out, Barbara. In fact, it might just be the hardest task of all."

"But I want to help her," she sobbed, clinging to him tightly. "How can I help her?"

"You can't," he replied. "She's beyond our reach now, but you *can* help others. See that no-one ever makes the same mistake as Tilly again. And help the rest of us, so that we might forget that the wretched place even exists."

CHAPTER SIXTEEN

January 1940...

ONCE BARBARA HAD FINISHED her tale, Harry sat in silence for a moment. Staring at Father Neville's bandaged hands, he tried to make sense of all that he'd just heard; as much as he wanted to exclaim that it was scarcely credible, he worried that he would be doing Barbara a great disservice if he expressed even a scintilla of doubt.

As far as he could tell, she certainly seemed to believe everything she'd just told him.

"So you see," she continued finally, speaking through gritted teeth, "once the pair of you had resolved to go out to that place, there was nothing anyone could do to save you. It's just a miracle that she claimed only one of you and not the other. I suppose in a way that's similar to..."

Her voice trailed off, and she took a moment to pull herself together before slowly getting to her feet.

"If you go out there again," she went on, "now that you know full well the consequences, it will be as if you are spitting upon the grave of my friend Tilly."

"I assure you that we intend no -"

"Spitting!" she hissed angrily. "On her grave! Do you understand?"

"I understand the strength of your conviction in this matter," he replied, choosing his words with care, "and I assure you that neither Father Neville or I ever intended to cause any upset."

"Perhaps *you* did not," she said, keeping her eyes fixed on him. "I can see the innocence in your eyes, and it's clear to me that you knew nothing of that place. But him..."

She turned and looked down at Father Neville for a moment.

"You cannot tell me," she went on, "that he was ignorant of the tale. It's clear to me that he knew exactly what he was getting himself into, yet he was filled with so much arrogance that he believed he was somehow better able to deal with it."

"I must disagree," Harry replied. "Father

Neville is a good man and by no means arrogant."

"You don't know what you're talking about," she said as she headed to the door. "Mark my words, he knew. I don't know how, and I don't know from whom, but he went out there willingly to try to confront the anchoress of St. Jude's. Now look at him. He's on the verge of death and I'm not sure he'll survive another night. Tell me again, when you went out there with him, did you both actually enter the church? Or was he the only one who went inside?"

"We both did," Harry admitted.

"Then consider yourself very lucky to have survived this long," she told him. "*If* you have emerged unscathed, then I can only assume that it's because the anchoress was entirely focused on your associate. I'm certain that you won't be so lucky a second time. Now be told, Father Stone... do not go anywhere near that place again. Find your scrap metal somewhere else, anywhere else – even strip it from this very pub if necessary – but steer clear of St. Jude's."

Stopping for a moment, she turned to him.

"I still sense Tilly from time to time," she went on. "Although she's dead, sometimes I feel as if some aspect of her lingers. And no matter how much I try to tidy them away, from time to time I still find nails around the place. Perhaps there's some other explanation, but I can't shake the fear that in some way she's reminding me of her presence. And of my role in all the terrible things that happened to her."

"Who is this anchoress you speak of?" he asked as she walked away. "You mentioned her a few times, but I don't quite understand. Who is she and how does she inspire such fear in the people of this village?"

Hearing a gasping sound, he turned to see that Father Neville was stirring.

"It's alright," he told the older man, taking a cup of water from the side and moving it closer to his lips. "Do you want to drink?"

He waited, but now he realised that although he had moved a few times, Father Neville was in fact still not conscious. Instead his eyes remained closed and he seemed to be lost – trapped, even – in some kind of nightmare. And the more he watched the man's lined and weathered face, the more Harry found himself wondering just what could be going on in his mind, and what had been going through his thoughts when he'd tried to gouge his wrists open.

"I shall leave this here," he said finally, setting the cup back down as he realised that he had never in all his life felt so utterly useless. "You can... you can drink it when you wake up."

"*If* you wake up," he almost added – but did not.

***

"It's someone for you," John said, holding the telephone receiver as Harry made his way into the pub's back room. "They only just called and I heard you coming down the stairs, so I told them to wait a minute. I'm not sure that went down very well."

"Thank you," Harry replied, taking the receiver.

As John left the room, Harry turned to watch him go. Ever since he'd first set foot in the Red Lion he'd felt as if the welcome was a frosty one, and now he was perhaps starting to understand why. If John and the others shared even one tenth of Barbara's feelings about St. Jude's, they were probably desperately opposed to the idea of anyone going out there. At the same time he told himself that some local superstitions were truer than others, and he still couldn't quite be sure that things had happened exactly as Barbara had described.

If she was correct, then why in the name of all that was holy would Father Neville have behaved as he had?

"Hello?" he said as he put the receiver to his ear. "This is Father Stone speaking, I -"

"Is Father Neville not able to come to the telephone?" the voice on the other end of the line asked, interrupting him with a sense of urgency.

"No, I'm afraid not," Harry replied. "As I mentioned before, he -"

"Very well," the voice continued, sounding much more hurried and tense than earlier, to the extent that Harry wasn't even entirely sure that it was the same person. "Have there been any other developments?"

"There has hardly been time for any developments," he admitted. "Father Neville is resting here at the Red Lion for now, but it is quite clear to me that he should be moved as soon as he is well enough. He is ailing and certainly not out of the woods yet. I think that tomorrow at the latest I should take him to -"

"No," the voice said firmly.

"I beg your pardon?"

"Under no circumstances are you to leave," the voice continued. "That is a direct order from the highest authority. You and Father Neville are to remain in the village and await further instructions."

"I'm not sure that I follow," Harry said cautiously, convinced that he must have missed some terribly important part of the order that would make the rest make sense. "What -"

"Do you think Father Neville will be in a fit state to speak tomorrow?" the voice asked.

"I cannot say for certain," Harry admitted, "but it seems to be the common consensus here that he is gravely ill. If he were to rise from his bed between now and the end of the week, I would consider that to be quite the miracle. Which is to say that, no, I do not believe that he will be able to speak to you tomorrow."

He waited for an answer, but in truth he was starting to question exactly why Father Sloane refused to speak to him directly and why instead he was always forced to talk to this intermediary. For a moment he found himself wondering exactly what he hadn't been told and whether Father Neville might have been keeping a few secrets; he quickly told himself, however, that he absolutely must not think such thoughts at any cost, and he tried to focus on the belief that Father Neville's honour and wisdom must not under any circumstances be impugned.

"You have your instructions," the voice on the telephone said. "I shall relay your comments to Father Sloane. In the meantime, under no circumstances are you or Father Neville to try to leave the village or its surrounding area. Is that clear?"

"It is," Harry replied, "but might I ask why the -"

Before he could get another word out, he heard a clicking sound that indicated the end of the call. Somewhat shocked at the abruptness, he lowered the receiver and tried to make sense of everything he had just heard. Quickly, however, he came to the conclusion that he simply was not privy to all the necessary information, so he told himself to merely obey his instructions and wait in the hope that Father Neville would soon wake up.

Just as he was about to go through to the main bar and seek out a sandwich, he happened to glance at the little wooden shelf directly beneath the telephone. He felt sure that there had been nothing there before, yet now he reached out and picked up a single black nail – just like the nail he had previously found upstairs.

***

Upstairs in one of the bedrooms, Father Neville remained flat on his back with his eyes closed. Since Harry had left the room, nobody had been to check on the ailing priest, whose only recognition of the outside world seemed to be a few occasional gasps that rose from his lips. He turned his head slightly sometimes, as if locked in a nightmare, while his bandaged hands and wrists remained crossed over his chest.

Had anyone stopped in the doorway and looked through at the priest, they would likely have seen only the man himself on the bed. For reasons perhaps known only to the Lord, they would undoubtedly not have been able to see the second person who had joined Father Neville in the bed from the moment he had first been placed there: curled up next to him, with a comforting hand resting on his chest, Tilly Whitten's ghostly figure was doing her utmost to keep him company and to help him drive away the worst of the nightmares that even now were filling his mind.

Again, though, it must be stressed that nobody else had seen Tilly in this way or had expressed any indication that her presence had been noted. Even Barbara had seemed unaware. Tilly was merely curled up on the bed next to the priest, keeping a hand on his chest as if to try to let him know that no matter what had happened to him, and no matter the anguish now filling his mind, he was not alone.

CHAPTER SEVENTEEN

AS SOON AS HE reached the graveyard surrounding St. Jude's, Harry stopped in his tracks. Ahead, the wooden door had been left open, as if Father Neville had rushed away from the place in a hurry.

Until that moment, Harry had told himself that he had plenty of time to come up with a plan. After his conversation on the phone with someone from Father Sloane's office, he'd been left with a feeling of utter helplessness. Father Neville was still unconscious and Barbara's rather vague warnings had failed to answer many of his questions. Finally he'd resolved to simply get on with the task at hand, to carry out the survey of St. Jude's so that at least – when Father Neville eventually woke up – the bulk of their work would be complete. As for any lingering concerns about a mysterious ghostly presence at the church, he'd told himself while cycling away from the village that he could figure that out later.

Now, however, he found himself feeling increasingly concerned as he stared at the open doorway and wondered exactly what had happened inside the church to leave his superior in such a dreadful state. He knew Father Neville to be a strong, stalwart man who was in no way given to panic; the fact that this very same man had been driven to cut his own wrists thus left Harry with a sense of grave concern, yet he still couldn't bring himself to believe all the hushed warnings that had been uttered by Barbara.

Superstition, he told himself, was not going to stop him getting to work. And he wasn't going to be swayed by the words of a young woman who seemed, at best, rather hysterical.

Forcing himself to keep going, then, he strode as confidently as he could manage toward the church. He slowed to examine a couple of gravestones, but he knew deep down that he was only playing for time. As he reached the front door he briefly considered stopping again and trying to rationalize his choice further, but instead he made himself step across the threshold and into the church.

***

After just a couple more paces, Harry stopped and saw perhaps the strangest sight that had yet confronted him during his twenty-nine years in this world.

One of the pews at the rear of the church had been broken apart – kicked, it seemed – and two lengths of wood had been ripped away; these lengths had then been tied together using a length of cord taken from a curtain next to the door, and the result had been the creation of a crude but rather large crucifix. What had become of this crucifix next was not clear, although a small amount of blood was drying on the wood. In the end the crucifix had evidently been discarded on the floor just a few feet from the door, as if dropped by a man fleeing in haste.

A man such as Father Stanley Neville.

Reaching down, Harry picked the crucifix up and turned it around. It had clearly been made very quickly, and when he pulled gently at the cord he found that it came away easily enough; the bar of the crucifix fell down and clattered against the floor, leaving Harry holding nothing more than a piece of broken pew.

What, he wondered, could have driven a sane and rational man such as Father Neville to cause such damage?

Setting the remains of the crucifix aside, he began to make his way along the aisle. His footsteps rang out loudly in the church – perhaps a little too loudly for his liking, although he knew he should have no reason for concern – and he was rather relieved when he stopped at the crossing and there was no further need for his footsteps to cause any noise at all.

He looked over at one transept and then at the other, and then he observed the altar up ahead.

Here, at least, there was no sign of anything amiss. He turned and looked all around, and from this particular vantage point the entire church seemed to be utterly unharmed, at least so long as he ignored the damaged pew at the far end. This view calmed his worries somewhat, and as he began to make his way over to the north transept he told himself that he had perhaps allowed Barbara's fantastic tales to burrow a little too deeply into his thoughts.

And then, as he passed the raised wooden pulpit, he froze as he realised that here too something was wrong.

He had scarcely paid any attention to the pulpit during his first visit to the church, yet he felt sure that he would have noticed if – as now – the wood had been so terribly scratched and damaged. Reaching out, he touched one of several thick grooves that had been cut into the wood, grooves that in some places had almost broken through to the other side. It was, he caught himself noting, as if some ferocious beast like a lion or a tiger had attacked the thing, and at the top some more shards of wood had been broken away.

Stepping around the pulpit, he noticed more signs of a confrontation. When he saw the steps leading up, however, he realised that at least the pulpit's entrance had been left unmolested. Whatever force had seen fit to attack the pulpit's exterior had been unwilling or unable to actually enter and cause yet more damage.

Making his way into the pulpit, Harry took a moment to look down at the broken top. His imagination was already running into overdrive and he was starting to imagine Father Neville hiding in the pulpit, perhaps cowering on the wooden floor as some terrible force attacked from all sides. Would the power of prayer have been enough to keep any sinful entity out? He quickly dismissed the idea as frivolous and foolish in the extreme, yet as he climbed back down from the pulpit he couldn't help but wonder what other explanation might make sense.

Had some terrible beast, perhaps escaped from a zoo, broken into the church and attacked Father Neville? And then had it... had it rushed away into the Welsh countryside, never to be seen again?

Stepping over to the altar, he soon realised that his earlier estimation had been incorrect. While he had believed the altar to be untouched, now he saw to his horror that several thick boot prints had been left on the surface, as if somebody had been possessed of sufficient temerity to actually climb up and stand on this holiest of spots. The idea scarcely seemed possible, yet the boot prints were clear for anyone to see. Although he knew for certain that Father Neville would never in a million years do something so sacrilegious, nevertheless he briefly wondered whether there was any calamity that might compel even a man of the Lord to act in such a way.

Unable to comprehend what might have happened, he stepped around past the altar and looked toward the sacristy, and in that moment he saw that something else was amiss. Making his way closer, he spotted a considerable amount of white dust on the floor, accompanied by thick marks – almost grooves – that had been worn into the stone wall. A small trowel had been left on the floor nearby, and the obvious implication was that somebody had used that trowel in an attempt to wear through the wall itself.

Reaching out, he touched the rough surface, and he felt sure that there was no reason why anybody would ever launch such a furious assault, but he also knew that the wall had been undamaged just twenty-four hours earlier.

"Why?" he whispered as he imagined Father Neville frantically hacking at this exact spot. "What could have possessed you to do such things?"

For a moment he imagined Father Neville racing around in the church, which of course would have been dark during the night – save, at most, for the light of a solitary candle. At some point the older man appeared to have worked hard to wear down a patch on the wall, then he'd stepped onto the altar before taking refuge in the pulpit from... well, there Harry's mind drew a blank, for he couldn't imagine what might have driven Father Neville to such extremes of fear. And then, somehow, the man had made his way along the aisle toward the door, only to break apart a pew and use the pieces of wood to construct a crude crucifix.

Then he'd left the church and had walked back to the village, arriving shortly after sunrise only to try to cut his own wrists open.

"This makes no sense whatsoever," he said under his breath as he began to wonder whether some mad vagrant had invaded the church, and whether it had been the vagrant who had done all these strange things.

If that had been the case, however, why would Father Neville have reacted in such an unusual manner?

Telling himself that perhaps these questions

should wait until – hopefully – Father Neville emerged from his sleep, Harry took out his notebook and tried to work out where he should start with the day's activities. He very much wanted to present Father Neville with an extensive list of metal and other precious items in the church, so he walked back over to the altar and supposed that this would be the best place to commence his work. He opened the notebook and turned to a new page, then he carefully wrote the date at the top and underlined it, and then he looked down at the metal railing that ran along the edge of the nearest wall.

"Stop!"

Startled, he turned and looked back along the aisle, and to his astonishment he saw Barbara standing in the open doorway at the far end.

"Are you out of your mind?" she shouted, and now her voice was filled with terror. "Get out! Get out of this church while you still can!"

CHAPTER EIGHTEEN

"WHAT ARE YOU DOING here?" Harry asked, shocked by her sudden arrival. "I thought -"

"Did you not listen to a word I told you this morning?" she shouted, sounding as if she was closer than ever to rage. "How could you possibly hear all of that and still come out here?"

"I -"

"Are you an idiot?"

"Well," he stammered, "no, at least I would hope not, I merely -"

"Then what the hell are you doing here?"

"I have a job to do," he said awkwardly, holding up the notebook as if he believed that this would somehow serve as proof. "I -"

"Did you not see what happened to your dear Father Neville?" she continued, and now the anger in her voice seemed to have become tinged with bitterness. "Did you not see how he's fighting for his life right now? Does that not matter to you at all? Do you want to end up in the bed next to him – or worse?"

"I was given my instructions and I intend to carry them out," he replied. Again he held up the notebook; again he seemed to think that this prop was enough to justify his actions, although he was feeling a little less certain now. "When Father Neville wakes up, I want to show him that I have completed the task so that he no longer has to worry. I telephoned Father Sloane's office and was told in no uncertain terms to stay here."

"You were told?"

"Yes."

"By who?"

"By... the authorities."

"What authorities?"

"The church authorities?" he replied, although he immediately wondered why he had allowed that answer to sound more like a question. "The church authorities," he said again, trying to sound more definite.

"And you just do as you're told, do you?" she continued.

"No, but -"

"If the church authorities told you to dive off the top of this place, would you do it?"

"I consider it highly unlikely that -"

"You're driving me out of my mind!" she snapped.

Letting out a sigh, she turned as if she meant to walk away. Almost immediately, however, she turned to look through at him again.

"I told you about Tilly," she continued, and now she sounded close to tears. "I told you what happened to her here."

"You did, and -"

"But you still came out here?" she shouted, before sighing again. "Seriously? When my uncle told me that you'd asked to borrow his bike, I assumed there must be some mistake. I told him that while you might seem like a somewhat weak man, you would never be so foolish as to ignore all the warnings!"

"Well," he said, feeling a little stung by her words – but quickly reminding himself to ignore his own sense of pride, "I wouldn't say that I'm weak, exactly."

"Please come out of there," she added. "I'm begging you. Can't you sense the evil in the air? Can't you sense her presence? I know she's unlikely to come out during the day, but still, you risk attracting her attention. Father Neville made the mistake of thinking that he could handle her, and you've seen what has become of him. You are not even as well prepared as he was, so please, come out immediately. Before it's too late."

As if she absolutely could not step across the threshold and enter the church, she held out a hand toward him.

"Please," she continued.

As much as he wanted to tell her that she was fussing over nothing, Harry felt as if he should at least try to be a little more conciliatory. After glancing around, then, he slipped his notebook away before making his way along the aisle. The sound of his footsteps filled the air until he walked around the damaged pew and stopped in front of the door. Barbara immediately reached out and tried to grab his hand, but she was a little too far away and once more she refused to actually set foot inside the church.

"Who are you talking about?" Harry asked.

"Just come outside."

"You have referred to a woman before," he continued, "yet it should be plain for you to see right now that there is no woman here. I have looked around quite extensively and nobody is hiding anywhere."

"The anchoress is hiding," she said firmly. "That's what she has been doing for all these years. Hiding... and waiting."

"Anchoress?"

"You know what an anchoress is, do you not?"

"Of course I do, but that's beside the -"

"Tell me," she said, cutting him off once again. "Tell me what you *think* an anchoress is."

"An anchoress," he replied cautiously, "is a female anchorite, a person who has chosen to live entirely apart from the rest of the world. She seeks shelter in a church, usually in a confined room where she can spend the rest of her life seeking a closer connection to God. She is fed by the members of the church, one of them might speak to her briefly once a year, but otherwise the anchoress – or anchorite – is dedicated entirely to the task of religious thought. Any anchorite or anchoress is a person of great piety, but I am not aware of there ever having been one at St. Jude's."

"That is where you are wrong," she told him, spitting each word out with furious determination. "There *was* an anchoress here once, many years ago. And she's still here. Even all these decades after her death, her spirit haunts this church." She paused for a moment, as if she was scared to speak the next words. "And she is vengeful."

***

"She went *where*?" Seth Wallace said, clearly shocked by the news as he stood at the bar of the Red Lion. "Are you sure? Barbara of all people?"

"She won't have gone inside," John muttered as he set a pint of beer down. "Not Barbara. There's no force in the world strong enough to drag her into that place."

"But the priest, though," Seth continued. "First one and now another."

"Evidently she thinks that she can dissuade him from continuing. I don't know, personally I wouldn't go out there for all the money in the world. Barbara's different, though. She's always been a kind and caring young woman. If she thinks she can help Father Stone – and that he needs help – she'll surely try her best. I'm starting to think I shouldn't have let the fellow borrow my bike, but then is it right to turn down a request from a man of the cloth?"

"I know Barbara's kind and caring," Seth said, "but... I mean, even kindness has limits, does it not?"

"I don't like it any more than you do," John said firmly as another customer wandered into the pub. "I always knew something like this would happen, though. After all that fuss with young Tilly, there were many people in this village who thought St. Jude's could be shut up and forgotten about. Not me, though. I know how the world works and I know that some damn fool'll always come along who thinks his ideas are better."

"Are you talking about those two priests?"

Humphrey asked as he joined them at the bar.

"If you ask me," Seth continued, "any fool who wants to go to St. Jude's should be allowed to do so, but on one condition. Whatever happens to 'em out there, they're not to drag it back into the village where it can hurt anyone else. And they're not to go begging for any sympathy or pity, either." He glanced at the ceiling. "That older priest's in this very pub, isn't he?"

"He's unconscious," John replied. "I wouldn't be surprised if he fails to last another night."

"Is he that bad?" Humphrey asked.

John nodded.

"What I mean," Seth said, "is that anything that happens in that church should *stay* there. And if it was up to me, I'd have that priest upstairs carted out and taken back to St. Jude's, then I'd throw him in and lock the door. If he wanted to be a bloody idiot and go poking around in something that doesn't concern him, then he should bloody well be the only one to deal with the consequences."

"You might be right there," Humphrey admitted. "So far it seems that nothing from the church can actually reach us here, but this priest seems to be testing that idea to its limits." Now he too looked at the ceiling. "It's tempting fate, that's what it's doing. Memories aren't long enough, not when we're talking about something that can outlast generations. This is what I've been worried about from the start. As time goes on, new folk arrive who don't remember the worst things. They weren't around to see what happened to Tilly Whitten, or they never heard about the anchoress from anyone who actually saw her in the flesh."

"And then the whole thing becomes a joke," Seth interjected, continuing his friend's train of thought. "A big laugh. Sometimes to be prodded now and again. That's when you get kids going out there for the thrill."

"Like young Tilly and Barbara," Humphrey reminded him.

"Like young Tilly and Barbara," Seth agreed, before turning to John. "What's the matter with you, anyway? You've gone awful quiet all of a sudden."

"I just don't like Barbara involving herself in the priests' work, that's all," John said darkly. "I remember what she went through when she was just a child. Her own parents damn near denounced her, and I'm not sure where she'd be now if Bea and I hadn't taken her in. I remember the screaming nightmares she used to have, too, when she first came to live with us. Just when I thought she was getting back on her own two feet and starting to move past all the unpleasantness, these priests arrive and bring it all back out into the open. And for what? Some metal?"

"It's a rum deal, that's for sure," Humphrey grumbled.

"I just hope that's *all* it is," John added, before looking up at the ceiling as he too contemplated the room in which Father Neville was recuperating. "And I hope I'm wrong, too, because there's something about that older priest that I don't like. I can't be sure, but I swear... I've seen him somewhere before. I don't think this is his first visit to the village."

AMY CROSS

CHAPTER NINETEEN

"IT ALL LOOKS SO very peaceful from this vantage point," Harry said finally, after a stretch of silence that had lasted for several minutes, standing in the graveyard and looking out at the immense peaks and troughs of the Welsh valleys. "I confess that this is a part of the world I have never visited before, but with which I am now very rapidly falling in love."

He paused for a moment before realising that he should perhaps correct his choice of wording.

"I am becoming fond of the area, that's all," he added, turning to Barbara and immediately seeing the fear in her eyes. "There's true beauty here."

Following her gaze, he looked once more at

the facade of St. Jude's looming high beyond the spot where he had stopped after leaving the church.

"Father Neville told me that I would take to this area," he continued, trying to keep the conversation on a more pleasant topic as he looked at Barbara again. "I believe he has been to Wales before, when he was a much younger man. He didn't quite go into any details, but he was certainly very sure that I would find the natural scenery to be peaceful. In this, as in everything else, he was most correct."

"Why are you really here?" she asked.

"I believe I have told you more than once," he replied. "We have been asked to -"

"There are hundreds, if not thousands, of churches all across the country," she pointed out. "Have priests been sent to check on all of *those* as well?"

"I do not believe so."

"Then why here?" she continued. "Why have you two been sent specifically to this abandoned, almost forgotten church when there are so many others that could be checked first?"

"I suppose its state of isolation makes it an ideal starting point," Harry suggested. "Given that it is not in use, and that it is so far removed from anywhere, perhaps it was felt that people would be less concerned about items being removed?" He paused for a moment as he realised that there were several faults with that line of reasoning. "Of course," he added, "we did have to travel quite far, and Father Neville did specify this particular church very quickly. Indeed, I believe it was he who came up with the idea of the whole endeavour."

She watched the church for a moment longer before turning to him again.

"He wanted to travel alone," Harry added, "but Father Sloane was absolutely insistent that somebody should accompany him. I don't quite know why. I suppose that's when I drew the short straw. Or the long one, perhaps. They probably felt that I was the most disposable, and that my absence wouldn't unduly affect too many other things."

He thought about that idea for a few seconds.

"Well, I don't see the need to dwell on such uncertainties," he went on. "I'm here now and I'm very much keen to get to work."

"I don't believe you," she replied.

"I beg your -"

"I don't believe that your bosses, or whoever sent you here, did so without knowing all about St. Jude's," she told him. "I think your Father Neville, for one, must have been fully aware." She looked him up and down for a moment. "I can believe that *you* don't have a clue, though."

"Me?" Feeling a little awkward, he took a moment to loosen his collar, which suddenly felt rather tight. "And why might that be?"

"You just seem a quite... credulous," she explained.

"I do?"

She nodded.

"I assure you that I would know if there had been any... hidden agenda," he continued, even though he wasn't entirely confident that this was true. "Father Neville and I have a very good working relationship and I can't for one second imagine that he would keep anything back from me."

"So he told you all about the anchoress?"

"He -"

In that moment, realising that he could no longer protest, he took a deep breath.

"Got you," Barbara said darkly. "It's interesting, don't you think? Why do you think Father Neville deliberately chose not to tell you the history of this place? You don't have a clue about the anchoress Margaret Crake, do you?"

"Who?"

"Margaret Crake," she continued, fixing him with a determined stare before looking past him and seeing the church's front door. "More than a century ago, she took up residence here at St. Jude's. Everyone in the area knows the story, even if most of them don't want to admit it. Mention her name in the pub or anywhere else in the village and most people will pretend to have no idea what you're talking about."

She paused for a moment as a shiver ran through her bones.

"But Margaret's story is burned into the minds of everyone here," she added finally. "Some even fear that telling the tale might encourage her spirit to return, but I know that's not possible. For in truth... she has never really left."

***

1825...

"Father, let me assure you that I have made up my mind and nothing shall deter me. If I cannot be accommodated here at St. Jude's, I shall simply seek charity elsewhere."

"It is not a matter of charity," Father Brook said cautiously as he sat with Margaret on a pew inside the church. "I must confess that I am merely surprised by this request. Margaret, are you sure that you have thought it through?"

"The world of man holds nothing for me," she told him. "I walk the streets of our village and see only coarseness and roughness... drunkenness... so much suffering... I cannot comprehend any of it and I feel as if day by day, week by week and year by year I am drifting further away from a connection to the Lord. Sometimes I even fear that..."

Her voice trailed off.

"Can I be completely honest with you, Father?" she added.

"Of course," he nodded.

"Sometimes I fear that the horrors of the world are going to cause me to turn my face away from the light," she went on, lowering her voice a little as if she worried that she might be overheard. "I must either strengthen my faith or let it shatter into a thousand pieces."

A moment later she glanced over her shoulder to make sure that nobody else had slipped unnoticed into the church and might overhear her. She watched the shadows, waiting in case some of them might suddenly move and spit out someone lurking in their depths.

"I know that it is not the matter of a single decision," she continued, turning to the priest again. "I must prove myself, and I am willing to do that over and over again. My only wish in this life now is to devote myself entirely to prayer and solitude. It is through this endeavour, I believe, that I might yet prove useful to the world."

"I do not believe that there has ever been an anchoress at St. Jude's," Father Brook admitted. "We are but a small parish, mostly unnoticed by others. If word were to spread that we had an anchoress among us, people might come from far and wide to witness such a thing."

"I seek not fame, Father," she said firmly, "nor virtue. It is private prayer that will occupy my mind, although I know that I shall be consulted from time to time on certain subjects. I do not claim to have any great insight into matters of the church, which I am sure would be better left to your good self, but I shall help where I can."

She hesitated yet again.

"Ten years have passed since I lost my Thomas at Waterloo," she added, and now her voice betrayed a hint of true sorrow. "I have no further interest in the material world."

"You understand, I hope," he replied, "that an anchoress has certain responsibilities. Never again shall you touch the flesh of another person. You shall not be permitted to leave your cell or -"

"I know all of this," she told him, clearly a little irritated by his persistent insinuation that she hadn't given the matter a great deal of thought already. Reaching up, she wiped away a solitary tear. "I have wrestled with this decision for several years and I know that there is no going back."

She hesitated, watching his every breath as she tried to discern whether or not she had managed to get through to him. Although she knew she faced an uphill struggle, and that as a woman she was far less likely to be taken seriously, she had studied

Father Brook for a while and had tried to fit her entreaties to his personality. She also believed that at the end of the day her genuine faith and hope would shine through and that the Lord would see that she became a true follower.

"It will take time to build a cell for you," the priest said finally, as if he was slowly getting past his reluctance. "Let me assure you, however. If you make this decision, there can be no going back. You shall be an anchoress for the rest of your mortal life, and as such you shall be considered dead to the world."

"That is all I ask," she told him. "It is all I have prayed for."

CHAPTER TWENTY

TEN YEARS LATER, AS she sat in her small cell in one corner of St. Jude's, Margaret Crake listened to the sound of voices drifting through to her from somewhere outside.

Although she had spoken to no-one other than Father Brook for almost an entire decade, she still enjoyed hearing occasional snippets of conversation from other people. Her heart was gladdened by the thought that the world was still going on out there, and that the people of the local area were living their lives free from the shadow of war and suffering. She had no desire to go back among them, of course, and after a moment she turned and looked across her little living area.

The cell was only ten feet by ten, and barely any taller. There was a simple wooden door that had not been opened in many years, and only a small window through which food and water could be supplied. She had specifically insisted that there should be no bed, since she was determined to avoid any comforts, and when she needed to sit she simply made do with the floor. A wooden chair had been provided against her wishes, but she rarely availed herself of its comfort. The walls themselves were made of stone and felt firm to the touch, and Margaret had long since moved past any hint of claustrophobia. As far as she was concerned, this retreat was the most perfect place in all the world.

Sometimes people would call to her from outside, but she always ignored them. As she sought to better understand her relationship with the Lord, she conversed only with Father Brook... and even then, she spoke to him only one time each year, whether she had anything to say or not. He conveyed the occasional question from members of the congregation, and Margaret in turn tried her best to provide thoughtful answers.

She had never once wavered in her devotion, although there was one aspect of her confinement that troubled her. Occasionally – just occasionally – a particularly irritating gentleman would linger outside in the graveyard and would try to rile her up with questions that she knew were intended merely to shake her faith.

On this particular day, he had returned,

although after his initial barrage of comments he had fallen quiet for a few minutes. She knew from bitter experience, however, that he was not done yet.

"How are you on this fine morning?" the man asked finally. "Have you made any progress?"

Resisting the urge to reply, Margaret knelt on the rough stone floor and began to pray for the man's soul.

"You're awfully quiet in there," he continued. "I'd be tempted to wonder whether you're still there at all, but I know you don't like to talk much. You save your tongue for Father Brook, do you not?"

She moved her mouth silently, asking the Lord to help this poor unfortunate soul so that he might gain the peace he so desperately needed.

"And how does he like that tongue?" the man purred. "Do you slip it between the cheeks of his arse?"

A shiver ran through Margaret's bones, but she had become accustomed to the man's foul language over the years and she knew he was only trying to get a rise out of her. Instead of reacting, she forced herself to focus on the need to pray and pray again for the soul of the poor wretch. Even if his mind was already too far gone to be entirely saved, she hoped very much that she might be able to nudge him back toward the right path.

"You're still a woman," he murmured. "Do you ever pleasure yourself in there? Does your hand ever reach down under the hem of your dress and start to dip into that slit between your legs? Does it dip into the sweet pink hole you keep hidden away?"

"He knows not what he says," Margaret whispered under her breath, making sure that even now there was no way the man would be able to hear her. "There must be some goodness in him somewhere, deep down. Please help him to find this goodness and encourage it to grow, so that it might overcome the dark and evil elements of his soul."

"I know what'd sort you out," the man snarled. "Give me five minutes in there and I'd get the job done. I'd turn you around and press you against the wall, and then I'd insert myself in your plump hole and pound you until you screamed for a very different master. Don't you think you'd enjoy that? And then I'd pull my weapon out and shove it into your deepest parts and I'd keep going until you could taste me in the back of your mouth and -"

"Stop!" she snapped suddenly, turning and looking over at the tiny window at the top of the far wall.

Immediately frustrated by her reaction, she watched the window. She knew it was too high up for the man to reach, but she felt sure that he was staring up at it from the wall's other side; she knew, too, that he no doubt meant every word of his threats and that he would carry them out in gross detail if only he could find a way through the wall or the door.

"So you *are* listening, eh?" the man continued. "Tell me, are your fingers gummy? Can you imagine what I'd taste like as I emptied myself into that pathetic hole you call a mouth? It'd be like a meal of oysters slipping down your throat."

"Lord, forgive me my weaknesses," she said, returning to prayer even as she heard the man still shouting invectives and foul suggestions from outside the church. She expected him to continue for many hours, possibly until sundown. "Give me the strength I need to be your humble servant in both this world and the next."

She could hear the man still snarling outside, throwing out words – Whore! Pussy! - that she knew were calculated to cut through to her, but she resolved to resist.

"Show him the mercy that he does not show to others," she continued, raising her voice now in an attempt to drown out his voice. "If there is but a glimmer of decency in his heart – and I am sure that there must be – then grant that glimmer a chance to grow and bloom."

***

At night the church was dark and silent, and these were the times that Margaret reserved for her deepest moments of contemplation. Her habit was to rest from sundown for a few hours, but she always woke around midnight – or at least she assumed it must be midnight, despite having no means of telling for sure – and entered into a state of profound spiritual consideration.

And it was in these moments that she felt most closely connected to the Lord.

On her knees once more, she kept her hands clasped in front of her bowed face and tried to imagine how wonderful the world would be if only its people could embrace the word of God. She thought of all war and hatred and hunger ending, and of all people working together to worship their master and build a better place. She felt sure that all the necessary parts were available, if only men and women around the world could set aside their differences and work for a common good. And although part of her worried that such a state of perfection might never come to pass, she clung to the hope that by some miracle the word of God might reach into every heart and bring comfort and hope to every life.

At first she barely noticed the sound of footsteps approaching her cell. Finally, however, she turned and looked at the wooden door as the footsteps stopped on the other side.

"Father Brook?" she whispered, wondering whether for some reason the priest had returned at such a late hour.

She waited, but now she heard no more footsteps. Instead, however, she noticed something else, a kind of low growling sound that seemed to be rumbling just beyond the door's bare wooden form.

"Father Brook?"

Slowly getting to her feet, and feeling a twinge of pain in both knees in the process, she brushed herself down before staring at the door. There was just enough moonlight shining through the tiny window behind her to illuminate the door's wooden panels, and Margaret couldn't help but feel a shiver run through her bones as she imagined somebody standing on the other side, somebody who evidently had seen fit to enter the church so late at night.

She wanted to call out again, but she reminded herself that it was really not her place to initiate contact with anyone. If some fellow had found a way into the church and had approached the cell then -

Suddenly a loud bang caused the door to shake, and Margaret immediately took a step back. Her heart was racing now and she told herself that there was no reason to be fearful, yet she was unable to shake the sense that something dangerous was waiting out there on the other side of such a flimsy piece of wood. Had Father Brook forgotten to lock the church for the night? She was sure that -

Before she could finish that thought, something slammed against the door again, then two more times with increasing force.

Dropping back down onto her knees, Margaret clasped her hands together and began to pray for deliverance. While the footsteps had sounded human, the force smashing against the door now seemed more like some kind of animal, although she had no idea what could be causing such damage. She briefly looked at the door again and saw a split starting to form straight down the middle, and a moment later another impact caused the wood to shudder violently in its frame.

"Lord, protect me," she whispered, trying not to panic as she clasped her hands together tighter than ever – and as the force outside, whatever it might be, continued to try to beat the door down. "I am your humble servant. I ask for your protection as I seek greater answers to your mystery and -"

In that moment an angry, semi-human snarl rang out. Gasping, Margaret opened her eyes and looked at the door, fully expecting it to have been broken open. Instead she saw that it was back to normal, showing no sign of damage at all, and a few seconds later she heard footsteps slowly walking away back across the church. Not daring to move her hands apart, however, she waited until the sound of footsteps was entirely gone before bowing her head once more and returning to her private and most urgent prayers.

CHAPTER TWENTY-ONE

1885...

"I KNOW THAT THESE are difficult times," Father Wardell said as he stood in the pulpit at St. Jude's and looked out at the nervous faces of his congregation, "but I command you all to trust not only in the Lord but also in Her Majesty Queen Victoria."

A murmur of agreement rippled across the gathered villagers, although many remained silent and simply watched the priest with increasingly common expressions of concern.

"I might share with you some wise words that were offered to me just a few weeks ago," the priest continued, "when I was speaking to a learned visitor who passed this way. He reminded me that while politicians in London might continually argue with one another and make great howls of noise -"

Now some members of the congregation couldn't help but laugh.

"Ultimately that is *all* they do," he went on, allowing himself the faintest of smiles. "They produce noise. Not hope, not courage, not a vision of the future... just noise, and when they inevitably move on they are replaced by others who create their own brand of noise altogether. Now, far be it for me to stray into the questionable moral realm of politics -"

More laughter.

"- but let me add only this. Whether Mr. Gladstone or the Marquess of Salisbury might form the government one month from now, our fields will grow the same and our little village will continue quite unmolested. Let the politicians have their moments in the sun, for they are naught but -"

Suddenly a brief cry rang out from somewhere inside the church. Although Father Wardell very consciously did not turn to acknowledge this cry, the entire congregation turned their heads almost as one, staring in the general direction of the cell that they knew contained the anchoress. Even a young boy, who sat with a man who appeared to be his father, looked in that direction – as if he too understood that something was very wrong.

"They are naught," Father Wardell continued quickly, keen to distract everyone from the interruption, "and they who came before them were also naught. We are also blessed in our certainty that -"

He flinched as he heard another cry, this time one that lasted for a few more seconds and sounded particularly ragged. He knew that everyone in the church understood exactly where the sound had come from, but he also knew that no good would come of naming the source out loud. Far better, he had learned over the years, to ignore any brief disturbances and to instead allow the anchoress to steady her own nerves.

"We are also blessed," he went on carefully, choosing each word with care in the hope that he could regain the attention of the congregation's members, many of whom were still staring in the direction of the cell, "in our certainty that the Lord protects us. Our world extends barely as far as we can see, for we are only -"

In that moment another cry filled the air, this one sounding far more anguished them the rest. A murmur of questions spread through the congregation, and many of the gathered villagers were becoming visibly rather agitated. The cry, meanwhile, was lasting much longer than usual and was only now petering out to become a gurgling, rasping whimper. Father Wardell had heard similar noises coming from the cell for a while now, but he was sure in his belief that the anchoress was merely expressing some degree of anguish associated with her extremely advanced age. She was, after all, almost one hundred years old now – and she had been resident in the church for more than half that time.

He had spoken to nobody about his concerns, yet he had for a while now been wondering whether her mind was starting to fail.

"Let us pray," he continued, raising his voice just a little in an attempt to drown out the occasional wails and groans that now drifted out from the cell. "Please, I invite you all to bow your heads and contemplate the words of our saviour. Will you all join me now in offering a prayer for our next harvest?"

***

"We are indeed fortunate to have in our midst an anchoress," Father Wardell said as he led his visitor Father Kent across the graveyard. "There are many who have come to our church to beg an audience of her, although in truth she speaks to very few."

"She must be busy with her deep thoughts on a great many matters," Father Kent opined with the calmness for which he was so well known. "It was your predecessor Father Brook who accepted her here at St. Jude's, was it not?"

"Indeed, and I bless his memory every day for that act of foresight," Father Wardell said, opening the door at the front of the church and stepping inside. "I only hope that the poor man rests in eternal peace now. It is as if -"

Stopping suddenly, he looked past the rows of empty pews and immediately felt as if something was wrong. He could not quite put his finger on the problem, at least not yet, but on some deeper level he was aware of a change. He stepped forward as he looked all around, but after just a fraction of a second longer he looked toward the far end of the church and realised that every sense in his possession was ringing with alarm. Still, however, he was struggling to pinpoint the cause of this sensation, although after a few more seconds he realised that there was perhaps only one likely culprit.

"Please wait for just one moment," he said, before hurrying along the aisle.

As soon as he was close enough to the cell, he stopped as he saw pieces of broken wood on the floor. He picked his way past those pieces, but already he knew what he was about to find: the cell's door had been smashed open from the inside and when he peered through the gap, he saw that the anchoress Margaret Crake was entirely absent. Only her wooden chair remained. He wasn't sure how such an elderly woman could have summoned the strength to break down a door, yet that was clearly what had happened and he realised that she might well have been gone for several hours now.

"Father Wardell?" Father Kent said, following him over but stopping as soon as he spotted the damage. "What has happened? Is that -"

"The cell of the anchoress, indeed," Father Wardell muttered, turning and looking back across the church. "Shattered and broken as you see. The damage has been caused entirely from the inside."

"Do you think she has lost her mind?"

"I think she has spent the past sixty years in mostly silent contemplation of the Lord," Father Wardell replied. "Of late she has given me some cause to worry that her mind might not be as strong as it once was, but I confess that I have been delaying the moment at which I might step in and offer help. Unfortunately it would seem that this moment has now rather been thrust upon me."

"Where is she?"

Although he opened his mouth to reply, for a moment Father Wardell was utterly unable to advance anything even approximating an answer. He felt sure that the anchoress must by now have fled the church, which meant that there were two possibilities: either she had made her way out across the countryside, where she would no doubt suffer from her exposure to the elements, or she had gone toward the village. He could not even begin to imagine what might happen if she made it all the way into Laidlow, yet he was quite sure that the anchoress was in no fit state to mingle with any villagers.

"You must excuse me," he told Father Kent, before hurrying back across the church. "I must locate her at once."

Left standing alone next to the broken door, Father Kent briefly considered following Father Wardell out of the church. Indeed, he knew that he should absolutely offer his assistance in the task of tracking down the errant anchoress, but for a moment he could not help himself. Taking care to avoid getting snagged on any pieces of the broken door, he stepped into the cell that had for so many decades been the home of Margaret Crake and even he – a pious and devout man who spent much of his time considering his relationship to the Lord – couldn't help but wonder how anyone could live all alone in such a confined space.

Turning to look around, he realised that he could reach out and almost touch all four walls from the spot upon which he was standing. And then, as he was about to test that theory a little further, he saw thick scratches in the stone wall beneath a window set up high.

Stepping closer, he peered at the scratches and saw that they were attempts to write words.

Although he could not make out many of those words, he began to wonder whether the anchoress had been trying to inscribe some form of scripture on the wall – albeit for a purpose that he felt he might never understand. As he looked up at the small window, however, he began to wonder whether the poor woman feared something that might make its way through from the other side.

"Lord," he said finally, "forgive this woman her sins and give her the strength she requires in order to return to the one true path." He reached out and touched some of the crudely scratched words. "Deliver her from doubt," he added, "and show her the light that only you can provide. For what other solace can there be in this world?"

CHAPTER TWENTY-TWO

"HAS ANYONE... HAS ANYONE seen anything out of the ordinary?" Father Wardell asked as he walked along the winding lane leading into the village. "Anything at all? Pray tell me if you have, there is no need to be fearful but I must know if anything is amiss."

Various women, who had been in the process of cleaning the pavements in front of the their houses, turned to see the priest approach. The expressions of confusion on their faces, however, already indicated that they had seen nothing more troubling that morning than the usual muck and grime that regularly built up on the village's streets.

"Has anyone seen anything?" Father Wardell continued, not quite wanting to trouble anyone yet by mentioning that the anchoress might have left her cell. "Please, it's very important. There's no need to panic, nothing's wrong, but there might be a small... problem we need to address."

"Father," a man said, leaning on the gate at the front of his cottage and watching proceedings with a curious sense of amusement, "do you need help with anything?"

"Not at this moment, thank you," Father Wardell replied, barely able to contain a growing sense of panic now as he made his way toward the front of the village's pub. "Your offer is much appreciated, Charles, but I am quite certain that everything will be alright."

Stopping for a moment, he looked up at the sign of the Red Lion, which swung high above in a gentle breeze. Looking at the front of the building, he could already see that several people had gathered inside to drink their souls into torpor. He felt sure that the anchoress would never take refuge in such a slovenly place, yet he also understood that village public houses were often the best places for hearing news from the local area.

He took a few seconds to gird his loins, then he made the sign of the cross against his chest, and finally he forced himself to march straight over to the Red Lion's front door. At the same time, he braced himself for whatever foul and pungent aromas he was about to encounter.

"Forgive me for entering this den of

iniquity," he said under his breath as he pulled the door open and was met by a wall of smoke and the stench of stale beer. "I do this purely out of necessity."

***

"A woman?" the man behind the bar said, as the various customers – who had all fallen silent now – eavesdropped with apparent impunity. "What kind of woman?"

"It is a rather delicate matter," Father Wardell continued, trying to choose his words with care while feeling utterly frustrated that the landlord hadn't managed to read between the lines. "I fear to say too much, but let me mark that if you had spied this woman, you would most assuredly know of whom I speak. I really cannot fathom that there might be two women of such alarming countenance on the loose in the area at any one time. Or even in the world."

"Alarming countenance?" the landlord replied cautiously. "Do you mean to say that there's something wrong with her?"

"Those are not the words I would choose," the priest said delicately, "but the implication of my inference should be clear enough to all of you."

He turned and looked around at the various faces that were staring at him, and already he could tell that not one of these gentlemen had the faintest inkling about the subject at hand. He had tried the public house in good faith and had hoped to discern some information, but he was more and more of the opinion now that the anchoress most likely had fled out into the valley, in which case she might simply never be seen again. For a few seconds he imagined the poor emaciated woman stumbling around in the wilderness and dying some lonely death.

"I shall pray for you," he whispered. "May the Lord -"

Suddenly a terrified scream rang out somewhere beyond the public house. Several of the customers hurried to the front of the main bar to look out through the window, but the landlord headed in the other direction and made his way through to the rear of the building.

Supposing that the landlord – despite being a brutish and unintelligent-looking figure – must know best, Father Wardell followed him out into a small yard at the rear of the place, and then into an alleyway running between two of the busier roads.

"Help!" a woman shouted. "Get her away from me! Help!"

Pushing past the landlord, Father Wardell made his way along the alley until he reached the far end. There he stopped, only to see that two women were hurrying in his direction as if filled with the most frightful terror; one of the women tripped and fell, and her companion had to help her up as the priest hurried over to assist them further.

"What is the matter?" he asked.

"There is the most dreadful woman loose in the streets!" one of the women – the poor individual who had taken a tumble and who was now mired in dirt – exclaimed with fright in her voice as she turned and pointed back in the direction from whence she and her friend had just come. "She must be mad for she shouts at everyone she meets and tries to grab at them. She is most accursedly old and she's wearing nothing at all. Father, she's naked!"

As a few more cries went up in the next street, Father Wardell offered the women some words of consolation before making his way to the corner. He felt certain now that he had located the anchoress, and sure enough when he made his way around the corner he was met with the most horrific sight.

Margaret Crake was stumbling naked along the pavement, almost falling with each step but just about managing to reach out and support herself against various fences and walls. Whenever she got anywhere near another soul she reached out, as if to grab them, only causing herself to stumble even more desperately. She was emitting a constant low growling sound and her general appearance was utterly frantic – causing every man, woman and child anywhere nearby to pull back as far away from her as possible.

Festering pus was oozing from the space between her legs, dribbling thick milky white liquid down the insides of her thighs. As she reached her hands out, she exposed blackened and split fingernails that looked in places to have become forked, while one side of her face had seemingly collapsed: her left cheek had sunk inward and the teeth on that side of her mouth had as a result worn through the flesh until their black and yellow tips were partially exposed, swimming in pale red blood that ran down to mingle with glistening saliva on her chin.

Finally spotting Father Wardell, she quickened her pace in a desperate attempt to get away from him.

"What are you doing?" he barked, rushing toward her. "How did you get all the way into the village?"

"The voice!" she gurgled, grabbing him by the shoulder and immediately putting all of her – not particularly great – weight against his body. Every attempt to speak caused her exposed teeth to chew a little more through her own cheeks. "You must stop the voice! It came through the spaces where the silence should have been!"

"What in the name of the Lord has happened to you?" he replied, scarcely able to believe such a horrendous sight – and rapidly becoming aware of a putrid sweaty smell.

"I opened the door for the Lord, but the Devil stepped through instead!" she sobbed as tears began to run from her eyes. "What did I do wrong? Have I wasted my entire life for *this*?"

"Margaret," he continued, struggling to work out what to do next as more and more people began to gather in the street to watch from a safe distance. "You must come back to St. Jude's at once. Do you understand? You must not be out here like this."

"St. Jude's?" she stammered, glaring at him with a terrified expression in her eyes as thick lumps of snot hung in her nostrils. "You want me to go *there*? *Again*? Do you not know what lurks in the grass? Snakes and priests, Father! Snakes and priests!"

"Can somebody fetch a coat?" he called out to the growing audience. "Do you have no hearts? Why do you stand gawping at this poor woman when she so clearly requires assistance! Find her a coat or something else to wear!"

A couple of men hurried into nearby cottages, but already Margaret was struggling to stay on her feet. Clutching at Father Wardell's arms, she somehow managed to keep herself up.

"He says the most dreadful things," she whimpered. "He has been coming to me almost since I first set foot in that place. Why can he never leave me alone? Why must he always taunt me? And the boy spoke such troubling words. What of the boy?"

"Here," a man said, hurrying over with an old black dress. "Father, you may keep this for her. It belonged to my wife's mother and she has been dead these last six months."

"It is better than nothing," the priest said, attempting to slip the dress over Margaret's thin frame in a bid to at least partially cover her nakedness. "Now I shall require some way to transport her back to the church, for I fear she cannot possibly make the return journey on foot."

"I shall find a cart," the man replied, turning and hurrying away to do just that.

"Why must there be such evil in the world?" Margaret whimpered, hunching forward now as if she was in the most terrible pain. "I sought only innocence and purity, yet instead I was met by a voice that spits the foulest things. Father, I fear that I am not strong enough. I have wasted my life and I have been found wanting, and now the Lord will surely see me for the failure that I am."

"Let us get you back to the church first," he replied, still trying to force her into the dress, "and then we shall decide what else must be done. Do you understand me, Margaret? I don't know what has occasioned this outburst from you, but I promise we shall set you back onto the one true path. I only wish that I had better attended to your needs sooner. In hindsight it is clear that your suffering was beyond anything that might ordinarily be expected of one in your position."

"Just make it so that I do not hear the voice again," she said, looking around as her eyes darted from left to right in their sockets. "I cannot bear to hear such things."

The dress began to fall, once again exposing her thin, ridged back. As he tried to put the dress back into place, Father Wardell marvelled that anyone could even hold their frame upright in such a terrible condition, but a moment later he saw a man driving a horse and cart around the far corner and he realised that at least they were both to be spared the long and agonizing walk back to St. Jude's.

"All will be well again," he told the old woman as he adjusted his grip, holding her up a little better. "You shall see, Margaret. It is perhaps only natural that you have these struggles. Let me assure you that from now on I shall make extra efforts to support you, and to make sure that you can never again weaken in this manner."

"You can't help me," she sneered angrily, glaring at him. "You're just a priest. In your ignorance and innocence, you serve the Devil! All you priests are servants of Satan! May he bite off your rancid cock when you shove it in his mouth!"

CHAPTER TWENTY-THREE

"THERE," GEORGE SAID AS he set his tools down and stepped back. "Even if I claim so myself, Father, I think I've not done a bad job with this at all."

"Indeed you have not," the priest replied, enjoying the peace and quiet now that the handyman's work was complete. "I only wish that I had seen to it that this was done many years earlier. I would have saved many of us a lot of trouble."

Before them, the space that had once held the wooden door leading into the cell had now been replaced by an entirely new section of wall. Having realised that Margaret might once again break free from her cell, Father Wardell had cast about for ideas and had learned that in many cases the dwelling of an anchoress had no door at all, and that it was by no means uncommon to brick them into their spaces so that escape might be truly impossible.

Following Margaret's shocking journey into the village, he had resolved to seal her away permanently. The cell's only openings now were a small gap that allowed for the provision of food and water – but which was barely large enough to permit a hand inside – and an even smaller window at the top of the far wall so that the anchoress would not entirely forget about the outside world. The woman was now well and truly cut off from the world and no amount of strength could possibly break down a stone wall. Indeed, as he admired George's work, Father Wardell couldn't help but feel that with a little more paint it might be possible to hide Margaret's cell entirely.

"Is this really what the anchoress wants?" George asked cautiously. "To be cut off, with no hope of leaving again?"

"She willingly submitted to this life," the priest replied confidently, "and she chose to become dead to the world. That is not something any mortal man can undo. The Margaret Crake who made that decision all those years ago would want nothing less. Her wishes must be respected."

"As long as she doesn't go running around naked in the village again, scaring people," George said as he began to put the last of his tools away.

"She right near scared my Rita half to death."

"The anchoress is so very old now. Older than perhaps she expected to become. I know of no other moment of weakness in her life and I am sure that the Lord will see to it that her mind is calmed. She seems to be catatonic for now, but I have dressed her appropriately and I am sure she will recover in the fullness of time. A little, at least."

Once he'd gathered his tools together, George carried them toward the door, although at the last moment he hesitated. Turning, he looked back at the cell's wall and he saw Father Wardell touching the stones, and he realised that there was yet one more question on his mind.

"And what when she dies?" he called out. "Forgive my rather morbid thought, Father, but... as you yourself pointed out, she is of an advanced age. Even with all the grace of God, she cannot have much time left in this world of ours. When the inevitable happens, will you be calling upon me to open her chamber up again so that she might be buried outside?"

"There will be no need of that."

"But if -"

"There will be no need," Father Wardell said again, turning to him. "Everything has been prepared for, George. Your work here is done. As for the spiritual aspect of these things, I trust that you will leave such matters to those who are better prepared to make the correct choices. I shall tend to the anchoress as necessary."

"But -"

"George, be told!"

"I'm sure you will do what's best, Father," George replied, finally understanding that he was to remain silent. "I'm sorry, I didn't mean to doubt you, not for one second. I was merely wondering, that's all. I just thought I should let you know that it didn't feel entirely right to seal her in, not after you even had me brick up the opening to the outside world. So I -"

"Did you leave the final stone?" Father Wardell asked, interrupting him.

"Yes, along with -"

"Then that is all I need of you," the priest said firmly. "Thank you for your help here, George. You may go now."

***

"And I'm telling you all," George said a few hours later, once he'd resumed his usual position propping up the bar at the Red Lion, "it was quite the queerest sight I ever did see. She's in a cell that's barely large enough to turn around in. You'd struggle to swing a cat in there, and she's sitting upright on a chair."

"A chair?" the landlord replied. "I don't

think she had a chair before, not from what I heard. Sounds like in her advanced years she's finally been afforded a little luxury."

"She had a chair, according to the priest," George explained, "but she didn't use it. He's put her in a black dress now too, with a veil. He said it was to give her some dignity. I heard someone in the village gave it to her, to cover her up."

"The sight of her in the street was almost enough to put me off women for life," one of the other customers murmured. "I feel nauseous just thinking about it."

"She's just sitting there," George continued. "I was bricking her in, sealing her up alive, and she was just... sitting there while I did it all. Sometimes she looked at me with those milky old eyes of hers, I could just about see them through the black veil, and I don't mind admitting that I got the right shivers. I almost wanted to down my tools, only the priest was watching my every move and he kept telling me that there was no need to be concerned. I think he sensed my discomfort, so to speak."

He paused as he thought back to his awful task.

"I remember seeing her face as I put the last stone in place," he added. "She was still watching me. I don't mind admitting that I whispered a little prayer for her soul as I slid the stone in and set it firm. I wanted to make the roof section of the cell a little more secure, but to be honest I couldn't stomach the idea of sticking around much longer. You don't think I did anything wrong, do you? The priest told me several times that it was all very necessary. Priests... I mean, they're never wrong, are they? You can't expect an ordinary man such as myself to question a priest's decisions."

"The anchoress has been there for almost as long as I can remember," the landlord replied. "She submitted to this existence by choice. It seems all very right and proper, if you ask me."

"Did she really just sit there?" his son John asked, having listened from the doorway.

"Haven't you got jobs to be doing?" the landlord replied, turning to him.

"I was helping our visitors down with their cases," the boy explained with obvious displeasure, just as the travelling teacher and his son made their way down the staircase behind him and out through the back door. "They're off now, and then I'll help Mother clean their room."

"Be sure that you do," the landlord murmured. "Go on, then. Away with you, and mind you keep your nose out of business that doesn't concern you."

As John sloped away, the landlord turned to George again.

"That boy'll be the death of me," he sighed. "He's got a lot of learning to do before he's fit to even *think* about taking this place on eventually."

"I keep remembering about her eyes," George said darkly. "Fixed on me, they were, as I put those pieces of stone in place and -"

"Then *stop* remembering her," the landlord replied, interrupting him. "You'll only drive yourself mad if you keep on like that. I know people keep saying that we should be honoured to have an anchoress in our local church, and they might be right. How would I even know? But it seems to me that here in the village, it doesn't have a lot to do with us."

"I don't like the thought of going to church and knowing she's in there," George told him. "I've been speaking about the matter to Victoria and she and I might make the slightly longer journey to St. Swithen's from now on. It's a good church and at least..."

"At least," one of the other denizens of the pub said, finishing the thought for him, "there's not some mad old woman bricked up in one of the walls."

"Do you think it even works?" George asked. "Do you think she's... communing with God, or whatever they reckon goes on in there? Because I'm not so sure. She didn't look much like she'd been communing with God while she was running around naked."

"That's not for us to question," the landlord

said firmly. "If I've told you once, I've told you a thousand times, and no exaggeration. What happens to the anchoress is a matter for her and the priest, and the rest of us should just accept it. And who knows? Perhaps she might come to some grand conclusion on the important questions of life, in which case we might all benefit."

Seeing that George had finished his pint, he took the glass and began to refill it.

"You'll be needing one more before you go home, George," he added. "I can tell already, Victoria won't want you bothering her with all these questions once you step through your front door. Better to drown 'em out so you're nice and docile, just like she's used to."

"I hope you're right," George muttered, turning to look at the window as he thought of St. Jude's out there in the distance. As the sun continued to set, he thought too of the anchoress in her little cell. "May God have mercy on her soul, that's all I can say for sure. I only hope that her decision to stay in that tiny place is the correct one. Because if she has another crisis of faith, and if she decides she wants to escape again, she won't have any luck. From this day forth she's trapped in there forever."

***

As he made his way past the apse, Father Wardell was rather satisfied by the sound his footsteps made. They were good, firm footsteps, the kind of footsteps that could only be produced by a confident man with God on his side. Indeed, he felt they were the finest footsteps he'd ever heard, and he felt sure that they would impress even the loftiest of bishops.

One day, he might even rise to the level of bishop himself. He felt that he certainly had the footsteps for it.

Stopping for a moment, he looked at the small opening in the wall ahead. With the sun slowly dipping outside, the interior of the church was starting to fall dark. He knew that the time would soon come for him to retreat for the night, so he made his way over to the wall and reached up. As soon as he slid the small metal plate out, he saw that the food and water he'd offered to the anchoress had gone entirely untouched.

"You must sustain yourself," he said, confident that she would be able to hear him. "No good will come from anything else."

He waited, and although he had expected no reply, he still gave her ample chance to speak. He imagined her sitting on her chair on the other side of the wall, no doubt lost in some deep contemplation of a devout nature, and in some ways he admired her a great deal. Not that he could ever do the same thing, of course; the idea of becoming an anchorite filled him with dread and he quickly told himself that he did far more good by being out in the world and conversing with his parishioners. The anchoress of St. Jude's, however, comforted him with her presence and he could only hope that she might gain some solace from the fact that her fate had now been decreed.

"I shall leave this for you overnight," he said, sliding the offering back through the small gap. "I pray that you will accept it, and I pray too for your continued connection with the Lord. You are a good woman, Margaret Crake. May the Lord have mercy on your soul."

CHAPTER TWENTY-FOUR

ONE YEAR LATER, AS soon as he slid the metal plate from the opening, Father Wardell saw that his worst fears were perhaps finally coming true. For seven days now the food and water had been left untouched. Although the anchoress had rarely taken anything that had been offered to her, now she seemed to be going entirely without.

"I fear..."

His voice faded to nothing as he looked down at the offerings. For a moment he contemplated the possibility that the anchoress was lost to the world, but he knew that he needed to be sure.

Setting the plate aside, he made his way to the sacristy and fetched a chair, which he then placed directly beneath the opening in the wall.

Every sound – from the bumping of the chair's legs against the floor to the creaking of his shoes as he stepped up – seemed so much louder in the sacred silence. Once he was on the chair, he craned his neck in an attempt to see through into the cell, although he quickly found – as he'd suspected – that he was unable to quite make out the spot where the anchoress was sitting.

Or was she hiding?

"Margaret?" he called out. "If you yet live, I ask that you give me a sign."

He waited for her to speak, or for her to even sigh, yet he heard nothing at all.

"Margaret," he said again, "it is Father Wardell. I know that you have thought long and hard about many matters of great importance, and I do not mean to interrupt, but I need to know... is there yet air in your lungs?"

Even as those words left his lips, he knew that there was no guarantee of the anchoress responding. Indeed, even before her attempted escape a year earlier she had barely spoken a word; instead she had seemed to withdraw into herself during her later years, and while he had hoped over time to gain some insights from her knowledge, he found that in fact she tended to speak only when spoken to – and even then, her responses were often just a single word or perhaps two at most.

"Margaret," he said for a third time, with a

little more force now. "Can you hear me?"

As much as he wanted to merely leave her alone, at the back of his mind he couldn't help but wonder whether she had arrived at the moment of death. His understanding was that she had now reached her one hundred and first year, an achievement that he believed was scarcely credible, yet he felt sure that she must be approaching the end of her life. Slipping a hand into his pocket, he carefully took out a compact mirror and held it up, and then he slid it into the opening and angled it so that he might finally be able to see the anchoress better.

He had to try a few times to get the angle right, but finally he saw a reflection of the simple wooden chair. To his great surprise, however, he realised that the anchoress was no longer on that chair – and that indeed there was no sign of her at all.

"Margaret?" he said yet again, as a sense of concern stirred in his chest. "Margaret, where are you?"

Knowing full well that she could not possibly have escaped from her cell for a second time, not now that the door had been filled in, he tilted the mirror again and saw one empty corner of the tight space. He tilted the mirror a second time, but he was becoming increasingly convinced now that the anchoress had somehow taken flight.

Telling himself that this was impossible, he began to consider the idea that a miracle might have taken place, that the Lord had seen fit to remove the anchoress and had taken her directly up to join Him in Heaven. Was it possible, he wondered now, that in His almighty wisdom He might have taken her body as well – perhaps as a sign?

"Margaret, I must know," he hissed, "are you still here? Margaret, say something!"

He tilted the mirror again and again, before stopping as he realised that he had now checked all four corners of the cell without spotting her at all. He could see the bare chair once more, and a growing sense of realisation crept through his chest as he understood that somehow the anchoress had indeed vanished. As much as he tried to come up with some possible explanation, he knew deep down that there was no way out of the cell. Not without divine assistance, at least.

And then, a moment later, he realised that he could hear the faintest scratching sound coming from somewhere below the opening.

"Margaret?" he said cautiously, pushing his hand a little further through the gap and tilting the mirror again. "*Are* you there?"

Straining now, he was struggling to keep hold of the mirror at all and the angle was narrowing. He tilted his head slightly and began to stand on tip toes, and after a few more seconds he was just about able to see the floor. As the scratching sound continued, he wondered exactly what could possibly -

Suddenly a shape lunged up from its hiding place on the other side of the gap.

Before he had a chance to pull back, Father Wardell felt teeth biting down hard on his wrist, crunching through the flesh with such force that he immediately dropped the mirror. He tried to pull back, but already a hand had grabbed his own arm and was pulling down with such force that he felt the bone might break at any moment. Hearing a snarling sound, he twisted his arm around and pushed against the wall, and now he felt teeth tearing through the muscle just above his wrist.

"Let go of me!" he snarled. "Let -"

In that moment he pulled harder than ever. He felt the teeth ripping through his arm and juddering against the bones of his wrist, but those teeth then fell away and the priest toppled back, slamming down hard against the stone floor. Clutching his damaged arm, he saw that a great deal of flesh had been torn aside, although mercifully no major blood vessels had been caught. After a moment he spotted something black and yellow in the blood; pulling it out, he found himself holding in his trembling hand one very rotten tooth.

"Priest!" a voice snarled. "Do you have any idea what I've found in here?"

Looking up, he was startled by the sight of Margaret Crake's furious eyes staring at him through the gap.

"I sought communion with the Lord," she sneered, spraying blood from her mouth, "but it was not the Lord I heard, not in the end. Another door was opened to a far darker force, and it whispered sweet truths into my soul!"

"Margaret -"

"Let me out of here so that I might spread the word!" she commanded, and now her voice was louder and more shrill than ever. "Let me out so that the word of the Lord can be cast aside to make room for the one true promise of our real master!"

"You have lost your mind," Father Wardell stammered, clutching his injured arm as he stumbled to his feet.

"I'll show you," she hissed angrily. "I'll show all of you! I saw beyond this world and I heard the words of truth, and do you know what they said to me?"

"You don't know what you're saying!"

"They told me that there is nothing," she groaned, although after a moment she started to laugh. "No Heaven. No God. Instead there is only a vast nothing, but there's no need to be fearful. Father, I bring glad tidings for I have finally understood the truth! This nothing of which I speak, this lack of God... it also has a name. And it will bring its name to the lips of all who dare listen!"

"Not me," he said through gritted teeth. "Margaret, I refuse to listen to a word of this sacrilege! You have been lied to by some malevolent force!"

"The void has a name," she went on, scratching at the edge of the opening even as her fingernails began to break away from their beds. "Do you want to hear its name, Father? Once you hear it, you can never go back! Have you never noticed how the name God is so weak and pathetic? *All* God's names are foolish. But this new name, the name of the void that waits to claims us all as its sons and daughters, is -"

"Silence!" the priest roared.

"You're scared!" she yelled.

"I am a believer!" he shouted back at her. "I believe in our one true lord, and so must you!"

"First I saw the void and I refused to believe it," she continued, still scratching at the opening. "Then I believed it but I thought it empty. And then, slowly, I realised that it had a voice. It came to my window and it spoke to me, it spoke of such awful things but I soon realised that this was only a reflection of my fears. The boy might be the only one who was even willing to consider the truth. I saw potential in his eyes. Bring the boy to me and I might yet be able to speak to him, but hurry – lest he becomes tainted by the same priestly tentacles that have soured so many souls."

Hurrying into the sacristy, Father Wardell grabbed the final stone that George had left behind, along with the bucket of materials that he would need in order to fix the stone into its rightful place. He raced back through to the apse and stopped as he heard a series of loud thuds, and in that moment he understood that Margaret Crake was dashing her own head against the walls of her cell.

"May you rest in peace, you mad woman," he said breathlessly as he prepared to do the one final thing that he had known would always be needed. "I can only pray that the Lord will forgive you the weakness that led you to stray from the righteous path, and that delivered you to the form of this abomination."

Reaching up, he began to slide the final stone into place – even as blood splattered at regular intervals through the closing gap and Margaret's head crunched against the other side of the wall.

CHAPTER TWENTY-FIVE

"IT IS SO GOOD to be here again," Father Kent said as he stopped at the end of the path and turned to look around at the graveyard of St. Jude's. "When I realised that I would be passing nearby, I told myself that I simply must come and visit you once more."

"An honour, as ever," Father Wardell replied. "In truth, we receive so few visitors here these days. Even the congregation -"

He caught himself just in time.

"Well," he went on, keen to cover his tracks, "these things always ebb and flow, do they not? I am sure that in time the congregation will recover."

"Are you experiencing difficulties in that regard?"

"No more than any other church might," Father Wardell explained, choosing his words with the utmost care. "In these uncertain times, some members of the congregation have chosen the comforts of St. Swithen's. While it might be a slightly longer journey, St. Swithen's seems to benefit from a more youthful priest."

"One cannot account for human weaknesses," Father Kent pointed out.

"Indeed one cannot," Father Wardell replied, absent-mindedly scratching his right wrist.

"Are you in discomfort?" Father Kent asked, looking down and seeing that a festering wound was oozing pus just above the wrist. "Father Wardell, that does not look good."

"It is fine," Father Wardell replied tersely, pulling his sleeve down to cover the foul sight. "Nothing that some medicine won't cure."

"And tell me, are you still blessed by the presence of an anchoress here at St. Jude's?"

"Alas we are not," Father Wardell said, having anticipated this very question for some time now. "It is my sad duty to report that in the months since your last visit, our anchoress Margaret Crake has departed this world. She remained devout until the end, she was a... true inspiration. I can only express my own gratitude for the fact that I was able to tend to her needs during her final years."

"Any priest would be grateful for such an opportunity," Father Kent said. "And is the anchoress buried here in the graveyard? I would very much like to pay my respects."

"Actually, there was a change of plan," Father Wardell told him, choosing his words with even greater care than before – and with no great degree of enthusiasm. "In her final moments, the anchoress expressed the clear wish that she preferred to remain in her cell, even in death."

"She did?"

"Indeed," Father Wardell said, nodding sagely. "And who am I to go against the wishes of one who is so holy? Of course I granted her this wish, and I made sure as well to hide the location of the cell so that it can never be disturbed by... prying eyes or minds. That was another of Margaret's wishes, expressed to me personally as we spoke for the final time."

"I imagine that her passing was peaceful, was it not?"

"Extremely so," Father Wardell lied, as he thought back to Margaret's heathen screams as he'd sealed the final gap in the wall. Again he reached down to scratch the bite mark on his wrist, which had still not even begun to heal. "There was a kind of beauty to the process."

In that moment he briefly remembered the way the anchoress had shouted and wailed inside her cell, and how this sound had lasted for almost a full day before finally she had fallen silent. Even then he had not been prepared to accept that she was truly dead, and he had waited a full week before telling himself that without food and water she must surely be gone. He still did not dare to open the cell, however, and he focused on the comforting thought that in death the anchoress had surely come to inspire the lives of many. Given the circumstances, he saw no need to spoil the legacy of Margaret Crake by divulging the sordid details of her final week – or the horror of her capitulation to dark forces.

"I should like to pray here before I leave," Father Kent said. "If I may, of course. I should like to pray one final time for the soul of your anchoress, that she might be delivered into the arms of the Lord."

"And I shall join you," Father Wardell replied, forcing a smile even though he had no desire to do anything of the sort. "Please, shall we go inside? I think you shall find that St. Jude's remains greatly conducive to prayer, rest and thoughtful contemplation."

***

As he and Father Kent remained on their knees before the altar, Father Wardell finally began to believe that his efforts at St. Jude's had been a success. While he had promised his visitor that the church was peaceful and restful, he had worried that these were mere words; now that they had begun to pray, however, he couldn't help but note that there was indeed something very pure about the atmosphere all around them.

It was almost as if a dark shadow had been lifted.

Opening his eyes a little, he couldn't help but look to his right, toward the stone wall that hid the cell near the sacristy. He knew that the body of the anchoress was still in there, but he had worked tirelessly to conceal the spot. While there were others in the nearby village who knew precisely where Margaret had spent her decades in the church, he supposed that over time this remembered knowledge would fade. He'd had a similar wall built on the other side of the aisle, so that the place would seem symmetrical, and he'd made sure that any traces on the outside of the building had been covered. He'd even gone to the trouble of having all the old plans for the church destroyed and new ones drawn up, just in case any fools ever arrived to disturb the scene.

He felt confident, in that moment, that within a decade or two nobody would ever be able to trace the location of the dead anchoress and her grave-like cell.

"There is nothing," he remembered Margaret snarling toward the end of her life. "No God. Instead there is only a vast nothing, but there's no need to be fearful. Father, I bring glad tidings for I have finally understood the truth! This nothing of which I speak, this lack of God... it also has a name. And it will bring its name to the lips of all who dare listen!"

Sometimes her words returned to him like errant dreams that flitted through his waking hours. At other times she returned in his nightmares, and he always felt a huge rush of relief whenever he woke up – always short of breath and drenched in sweat – and realised that she had not in fact returned from beyond the grave.

Hearing a rustling sound, he turned to see that Father Kent had opened his eyes too, and that he was looking toward the altar.

"I have commended her soul to the Lord," Father Kent said softly, "and I trust that she will be rewarded now that she has moved on from the pain and torment of this world."

"Amen," Father Wardell replied, and then the two men got to their feet.

"I fear," Father Kent continued, "that the noble tradition of the anchoress is rather dying off. There are few people around these days – men or women – who are willing to cut all ties with the material world and devote their lives to holy contemplation."

"There will always be exceptions."

"I hope so, but I have my doubts. Tell me, though... did Margaret Crake ever express any concerns or fears?"

"Not that I am aware of," Father Wardell lied.

"Nothing at all?"

"Indeed not."

"That is all the more remarkable, then," Father Kent said as they began to make their way back along the aisle, heading toward the door. "I have heard accounts of the lives of anchorites, and their female equivalents as well, and I have often wondered how they can maintain their states of mind for so long. I do not use the word lightly when I question whether such people are almost saints."

"That is not for us to decide," Father

Wardell pointed out, and he couldn't help but look down at his right arm and think once more of the rotten tooth he'd pulled from the wound. "They devote themselves entirely to their faith and the rest of us can only hope to learn from what they discover. Margaret Crake was part of St. Jude's for more than half a century and I am sure that her legacy will be substantial. Beyond that, it is difficult to ascertain any hint of this church's future but I am sure that it will be bright. As for myself, I am planning to move on."

"You're going to be leaving St. Jude's?"

"I feel that my work here is done."

"Has any attempt been made to find someone who will take the parish on? I fear that will not be easy, given that St. Jude's is rather isolated out here. Is there any chance of a merger with St. Swithen's?"

"Sadly not. That idea has already been considered and discarded."

"Then is anyone interested in St. Jude's at all?"

"Not yet, but in truth I cannot wait around for an appointment to be made."

As they reached the door, he let Father Kent go first before glancing back toward the spot where he knew the anchoress was entombed within her cell.

"I am sure St. Jude's shall not remain empty for too long," he added, even though he did not really mean those words. "My replacement will surely be found. It is time for the place to be given a fresh start. In fact, I intend to speak to somebody soon about precisely that prospect. I shall be going to London on Tuesday week, there to discuss the future of this very church. And I trust that my recommendations, when they are made most forcefully, shall be listened to with due care and attention. Indeed I shall refuse to fall silent until I have been heard."

With that, he stepped outside and shut the door. A moment later the key could be heard turning in the lock, and the two priests' voices began to move away from the church.

Finally there was only silence as row after row of empty pews faced the altar. Even the slightest sound, such as a spot of dust landing on the stone floor, might have been heard in that instant, such was the utter lack of any presence at all. Even over by the far wall, close to the doorway leading into the sacristy, there was not even the slightest hint of movement.

CHAPTER TWENTY-SIX

January 1940...

"THAT IS A MOST... troubling sequence of events," Harry said once Barbara had finally brought her tale to an end. Sitting on a low wall at one side of the graveyard, he looked out across the overgrown grass and considered her words for a moment. "It strikes me as a curious mix of fact and rumour."

"Everyone knows the truth," she told him, taking a moment to tuck some stray strands of hair behind her ear. "Okay, fine, some of the details might be conjecture but most of it's absolutely true. The old priest had Margaret Crake sealed up in her cell here once she was dead."

"That would be most inappropriate."

"It's still what happened."

"I'm not sure it would be allowed."

"Do you really think the priest cared?"

"Yes, I do!"

"Then you're -"

She sighed, as if she couldn't quite find the right words to express her frustration.

Harry looked at the church for a moment longer before standing up and turning to her. As confident and certain as she had sounded – as she always sounded, it seemed to him – he nevertheless felt as if she needed to be reminded of a few things; chief among these was the tendency for people to exaggerate and distort a tale with each telling, so that even the simplest of all stories might become twisted beyond recognition. That was true of even the most rudimentary sequences of events, and the passage of so many years undoubtedly added an extra dimension.

"Thank you for sharing your version of that tale with me," he said after a moment. "I shall -"

"My version of the tale?" she replied, clearly shocked by his attitude.

"Indeed, for that is what you have just relayed," he continued, striving to strike a friendly and conciliatory tone. The last thing he wanted was to offend her. "You have told me your version of something that happened long before you were even born. I'm quite sure that the tale has passed from voice to voice over the years, each time gaining some new little change that suits the intention of the teller. It's hardly a shock to realise that people enjoy... complicating these tales and adding little twists to them."

"Twists?"

"I do not claim to have ever heard of this Father Wardell fellow before," he went on, "but I have no doubt that he was a good man. The idea that anyone would have simply walled the body of a woman – and an anchoress, indeed – inside a small cell or chamber in any church is... I mean, it's ludicrous. It's out of the question."

"You don't believe that a priest did such a thing?"

"I don't believe that a priest could *ever* do such a thing."

"Ask anyone in the village," she replied darkly. "They all know it's true."

"Then they have all no doubt heard the same tall tales that informed your account just now," he insisted. "I must admit that I am amused by the creativity you have shown, and I do not seek to dismiss every aspect of the account, but you need to understand that I can't entertain the more sordid and unlikely elements. There *was* an anchoress here, that much is clear, but I can assure you that any priest would have made sure that she received a proper burial."

With tears in her eyes, she began to slowly shake her head.

"You really have wasted your time coming out here today," he continued, turning and starting to make his way back toward the church's main door. "I trust that you will have an enjoyable cycle ride back to the village. Your uncle no doubt has much for you to do."

"Where are you going?" she called after him.

"I have a task to complete," he reminded her, holding up his notebook for her to see as he stepped into the church's shadow. "I did not come here to listen to foolish stories. I came to accomplish a specific job and I intend to complete that job. Again, enjoy your cycle ride back to the village."

"You arrogant son of a -"

Stopping herself just in time, Barbara watched as he disappeared into the church.

"You arrogant sod!" she snapped finally, no longer able to maintain her composure. "How can you ignore everything I just told you? How can you possibly believe that you know best?"

***

A couple of hours later, on his knees in the eastern transept, Harry took a moment to note down some details about a section of lead piping that he'd discovered loosely attached to one of the walls. In truth he wasn't sure that a ten foot piece of lead was going to do much to help the war effort, but he supposed that it wasn't his job to make such determinations.

His job, as Father Neville had made very clear, was merely to note down the details so that other – far more qualified individuals – could make the decisions.

"Ten feet," he murmured under his breath, "by about -"

In that moment, hearing a brief cracking sound, he turned and looked back across the church. He saw row after row of empty pews, but otherwise there was no sign of anything at all. He hesitated, however, since he was certain that the sound had been very real, although after a few more seconds he realised that the sun was beginning to dip outside and that long shadows were spreading across the pews. The stained glass in the windows, meanwhile, was now filled with the very rich hues of an impending sunset.

Checking his watch, he realised that the light would soon fade too much. He knew that he could light a candle and continue his work after dark, but he'd promised himself that he would set off for the village in good time and he supposed that he still had the next day in which to finish his work.

Perhaps even the day after that, depending on how swiftly – or not – Father Neville recovered.

Getting to his feet, he flicked back through the notebook and saw that he'd got a lot done. More, in fact, than he'd appreciated. Indeed, he felt sure that he would need only a few more hours on the following day and then he would have everything done to Father Neville's satisfaction. And that thought, in turn, made him wonder whether there was any chance that his superior might have improved or perhaps even woken up during the day.

Putting aside any last consideration of staying late, Harry checked that he had everything with him and then he walked over to the central aisle. He was already considering the need for something to eat, and he supposed that one of the rather delightful sandwiches from the Red Lion might be just the sustenance he would require after his cycle ride back to the village. Already he was savouring the thought of cheese and relish, and perhaps a little -

Suddenly he stopped in his tracks as he heard the cracking sound again, and this time the disturbance lasted for a couple of seconds – long enough, indeed, for him to turn and look over his shoulder. As the sound faded away, he had already determined that it must have come from somewhere over by the door leading into the sacristy.

"Hello?" he called out, wondering whether

there was any chance that somebody had entered the church while he'd been working.

He waited, standing in a patch of evening light that was shining through a stained glass window, but already he was telling himself that the sound might have been caused by any number of things. A stray mouse, perhaps, or a bird that might have managed to get into a gap somewhere in the roof. In fact, there were so many possibilities that he felt foolish for allowing even the slightest flicker of doubt into his chest.

Convinced that he had been rather improperly influenced by Barbara's garish tale earlier, he turned and began to make his way along the aisle. His footsteps rang out against the stone floor but he was already almost at the door and -

In that moment he heard the cracking sound again, except this time it possessed an extra quality, almost as if something was very slowly splitting or twisting. The sound lasted even longer now, extending for almost ten seconds before finally fading out, at which point Harry slowly turned and once again found his eyes immediately focusing on the area around the entrance to the sacristy.

Why, he wondered, was some hidden part of his soul constantly drawn to watch that particular spot?

"Hello?" he said again, before making his way in that direction, determined to satisfy his curiosity – and to prove once and for all that there was no reason to be concerned.

Reaching the door, he looked through and saw nothing untoward. He waited, hoping that the sound might return and allow him to better judge its source, yet now he was met with only an ominous silence that seemed somehow to be growing stronger with each passing second.

Slowly turning to look over his shoulder, he now found himself looking at the wall next to the sacristy's door. There was nothing unusual about that wall at all, at least nothing that he could see, yet after a few seconds he began to notice that it was perhaps rather bare. Nothing had been placed against it, nothing had been hung on it... instead it had been left completely untouched, almost as if this was the one part of the entire church that over the years people had always shied away from.

Stepping closer, he reached out and touched the rough stone of the wall. He ran his hands across the ragged surface and wondered why he was drawn to this particular spot. A moment later, not really knowing why, he turned his head slightly and placed an ear against the wall. He waited for a few seconds, but he heard nothing unusual so finally he stepped back and told himself that there was absolutely no reason to be concerned.

Still, he lingered in front of the wall for a few more seconds before forcing himself to turn and walk away. Each step felt heavy and almost wrong somehow, yet he managed to keep going. Already the sun had dipped a little lower outside and the shadows cast through the windows were longer than ever as Harry's departing footsteps rang out through the otherwise silent church.

CHAPTER TWENTY-SEVEN

AS SOON AS HE stepped outside, Harry saw that he was not alone.

"What are you doing here?" he asked as he saw that Barbara was still sitting on the wall next to their two bikes.

"What does it look like I'm doing here?" she replied defiantly, watching as he locked the building's front door. "I wasn't going to leave you behind. I stayed to make sure that you left before sunset."

"I've been in there for several hours since our last conversation," he pointed out, making his way over to join her. "Three at least. Do you mean to tell me that you've been sitting here for all that time, in some way... keeping an eye on me?"

"I had to know that you left."

"But -"

"I *had* to know that you left," she said again, with much more force this time.

"This is absurd," he sighed.

In return she offered only a wide, flat smile of defiance.

He opened his mouth to reply, but for a few seconds he was genuinely stunned by the idea that she had remained in place for so very long. Indeed, he was starting to understand that Barbara had a rather unique ability to surprise him at almost every turn.

"What if I had not?" he asked finally. "What if, like Father Neville, I had lit a candle and resolved to work later?"

"You didn't."

"But if I had, would you have come inside and dragged me out?"

"Inside? Me?" She was clearly shocked by this suggestion and after a moment she turned and looked over at the door. "No," she added finally, "I couldn't have gone in there. Not ever. But I'd have... I don't know, I'd have thought of something."

"You'd have tied a lasso and thrown it inside so that you could drag me out?"

"Maybe," she replied, clearly not particularly amused by his attempt at humour.

"You really believe that story you told me earlier, don't you?"

"Every word," she said firmly. "I'm not the only one, either. I'm not going to try to persuade you again because it's clear you're never going to listen. Your mind's too closed."

"My mind is *closed*?"

Having always considered himself to be an inquisitive and thoughtful person, Harry was shocked by this suggestion.

She nodded. "But at least I can stay here and make sure that you get out safely."

"And are you going to do the same tomorrow?" he asked with a faint smile, equally frustrated and amused by her persistence. "Am I to have some kind of personal guard waiting while I tend to my work?"

"If you come out here, then yes," she said firmly.

His first instinct was to assume that she was joking, but he quickly realised from the determined expression in her eyes that she was deadly serious. As much as he wanted to reassure her and insist that there was no need for her to waste her time, he could already tell that she was extremely stubborn. Indeed, he had never met a woman like Barbara Dewhurst before, although in truth he had spent precious little time around women at all. They certainly seemed rather strange.

"It's getting late," he pointed out finally, not really knowing what else to say except the obvious.

"If we want to get back to the village before darkness, we should probably set off soon."

"You go first," she replied. "I'll follow a short distance behind. Just in case you decide to double back and go into the church again."

***

"So what made you become a priest?" Barbara asked a short while later, once the pair of them had stopped for a moment by the side of the road to watch the sunset a little way out of the village. "What makes a man like you decide to devote your life to God?"

"A man like me?"

"I'm sorry," she continued, leaning back against the wall for a moment. Now that they were away from the church, she was able to relax just a little more. "You're the first priest I've ever met who's under the age of about fifty."

"I felt a strong calling from an early age," he told her, before hesitating. For some reason that he couldn't quite understand, he felt unusually predisposed to the idea of telling Barbara the full truth. "My mother died when I was young. The cancer ate her away from the inside. The guidance of our local priest helped her through the worst moments, and I wanted to offer the same comfort to others."

"A noble cause. What kind of cancer was it?"

"I hardly see that it matters."

"So tell me."

"There is no need."

"Tell me."

He hesitated. "I believe it started in her uterus," he said cautiously, again wondering why he was being so open with this complete stranger. "By the end it was... everywhere."

"I'm sorry," she replied, and it was clear that she meant those words.

"So far I have mainly been working away from people," he admitted before frowning slightly. "Father Boughton and Father Sloane seem to think that I'm not very good at interpersonal relationships for some reason, although I think I'm rather handy. I just need more practice. For now, though, I mostly work on the administration side of things. I spend a lot of time with dusty boxes and piles of books."

"I suppose you might seem a little stiff."

"Stiff?"

"Awkward," she continued with a smile. "Don't take this the wrong way, Father Stone, but you never seem very relaxed."

"I think I'm very relaxed indeed," he replied, taking slight offence to that suggestion. "Father Boughton once said the exact same thing as you, however. He called me wooden. Why do people think that I'm not relaxed when I quite clearly am?"

He waited for a serious response, but instead Barbara seemed too amused to say much.

"I am still learning," he insisted.

"Can I ask another question?"

"I am happy to talk about anything that concerns you."

"Why aren't you out there?" she continued, eyeing him with a hint of caution. Another gust of wind blew against them both, and again she tucked some errant hair behind her ear. "Fighting, I mean. You seem fit and healthy, and obviously age isn't a factor. And you're clearly not a coward. Is it because of your job? Are priests exempt from fighting?"

"A number of my colleagues have gone out to France," he explained, picking his words with the utmost care, "but unfortunately I have a slight leg injury that means I have – for now – been chosen to remain at home and provide services here. You might not have noticed anything, but let me assure you that running is absolutely not one of my strengths. I can just about cycle, but even that becomes tiring after a while. I know people often suspect that I am using my condition as an excuse. Let me assure you, however, that I would be out there if I could."

"*I* don't think you're using anything as an excuse," she told him. "I can tell that you're a good man."

"You can?"

"Stubborn and arrogant, perhaps," she added with a faint smile, "and extremely credulous, but deep down a good soul."

"It's not for me to say," he pointed out somewhat awkwardly.

"That's alright," she continued. "It's obvious enough to me."

"I imagine that if things get much worse," he went on, "then I might well be called up. I have offered my services but so far I have been declined. I suspect they fear I might slow everything down."

"Perhaps they'll stick you behind a desk," she suggested. "You seem good at that sort of thing."

She paused for a moment, looking out across the fields, but her gaze quickly settled on the farthest visible point of the winding country road.

"I can still feel it, you know," she said finally. "I'm sure you think I'm quite mad, and you might be right, but I swear I can feel it no matter where I go. Even here, within eyesight of the village."

"Feel what?"

"The church," she continued. "In my day to day life at the pub, I can usually force myself to ignore it. As soon as I get out of the village, however, it breaks through and starts to make me feel... uneasy. Again, I know you won't believe me, but I swear that the church – or whatever's *in* the church – is radiating out for miles in every direction. It's why a lot of people avoid using the road that goes anywhere near St. Jude's. I sometimes wonder if I can ever be free of this sensation. I daresay that even if I went to the other side of the world, that church's influence might follow me."

After a moment, realising that he hadn't responded, she turned to him.

"You think I'm imagining things," she added with a slight hint of disappointment. "I can tell from your eyes."

"I'm sure you believe that everything you say is true," he replied, trying to be as diplomatic as possible. "However, you must acknowledge that human minds can be most impressionable. If you have grown up here in the village, hearing whispers about the mysterious anchoress of St. Jude's all through your younger years, it's really no surprise if the tale is almost... entwined in your psyche."

"Now you sound like one of those psychiatrists," she told him.

"I am nothing of the sort," he said quickly, as if the very idea offended him. "I am merely a keen student of human behaviour. But let me be the one to ask a question this time, even if it is one that I have alluded to before. If you are so troubled by the thought of St. Jude's, why do you not leave?"

"Leave?"

"The village. The county. You could even move to a city."

"I tell myself that I have no other options," she replied, "and that I can manage here. The truth, though, is that I can't shake the feeling that I *need* to stay. I always worry that over time people, even in the village, will start to forget even more of the story of St. Jude's. And what then? Would more people risk going closer? Would they consider reopening the church?"

"You see it as your duty to stay and remind everyone?"

"Yes," she insisted, before taking a moment to steady her nerves. "I suppose so, in a way. Besides, nobody else was ever going to go out there today and keep an eye on you, were they? They'd all just sit there muttering in the pub without actually doing anything."

"Well, I feel very lucky to have received your attention on this fine afternoon and evening," he told her. "I can only hope that I haven't kept you away from any more important duties."

"Uncle John'll be angry that I was gone all day," she admitted as she climbed onto her bike again, "but I know how to talk him round. Despite his rather tough exterior he's a softie at heart. Honestly, I don't know where I'd be without him. He took me in at a time when my own family could barely even stand to look at me. Ever since, he's given me invaluable training and I feel that I could almost take on the pub myself one day. I'm not sure what the locals would think about that, though. Women – at least unmarried women – don't tend to run such places."

"I'm sure the regulars will be happy so long as their beer is served in good order," he said as he too prepared for the last part of the ride back to the village. "And who knows? Perhaps one day you'll be able to add your own name to the long list of the Red Lion's licensees."

CHAPTER TWENTY-EIGHT

STANDING IN THE CORRIDOR upstairs at the Red Lion, John stared through into the room and watched as Father Neville continued to sleep.

Although he couldn't put his finger on the cause – and indeed wasn't even sure that a cause existed at all – John felt increasingly certain that this Neville fellow was no stranger. Having barely ever left the village in his life, John knew that there were precious few chances for the pair of them to have met; he also recalled Father Neville mentioning that this was his first time in the village, and he certainly wasn't about to accuse anyone – and a priest, no less – of lying, yet the niggling sense of familiarity remained and he felt certain that at any moment his brain was going to solve the mystery.

Finally, hearing footsteps, he turned to see that Barbara was making her way up.

"And where the hell have you been?" he asked. "I've been searching for you all afternoon!"

"I'm sorry," she replied as she joined him at the door. "I went out on a small errand that... well, I suppose it turned into a much larger errand than I anticipated. It looks like you managed without me."

"My back's playing up."

"I'm sorry," she replied. "It won't happen again, I promise."

"I had to clean the kitchen myself."

"Oh no!" she said with mock alarm. "How did you cope?"

He scowled at her.

"I *am* sorry," she said again, putting a hand on the side of his arm this time to show that she was serious. "Truly. I know your back is bad sometimes and I didn't realise that the kitchen needed to be cleaned today. I promise I shall pay more attention to such things in future. I meant it when I said that nothing like this will ever happen again."

She paused for a moment.

"Well," she added, "there's a chance it might happen again tomorrow. I'm afraid it all depends on Father Stone and his plans. If he insists on going out to St. Jude's again..."

"I see now," John murmured. "You've been keeping an eye on the fellow."

"Someone has to."

"Does he know about the stories?"

"He does now, for I have told him," she explained. "Not that he listened very much. I suppose that's the problem with priests, isn't it? They think they know everything. He's downstairs now making a telephone call and waiting for his supper, but he fully intends to go back out there tomorrow and finish his task. Don't worry, I didn't go inside the place. I'd never do that. I stayed in the graveyard and waited to make sure that he left."

"And did he... notice anything while he was in there?"

"Not that he has mentioned," she said with a sigh. "You know, sometimes I wonder what is to become of St. Jude's. It sits there year after year, but that can't go on forever. People get curious over time, and foolhardy, and there won't always be someone around to hold them back. Don't you think that eventually something ought to be done?"

"Depends on your point of view," he replied, stepping past her and heading to the top of the stairs. "Some folk round these parts reckon it's all fine just so long as whatever's in that church remains contained. That's my way of thinking, to be honest. So long as nobody goes out there and pokes about, we can hopefully just leave the place to rot."

"I'd love to believe that you're right," she said softly, looking into the room and seeing that

Father Neville was showing no sign of improvement. "Unfortunately it would seem that there will always be people who think they know best. I just worry that one day someone might come along and do harm to more than just their own body. What would the power of the anchoress be if she was eventually released from her confinement?"

***

"This is really quite intolerable," Harry said as he once again stood in one of the pub's back rooms with the telephone receiver against the side of his face. "I have telephoned twice now to speak to Father Sloane yet I am continually told that he is unavailable. Are you even passing my messages on to him at all?"

"Father Sloane is being kept abreast of all developments," the voice replied, and it was the same slightly rasping voice that had seemingly been stonewalling him from the start. "He has no further information that he wishes to convey to you at present."

"I just don't see what -"

Stopping himself at the last moment, Harry tried to work out how best to phrase his next question. As much as he always told himself to be respectful when dealing with figures of authority, a niggling concern had been troubling him for a while now and he felt that he needed answers.

"There are tens of thousands of churches in this country," he said finally, "and regrettably at least a few hundred of those are no longer in use. Certainly many of them are far more accessible than St. Jude's, yet I am aware of no other attempts to assess abandoned churches for possible metals and other items to be used in the war effort. Indeed, since I was first told about this mission, something about the whole endeavour has not sat right with me."

He waited for an answer, hoping that the person on the other end of the line might already understand where he was going with this query.

"So why," he went on, "were Father Neville and I sent all the way out here to the Welsh valleys to inspect this *particular* church when so many other options seem to have been available?"

Again he waited, but he heard only silence.

"Is there something about St. Jude's that makes it more notable than the rest," he continued, "or is... is there some other reason why we might have been sent here? After all, there appears to be no end to the stories about this place. For example, I was told just today about an anchoress who -"

"You have your instructions," the voice said firmly, cutting him off before he could get another word out. "Once your work is complete, wait for Father Neville to recover. If possible, allow him to direct your next move. If he has not recovered by one week from today, get in touch and arrangements will be made for you both to be extracted."

"Extracted?" he replied, puzzled by the use of this word. "Am I really to wait for up to a week while -"

Before he could continue, he heard the same clicking sound as before, indicating that the call had come to another abrupt end. Pulling the receiver away, he stared at it for a moment before hanging up just as he heard someone approaching the nearby doorway.

"Your supper's ready," Barbara said, before frowning as she realised that something appeared to be wrong. "Father Stone, is there a problem?"

"No," he replied quickly, before realising that she was perhaps the only person in the village in whom he might be able to confide. "Not really," he continued. "By which I mean, I'm not entirely sure. I know that I should not question anything, yet I can't shake the feeling that something here is not quite right."

"Why wouldn't you question things that don't seem right?"

"Because my superiors are in positions of authority for a good reason. They are far better placed than either of us to determine what needs to be done."

"You can't seriously be planning to go

through your entire life with an attitude like that, can you?" she asked with a sigh.

"What do you mean by -"

"If something feels wrong, then you need to act on that fact," she continued, stepping over to him. "Trust your instincts. So you keep ringing some kind of... office, right?"

He nodded.

"And they're not being open with you," she added, having lowered her voice a little. "That much is pretty obvious. You must realise that this has something to do with Margaret Crake. There's no way they just happened to send you and Father Neville to the one church in the entire country that's supposed to be haunted by the ghost of a long-dead anchoress."

"I was told that Father Neville selected the location for our work."

"And do you think that's true?"

"I have no reason to disbelieve the information," he told her, although he could instantly hear the doubt in his own voice. Indeed, he knew in that moment that if their roles in the conversation had been reversed he would never have believed a statement delivered with such a glaring lack of conviction. "Father Neville would not lie to me," he added with an equal lack of belief. "I just can't imagine that such a thing might be possible."

"I get it now," she replied. "You respect authority and you have a hard time questioning your orders. Sounds like you'd make a good soldier after all. But you're also smart, Father Stone, and you're *too* smart to let the wool be pulled over your eyes for long. Deep down you *know* that something fishy's going on here."

"I know no such thing," he insisted. "Did you say that my supper is ready? I really would like to eat soon so that I can go to my room and read over my notes from today."

"Father Stone -"

"And I would be grateful if you would refrain from attempting to involve yourself any further in ecclesiastical matters," he added as he stepped past her and headed to the bar area. "Thank you for your kind help today, it has been much appreciated. Further help will not be required tomorrow."

CHAPTER TWENTY-NINE

AS HIS HEAVY EYELIDS finally began to open after a period of deep rest, Father Stanley Neville found that his vision was blurred. He blinked several times in an attempt to clear his view a little, and he finally saw that he was in a small and rather dull wood-panelled room that was entirely unfamiliar to him.

He considered this development for a moment, yet already further sleep was trying to drag him down. After a few seconds, unable to keep his eyes open any longer, he allowed them to slowly slip shut as he let out a long, exhausted sigh.

Suddenly he gasped and opened his eyes again, while pulling to his left as if startled by something. Staring at the other side of the bed, he saw nothing but some rumpled sheets yet he felt absolutely sure that for a moment – just one brief and slightly blurry instant – a young woman had been resting on her side next to him. And as much as he wanted to believe that this vision couldn't possibly have been real, he felt sure that the girl had possessed no eyes of her own. Instead, both sockets had appeared to have been gouged out.

Looking around the room now, he saw no sign of the strange girl. He knew that she couldn't have vanished so quickly, and as he sat up he told himself that she simply couldn't have been there at all, that she must have been some lingering element of a long-forgotten and perhaps slightly feverish dream.

Taking a deep breath, he tried to calm his racing nerves. A moment later he realised that he could hear muffled voices coming from somewhere below, and when he looked at the window he saw not the familiar tops of London houses but rather swaying trees and – further off – several rolling fields beneath the light of a setting sun. He was still slightly puzzled, but as his foggy mind began to clear he remembered his journey to Wales with Father Stone and finally he realised that he must be in a room at the Red Lion public house.

But...

As fragments of his memory began to return, he looked down at his hands and saw that they were heavily bandaged up to and including the wrists. He had some dim recollection that he'd been bleeding in the bar area downstairs, and after a few more seconds he thought back to the sensation of a knife cutting through his flesh. For a moment he was unable to connect that memory to any other events, yet he could feel the fog starting to lift from his mind and finally he recalled one striking image from the night.

He'd clambered from the pulpit at St. Jude's as something – something dark and angry – had smashed against the side, almost toppling the entire thing. He'd heard a scratching sound, too, as if thick nails had cut through wood and stone.

"I went there," he whispered now as he began to understand. "I did it."

While he didn't yet have even one tenth of his memories of the previous few days, he at least knew now that he *had* tried to make contact with the anchoress – and given his poor physical condition and the fact that he'd clearly only barely survived the incident, he could tell that things hadn't gone well.

A moment later, hearing footsteps, he turned and looked at the open doorway. Had he been quicker with his wits he might have pretended to still be asleep, but he was too slow and Barbara immediately froze as soon as she saw him sitting up in the bed.

"Good morning," Father Neville said

uncertainly, before turning to look toward the window. "Or should I... should I say good evening?"

***

"I confess that I remember very little from that night," the priest continued as he slowly set his bare feet down against the guest room's rough wooden floor. "You'll have to forgive me. There are... moments that keep coming to me, but I'm somehow unable to string them all together."

"I'm just so relieved that you're awake," Harry said, before turning to head out into the corridor. "I shall call Father Sloane's office at once and -"

"Wait!" Father Neville called out.

Surprised by this command, Harry turned to face him again.

"Just... give me time to think," the older man continued, forcing a smile that in no way compensated for his obvious sense of panic and confusion. "Please, just a moment."

"Of course," Harry said uncertainly.

"I'll find something for you to eat," Barbara muttered, stepping past Harry. "You must be famished, Father Neville."

"I am. Most certainly."

"I'm sure," Harry continued once Barbara

had left the room, "that Father Sloane will be most relieved to hear that you've woken up. I wasn't intending to get you down there to speak to anyone on the telephone personally, I merely intend to inform them of this development."

"There'll be time for all of that later," Father Neville replied, sounding a little weaker already. "Tell me, young man, since the unfortunate incident with my wrists... have you been out to St. Jude's at all?"

"I have indeed," Harry replied eagerly, sounding rather pleased with himself. "I was there for several hours today, logging all sorts of information about various items of metal and other things that might be useful. I'm certain that I've done a much better job than before and that you'll be extremely satisfied with the results."

"I see, and did you notice anything... unusual?"

"I confess that when I first went to the church following your mishap, I found the place to be in quite a state. The pulpit has been badly damaged, and one of the pews was seemingly used in an attempt to create a kind of crude crucifix."

"Yes," Father Neville said softly, as if he was only now remembering this last piece of information. "I recall now. That worked rather well, at least for a few minutes."

"I beg your pardon?"

"Nothing," Father Neville continued, trying to stand up – only to wince as he had to sit again. "I feel as if I must have been in bed for a thousand years. Well, there's no time to sit around fussing about things."

He tried again to stand, and this time Harry hurried over to support him.

"There's work to be done," the older man murmured.

"I'm sure it can wait at least until tomorrow," Harry replied. "You must be feeling so weak. You lost quite a lot of blood and I think we should get you to a hospital as soon as possible."

"There'll be time for that later," Father Neville said, trying to step forward but quickly finding that he was too unsteady on his feet. "I need to get back out there."

"Back out where?" Harry asked, although he quickly understood the proposition. "It's dark outside," he continued. "You cannot possibly mean to go out to St. Jude's at such a late hour."

"There's no time to waste."

"Father Neville -"

"Do not tell me what to do!" the older priest snarled angrily, momentarily losing his composure before taking a few seconds to get his emotions under control. "I'm sorry, Father Stone, but you simply don't understand what is at stake here."

"I confess that I do not," Harry replied, "but

only because you will not tell me."

Reaching out, Father Neville supported himself against the side of the door. He was clearly in pain, but after a moment he shuffled forward as if he was under no circumstances going to listen to any entreaties to rest.

"This is the *perfect* time to go out there," the old man continued. "Night is when she is easiest to find. I located her cell and now I know what I must do. She might have bested me once but I will not let that happen again. I... I am better prepared now. I am better prepared than ever."

"Who are you talking about?" Harry asked.

Gripping the door's other jamb, Father Neville began to limp out onto the landing.

"Do you mean the anchoress?" Harry continued. "Do you mean Margaret Crake?"

As soon as he heard those words, Father Neville stopped in the doorway, yet he did not immediately turn and look back at the younger priest; when he finally did so, his watery eyes were filled with tears.

"How do you know that name?" he barked. "Who told you about her?"

"I have heard a story," Harry said cautiously. "It is really, I think, little more than that."

"A story?" Father Neville replied. "Well, if it was from anyone in this village, then I imagine it was the most ludicrous assemblage of rumour, gossip and downright invention. I'm quite certain that there's not a single sensible mind in this entire place. Ask each of the residents what really happened out there and you'll most likely get a full range of completely different accounts."

"But the core elements of the tale," Harry continued, finally determined to get to the truth, "concern an anchoress named Margaret Crake who struggled with her calling. Is that not correct?"

He waited for an answer, but he could already tell from the expression on Father Neville's face that he was getting close to the truth.

"And she is... I can't believe that I am saying this, but according to some versions of events she is walled up in a cell in the church. Is that also true?"

"You don't know what you're talking about."

"Then tell me!" Harry continued, surprising himself with the forcefulness of his plea. "Let us be completely honest here, Father. You are in no fit state to go out to St. Jude's tonight and you won't find anyone who'll take you, not this late. Please, I am not accusing you of deceiving me, but I fear some parts of our mission here have been kept from me."

He waited again, determined this time to get to the truth.

"Tell me," he added finally. "Tell me the real reason you brought me out here to St. Jude's."

CHAPTER THIRTY

"I'M SURPRISED THAT HE'S awake so soon," Barbara muttered as she cut another slice of cheese from the block. "I thought he would need at least another night's rest first."

Realising that her uncle hadn't answered for a few minutes, she looked across the kitchen and saw that he was looking up at the ceiling.

"Uncle John?"

"Hmm?"

Turning to her, he seemed momentarily lost – as if he hadn't heard a single word that had just come from her mouth.

"I'm sorry," he muttered, "but I still can't shake the feeling that I've seen that man before."

"You mean Father Neville?"

"It's the strangest thing," he continued. "I

can't have seen him, the idea simply doesn't make sense, yet I can't shake it at all. I don't know where or when, but I have come across the man's face at least once in the past."

"He claims he's never been here before, doesn't he?"

"Aye."

"And you have never been to London."

"I haven't been to many places."

"Is it possible that you're mistaken?"

"Anything's *possible*," he admitted, before hesitating again. "I felt it as soon as he walked through the door and the sense has only grown stronger since. I know it's wrong to say such things about a man of God, but sometimes when that Neville fellow speaks I catch myself thinking that he's... being economical with the truth."

"Or he's downright lying," she suggested.

"That thought has crossed my mind too," he replied with a sigh. "Then I wonder about that other priest, the young one. He doesn't seem much better."

"*He's* not a liar," she said. "I would wager any amount on his word. He might not be very worldly and he might be very trusting, but he tells the truth. Or what he believes to be the truth, at least."

Once again she waited for her uncle to reply, but she could tell that he was still chewing over the possibility that he'd met Father Neville before. And as much as she felt that this idea was unlikely, she knew her uncle well enough to be sure that he rarely made mistakes. If he believed that he'd encountered the priest some other time, then he most likely had. But that, Barbara knew, made no sense whatsoever.

"Wait," he whispered finally, turning to her again with a hint of shock in his eyes. "I think... I think I've got it! I know exactly where and when I met him before." He turned and looked through toward the bar area. "It was many years ago in this very pub!"

***

"I rather think," Father Neville said after a moment's contemplation, once he'd finally given up on his attempt to stand and had instead sat on a chair next to the dresser, "that you need to remember your place, Father Stone. You are still very much the junior member in this particular expedition."

"I am very aware of that fact," Harry said firmly. "Believe me, it has remained very much at the forefront of my mind. Yet I fear that I have been left somewhat in the dark. I must ask you very directly, Father Neville, whether our mission here is *solely* to document possible metals and other items for the war effort."

"That is why we are here, yes."

"But is it the only reason?"

"You heard Father Sloane!" the old man insisted, sounding increasingly exasperated. "You were in the office with him just the other day!"

"But why *this* church?" Harry asked, determined to get to the truth. "Of all the churches in the country, why did you bring us here?"

"Father Sloane directed us!"

"I know you made the recommendation," Harry continued, feeling increasingly frustrated by these attempts at obfuscation. "Father Sloane indicated as much. I also know that he seemed... reluctant to agree, but that ultimately you seemed to persuade him."

"I'm tired," Father Neville replied, shaking his head. "It's late. I wish to terminate this tiresome conversation."

"Is it to do with the anchoress?" Harry asked. "It has to be. We're here because of the anchoress and the search for metal is at best a cover story."

As soon as those words had left his lips, he regretted being so direct – yet he also wondered whether he might finally be about to get an honest answer. At the same time he could feel that his heart was pounding now; he had never been so direct in his life and he was finding that the experience wasn't entirely pleasant.

"You know nothing," Father Neville said bitterly. "Less than nothing! You're just a fool who fails entirely to understand how the world works! Your task here is to follow instructions! No more and no less!"

"But I am not permitted to know *why* we do these things?"

"No!" Father Neville shouted. "No, you are not!"

Although he wanted to continue the discussion, Harry realised that he might be better to wait until the morning. At the same time, he was worried that the older man might try to sneak out on some foolhardy dash back to the church; in his mind's eye he imagined his fellow priest's weak figure stumbling along a dark country lane and perhaps collapsing due to sheer exhaustion.

"Get out of here!" Father Neville barked, pointing toward the door. "You say that I need to rest, yet you stand here peppering me with questions! If you don't leave this room immediately, I shall be minded to tell Father Sloane that you have sabotaged our mission here!"

"I have done no such thing," Harry replied, before taking a step back. "I shall retire for the night but at some point you must tell me what we're really doing here. I want to help, but I can only do that if I know the truth."

"You won't get the truth from *him*!" a voice

called out, and Harry turned to see John making his way up the stairs with Barbara just a few steps behind. The landlord's feet were stomping noticeably louder on each and every wooden board they reached. "He hasn't been telling the truth since the moment he first walked into this pub."

"What are you talking about?" Harry asked.

"I'm talking about this Neville fellow's real intentions," John said, barging into the bedroom and looking down at the elderly priest. "I'm talking about his false claims to have never been to Laidlow before."

"Leave me alone!" Father Neville gasped, gesturing for him to go away. "I am not up to this right now!"

"You don't recognize me, do you?" John continued. "Or perhaps you do and you're just good at hiding such things. It took me a while to work out where I'd seen you before, but I finally understood. Perhaps you were too young back then, or perhaps you didn't notice me all those years ago, but *I* noticed *you*. It's all starting to make sense now."

"You are mistaken!"

"I am not, Sir!"

"Father Stone," the priest continued, "get this oafish man out of my company! I don't know what he's thinking, storming in here like this and disturbing my attempts to recuperate! Have you all forgotten that I'm not well?"

He made a point of wiping the back of one hand against his own brow.

"I'm really not well at all..."

"It was a long, long time ago," John continued, keeping his eyes fixed firmly on the old man. "We were both so young back then, weren't we? A lifetime has passed for both of us, and in truth we barely even met back in the day, did we? I'm not surprised you don't remember me, I'm sure that at the time you thought I was nothing but a servant whose job was to carry your bags up and down the stairs."

"Nonsense!" Father Neville spluttered. "Pure errant nonsense!"

"You can try to hide the truth," John said, "but I'm absolutely certain that I'm right."

"Can someone please explain what is going on here?" Harry murmured.

"I'm so lost," Barbara added. "Uncle, why are you acting in this manner? Even if you remember Father Neville from many years ago, I fear that you're being rather rude to him."

"I'm treating him with the contempt he deserves," John sneered. "Anyone else would have thrown him out of this pub by now, but I have too much respect for the priesthood to do that. This particular specimen, however, is beneath contempt and should be treated as such."

"That is too much!" Harry said, stepping

toward him. "I'm sorry, but I must ask you to leave. Father Neville is tired and needs time to recover."

"Are you going to explain or shall I?" John continued, and for a moment he looked as if he was on the verge of dragging the elderly priest up from the chair. "It's all so obvious now, I can't believe that I didn't make the connection before. I'm sorry, Father Stone, I don't mean to cause trouble but I have always abhorred liars and I will not have one twisting his words under my roof. It's time for the truth to come out."

"Leave me alone," Father Neville whimpered, seemingly close to tears now. "I have never been spoken to in such a terrible manner in all my life. You must leave me alone immediately!"

"Fine, then *I'll* tell them all," John said, turning first to Barbara and then to Harry. "Father Neville *has* been to Laidlow before, but back then he was merely Stanley Neville. He came here with his father and stayed in this very pub. It must have been fifty-five years ago, by my reckoning, but I remember it all as if it was yesterday. There have been many sorry moments in the history of our village, but those days were some of the darkest of all. And it's all because of this wretched fellow and his lying, cheating excuse for a father!"

CHAPTER THIRTY-ONE

1885...

"JUST A FEW DAYS," William Neville said, standing at the bar in the Red Lion pub. "That's right. Just long enough for me to spread the good word."

"And what good word might that be?" Henry asked as he made a note of the visitor's arrival in his ledger.

"There are truths about the world that are hidden from most good people," William continued with the slightest hint of a smile on his lips. Reaching into his pocket, he pulled out a tattered pamphlet and placed it on the bar. "As a matter of fact, I explain them all in here. You might be surprised to learn that I am a writer as well as a teacher, and I believe I have been put in this world for the express purpose of getting the truth out to the common man."

"You have, huh?" Henry said, before taking a key from the hook behind the bar. "You and your son'll be in the first room to the left once you go up the stairs."

"Do you have somebody to help us with our cases?" William asked as he took the key.

"My son John will be able to do that."

"This seems like a lovely little village," William continued, examining the key for a few seconds before slipping it into his pocket. "I shall very much enjoy meeting the locals and telling them all about the true vision I have experienced."

"Is that so?" Henry replied, making little effort to hide a sense of great scepticism. "I'm sure us common men will be fascinated."

"I'm accustomed to people doubting me." William said confidently. "I do not blame them in the slightest, for what I have to teach them is truly startling. All great teachers are met with scepticism at times. Even Christ."

He turned the pamphlet around on the bar so that Henry could more easily see the printed title.

"If my task had been made easy," William continued, "it would perhaps not be worth doing at all."

Looking down at the pamphlet, Henry saw

that it was titled *A New Way to Reach God*, and he felt a shudder run through his bones as he realised that this latest arrival was just another lunatic self-proclaimed preacher. He'd heard of such people before, and he understood that they were always trying to start their own brand of religion, although as far as he was aware they usually faded away and caused no real harm. Still, he'd been able to pay for the room upfront, and that was all that really mattered.

"If you need to extend your stay," Henry said finally, preferring to stick to practical matters rather than engage in any kind of esoteric discussion, "just let me know the night before. I can't imagine that there'll be any problem."

"That is good to know," William said, "but we have a very strict schedule and we must stick to it."

He stepped aside and looked toward his ten-year-old son, who had been waiting patiently next to the cases.

"Isn't that right, Stanley?"

Pale and thin, and wearing shabbier clothes by far than his father, young Stanley Neville merely nodded as if he knew that he had no real role to play in the conversation. He'd been hanging back so far and hadn't said so much as a word since he and his father had arrived at the Red Lion. Even now, as if embarrassed that any attention had been drawn to him at all, the boy quickly looked down at his own rather ragged shoes. He seemed positively emaciated, as if he was rarely given a proper meal.

"Tell your lad to take our cases up to our room," William continued. "Stanley and I have no time to waste. We always like to recruit at least three new followers from every village we visit!"

***

"- from some damnable heretic!"

With that the cottage door slammed shut in his face, and William Neville took a step back while still holding the proffered pamphlet in his right hand.

"Right, then," he said, taking a moment to regain his composure before leaning down and pushing the pamphlet through the letterbox. "Perhaps you'll find time later to peruse my writing in a little more detail. I'm sure you'll find it far more interesting that you can possibly anticipate. Assuming you can read at all."

Making his way back to the street, he set off again to the next row of cottages with his son Stanley shuffling along as usual just a few paces behind. As he walked, he took care to straighten his suit, trying to make it look a little less shabby.

"This place is harder than most," he said under his breath. "Did you see the anger in their eyes, Stanley? It's as if they're so desperate to avoid learning the truth. Are my ideas really so very difficult to comprehend? I merely argue for a new way of approaching our relationship with the Lord."

He pushed open another gate and stopped for a moment as he prepared to once again launch into his speech.

"Sometimes I wonder whether it is my fate to end up crucified," he added loftily. "Would these heathens really do something like that? Would they refuse to listen to the word I am attempting to preach? Must I end up suffering like Christ?"

He looked down at his own wrists.

"The idea of the Lord literally inhabiting the bodies of his worshipful congregation shouldn't be *that* shocking," he continued. "You know, Stanley, sometimes I think that I should have gone to America when I was a younger man. Out there they're far more open-minded when it comes to new things. Not like the stick-in-the-muds of merry old Britannia. I think I could have really made something of myself out there in the wilderness of somewhere like California or Texas. I should have placed myself more firmly among other free-thinkers. I might even be rich by now."

Stanley stared at his father before looking down once more.

"It might have done *you* some good too," William continued, before shuffling toward the cottage's front door. "Lord knows, you've certainly not inherited my gift for speaking to people, have you? In fact, you don't seem to have much personality at all."

Left standing on the pavement, Stanley turned and looked along the street. So far Laidlow just seemed like yet another in a long succession of dull little villages, and there was no obvious reason to think that it was in any way different to the countless other places they'd visited on their travels. For almost two years now Stanley had been traipsing around with his father, listening to the old man's lectures on some new religion he believed he'd been born to start, and any sense of adventure had long since been counterweighted by a weary inability to stay in the same place for more than a few days at a time.

Sometimes Stanley saw other boys in actual houses with both their parents, and he told himself that he'd give anything to have lived a life like that. Instead -

Suddenly hearing a shriek, he turned just in time to see that another door had been slammed in his father's face. There had been a time when Stanley had believed that *perhaps* his father was a genuine prophet of sorts, but he'd finally come to the conclusion that he was nothing more than a travelling charlatan. Occasionally William was able to persuade people – usually old widows – to part with some money, usually after spending the night in their homes while Stanley slept in the street, but for the most part both father and son were becoming increasingly poor and scorned.

Although he didn't want to be disloyal, Stanley couldn't help but wonder just how long this type of lifestyle could possibly last.

"There's another one who refuses to listen," William said as he rejoined his son, while holding up another pamphlet. "I won't waste more paper by putting one through *her* letterbox. Do people not understand the costs involved in printing these things up? I still haven't quite got enough to pay for the next batch."

Not really knowing what to say, Stanley turned and looked along the street again.

"Oh," William continued, "to be blessed with an intelligent son... what would I not give? Instead I have to suffer the company of this halfwit all the time."

Looking up at his father again, Stanley could already tell that he was once more to be blamed for the failures of their mission.

"You don't inspire anyone, you know," William went on, and now his voice was positively dripping with an unprecedented sense of disdain. "How do you think it makes me look when I can only drag around a solitary boy? By now I should have a dozen or more followers, each of them willing to follow me to the ends of the Earth if necessary. I should have wives and disciples! Instead I have this... pathetic sight."

He hesitated, as if he was trying to think up some new way to express his disgust, before finally – and with no warning – he kicked the boy hard in the shin and then clipped him around the ear.

Wincing, Stanley stepped back, but he knew to refrain from showing too much pain.

"Go back to that public house and wait for me there," his father sneered. "Go on, get out of here! The less I'm seen with you, the better!"

Relieved that he was to be given some time alone, but not wanting to reveal this reaction to his father, Stanley turned and hurried away along the street. Glancing over his shoulder, he saw that William was watching him – and he understood in that moment that he was likely to receive a good hiding once his father returned in the evening. Still, that was something to worry about later, and for now he was determined to enjoy some peace and quiet.

And one day, he promised himself, he would be able to run away from his father forever and never look back.

CHAPTER THIRTY-TWO

ANOTHER STONE HIT THE ground just a few inches too far to the left, failing to dislodge its target and instead skittering away until it hit the bottom of the wall.

For almost an entire hour now, Stanley Neville had been sitting in the yard behind the Red Lion, and he'd taken to amusing himself by throwing stones at small targets that he himself had constructed. This was one of his favourite ways to pass time, and he felt sure that he was slowly getting better with his aim, and he could only hope that his father wouldn't be returning any time soon.

After all, his father's presence always brought some mix of drama and trouble.

Hearing a shuffling sound, but already perceiving that it was too slow to be caused by

William, the boy turned just in time to see the landlord's son John entering the yard. He instantly bristled; something about the boy struck him as loutish and crude.

"What are you doing?" John asked.

"Nothing," Stanley replied, immediately tensing.

"It looks like you're doing *something*," John remarked, stopping to look at the little targets. "I thought you were out with your father, knocking on all the doors in the village."

At this, Stanley merely shrugged.

"What's wrong?" John continued. "Haven't you got a tongue in your mouth or a brain in your skull?"

"I haven't got anything to say, that's all," Stanley replied.

With a faint smile on his lips, John walked over to the targets and kicked them. Stanley immediately got to his feet, feeling a rush of anger in his heart, but as he clenched his fists he told himself that there was no need to get into a fight. After all, he'd been in fights before and he'd always been beaten – first by his opponent and later by his father, who believed that young men with good souls should never lower themselves to the level of common brawling. And that, if they did, they should always win.

"Your father's a fraud and a liar," John said

after a moment. "That's what *my* father says, anyway."

"Then your father doesn't know anything," Stanley replied.

"He knows how to run this public house," John said, making his way across the yard so that he could square up to the boy. "He doesn't have to spend his life travelling from village to village, attempting to sign people up to some fantasy religion he's invented."

"It's not a fantasy," Stanley said, although he sounded quite uncertain. "It's all true."

"No-one in their right mind thinks that," John sneered. "What's wrong with the old religions, anyway? At least they've stood the test of time. There's no need for people to try to invent new things when the old ones work just fine."

"Shows what you know," Stanley sneered, feeling an uncommon urge to defend his father. "You're just a stupid little manual worker in a public house in the middle of nowhere. You're not destined for greatness or anything worthy. You're pathetic!"

He waited for John to reply, but after a moment the older boy merely burst into peals of laughter. Enraged, Stanley stamped a foot against the ground before finally retaliating in the only way he'd ever learned: he kicked out hard, slamming his heel against John's shin with such force that the other boy let out a pained gasp and stumbled back.

"You little piece of shit!" John snapped, lunging at him but not quite managing to grab his collar as Stanley pulled away. "Come here and I'll teach you a lesson you'll never forget!"

As the older boy tried again and again to grab him, Stanley raced out of the yard and scampered away along the alley. Reaching the far end, he swung around the corner and kept going, swiftly taking a few different lefts and rights until finally he stumbled out onto another street and swung around to check that he wasn't being followed. Struggling to get his breath back, he watched the end of the alley and after a few seconds he allowed himself a faint smile as he realised that he'd managed to lose his pursuer.

"Idiot," he sneered under his breath, as all his earlier bravado began to flood back into his chest. "There'll be a special place in Hell for the likes of you when the day of judgement finally comes."

***

A short while later, having supposed that he really shouldn't risk returning to the Red Lion until he had the protection of his father, Stanley Neville made his way along another street at the edge of the village while absent-mindedly tapping a broken branch against various walls as he passed.

Deep down he knew he shouldn't have started a fight with that boy in the pub's yard, but he'd been unable to stop himself. He couldn't help getting angry whenever someone treated him like dirt, and something about John's slightly pudgy face had filled him with a kind of screaming rage. Now that he was sure nobody was trying to hunt him down, he was feeling a little more confident and he told himself that it was John who'd been the lucky one.

"Try that again," he murmured as he allowed himself to become cocky again, "and I'll beat the grin off your face. You're no better than -"

Suddenly hearing a shuffling sound, he spun around. He was terrified that John might have caught up to him, but instead he found himself staring at the utterly unlikely sight of a naked old woman who was watching him from the other side of the street.

For a moment, Stanley could only stare at the woman. She was painfully thin and had long, stringy white hair, and she appeared to be swaying slightly as if being nudged by the slightest of breezes. Her eyes, however, were very much fixed on Stanley and he couldn't help but feel as if she was almost trying to see *into* his mind, as if she believed she could peel back the layers of his flesh and bone and read his thoughts.

Feeling more than a little uncomfortable, he

looked both ways along the street but saw no sign of anyone else. A few seconds later, hearing a scrabbling sound, he turned and gasped as he saw that the strange woman was limping toward him.

"You there," she croaked, struggling to get the words out. Raising her left hand, she pointed with a gnarled finger topped by a cracked and slightly broken nail. "Boy. You there. You have your mind already half open."

"I... what?" Stanley replied, confused by her words.

"Your mind is already half open, if not more, to new things," she continued, stopping in front of him – and still swaying slightly. Now that she was closer, a pungent stench of stale sweat and other bodily fluids hung in the air. "Don't be afraid. It's a wonderful thing. It means that you're more likely to listen to the truth."

"What truth?" Stanley asked, scrunching his nose up.

Slowly, and with evident pain, the old woman lowered herself down until she was on her knees. Her tired old bones clicked with almost every move. Now she looked directly into the boy's eyes as if she was searching for something, for something important that perhaps only she could see.

"I have heard the voice so many times now," she said, reaching out and putting a withered hand on one side of his face. "It takes a different form always, but it's consistent in its teaching."

Although he wanted to pull away, Stanley told himself to remain calm. The woman's breath was foul but something about her eyes struck him as being extremely intelligent.

"It comes to my window sometimes and mocks me," she continued, tilting her head slightly to one side. "At first I was horrified, but over the years I came to understand that it was trying to teach me something. The more I began to consider the true meaning of existence, the more the voice started to soothe me, until finally I realised the lesson it had been trying to teach me all along. There is a vast void of nothingness beyond this life, and that void has a name."

"I don't know what you mean," Stanley replied.

"Oh, but you do!"

She squeezed his cheek a little harder.

"Oh you do," she gurgled. "Your mind is already open to it. All those foolish priests think they're the guardians of knowledge, but I have spent almost my entire life seeking out the real truth. Priests, though... priests are the enemy of us all, for they try to construct a prison around our minds, a prison made out of lies and malignant half-realities. Do you understand?"

"My father preaches something similar,"

Stanley said cautiously, although in truth he hadn't quite yet worked out how to connect the old woman's raving claims to his father's pamphlets – even if he felt sure that a connection existed. "He believes in a new -"

"A new possibility!" the woman snarled, leaning closer to his face. "That's right! The void waits to claim us all!"

"I don't know anything about a void," Stanley replied, trying to turn away – if only to get away from the stench erupting from the back of the woman's throat. "I just -"

"But you're so close to understanding it all," she continued, speaking a little faster now as if her excitement was growing. "You're the first one I've found who might yet see through to the reality! I thought that in my silent contemplation I would grow closer to the Lord, but instead I found that another voice began to peel away the layers of my mind so that it could speak to my one true core! There is something out there, something waiting, that is so much greater than anything mankind can dream of, yet *I* have begun to see its true shape! I alone can draw the truth into this world! But I must get past the priests first!"

"You -"

"They're guardians of ignorance! They're warriors standing against what is real!"

"You're hurting me," Stanley said,

struggling to hold back tears as the woman squeezed his cheek even tighter.

"Let me teach you the true word!" she hissed. "It will take time but I can open your eyes and your mind to a truth that comes to us from the void of nothingness. I only ask -"

"Who are you?" a voice gasped suddenly. "What are you doing with that boy?"

Startled, Stanley turned to see that two women had emerged from a nearby cottage, and that they were now staring in shock at the scene.

"Don't interfere!" the old woman snarled, letting go of Stanley's cheek and stumbling toward the new arrivals, then quickly starting to push them back. "This is nothing to do with you! Nothing at all! Your pathetic and weak minds would burst if you heard even one sliver of the truth I have uncovered!"

"Don't touch me!" the younger woman replied, trying to shove her aside. "I don't know who you are or what you're doing here, but if you don't leave me alone I shall fetch my husband to deal with you! You look diseased!"

"You will fetch no-one!" the old woman shouted, lunging at her and grabbing her face, seemingly trying to gouge out her eyes with her cracked thumbnails. "Silence! If you won't shut your infernal mouth, I shall rip out your tongue and shut it for you!"

The other woman screamed and stumbled back as the old woman somehow forced her victim down to the ground. Stanley could only stare in shock as the naked figure tried to dig out the eyes of the woman who was now on her knees, but a moment later he turned and ran as he realised that several men were racing out of nearby cottages to see what was causing all the commotion.

"Help!" the woman on the ground shouted finally. "Get her away from me! Help!"

CHAPTER THIRTY-THREE

"YOU DON'T UNDERSTAND," STANLEY sobbed a few hours later, standing in the guest room upstairs at the Red Lion, "I didn't do anything wrong. The old woman just -"

Before he could get another word out, his father's hand slapped him again – harder, this time, and with enough force to almost knock him off his feet.

"When I tell you to be quiet," William Neville sneered, "I do not expect you to immediately start answering me back. Is that clear?"

"Yes, Father," Stanley whimpered.

"As if I haven't had a hard enough day already," William continued, "I now have to deal with a son who apparently can't amuse himself for so much as an afternoon without finding his way into trouble. Not only did you apparently get into a fight with the landlord's son, you also were caught in the company of some deranged old hag who had to be dragged away kicking and screaming."

"She said -"

"I don't care what she said!" he shouted angrily as rain began to batter the window and darkness continued to fall outside. "I don't care about any of it! Only one thing matters, and that's my ability to spread the word! I've been working hard all afternoon and how do you repay me? Do you realise how it looks when we draw attention to ourselves in this way? It's hard enough as it is, I barely get any donations, and then you go and make it a hundred times more difficult!"

"Father -"

Before Stanley could get another word out, they both heard a knock at the door. They turned to look, and William immediately pushed his son aside before making his way over and pulling the door open.

"That's him!" a man snarled, stepping forward – only for Henry to hold out an arm to hold him back.

"Gentlemen," William said with a slightly condescending smile, "I'm sorry, my son and I were just -"

"That's the thief!" the man continued, pointing at William. "He was seen sneaking into the backs of several cottages this afternoon and now items are missing."

"Absolutely not!" William replied, although his defiant refusal carried more than a hint of theatricality. Indeed, he seemed unusually prepared for the accusation. "I resent the implication! I am a teacher and a man of high intent, not some common thief!"

"A few people have made the same claim now," Henry said darkly. "It's been a busy day in Laidlow and nobody's much in the mood for foolishness. Mr. Neville, I'm not going to turf you out into a rainy night, not with a boy in tow. But I shall be obliged if you'll pack your things and leave first thing in the morning."

"I -"

"You're no longer welcome at the Red Lion," Henry added, interrupting him before he could get another word out. "If you leave willingly tomorrow, that'll be the end of it. If you refuse... well, I already know several men who'll happily force the issue. Indeed, they're minded to press their business sooner rather than later."

"You can come into the room right now and search for whatever you think is missing," William replied, stepping aside and gesturing for them to do just that. "I have nothing to hide! Strip the place down if you must!"

"I've spoken to these gentlemen," Henry

continued, "and they've agreed to hold off for tonight. If you're still here past lunchtime tomorrow, however, your safety can no longer be guaranteed. Have I made myself clear?"

"You've demonstrated a refusal to stand against the mob," William sneered, "but fine, my son and I shall depart first thing in the morning. Clearly the people of Laidlow are not ready to open their minds and listen to the truth about their lives. My son and I shall go to a place where the locals are more receptive."

"See that you're gone as early as possible," Henry muttered, turning and leading the angry man away. "Sticking around wouldn't be smart. Not smart at all. While you're in my pub, I can keep the mob at bay. Once you're out of here, you need to leave fast."

John was the only one out on the landing now. He fixed Stanley with a dark, angry stare before William swung the door shut.

"Did you hear that?" he barked at his son. "These feckless ingrates are too unintelligent and uneducated to even listen to what we came to tell them. That shall be their loss, then. I have never been welcomed so poorly in all my life." Clearly angry, he marched over to his satchel in the corner. "Pack your things. We shall be leaving first thing in the morning! There must be *somewhere* out there that will welcome us!"

***

The weather the following morning had taken a decided turn for the worse. As William and his son Stanley lugged their cases along the rough road leading away from Laidlow, they could see their own breath in the cold air and they were already starting to shiver. The road ahead looked grim and foreboding, with no hint of another village or town up ahead.

"It should be... about twenty-five miles to the next place," William called back to his son. "If we hurry, we can be there in... I should say ten hours ought to do it."

"Ten hours?" Stanley replied, shocked by this suggestion. His shoes were already falling apart; one was missing its sole entirely. "That seems like a long time to go without any food or water."

"I never once promised you that this would be an easy life," his father insisted, "it's more -"

As his case caught against a rock, he let out a few curses under his breath.

"We are proving our devotion to the cause," he continued angrily. "Let the world throw all its hardships at us. Let the uneducated and mindless cast us out. Let the ignorant and ugly spurn our truths! We shall allow nothing to stop us!"

"But... is it true what they said?"

Stopping, William turned to look at his son.

"Nothing," Stanley said, realising that he'd gone too far. "I said nothing. I'm sorry. Can we just keep going?"

"What did you ask me?" William sneered. "Are you referring to those heathens back there, to the ones that dared to accuse me of thievery?"

"No, Father."

"Then to whom *were* you referring?"

"I... don't know, Father."

As those words left his lips, Stanley couldn't help but notice the leather pouch that always hung from his father's belt. After leaving any village, that pouch was usually fuller than when they'd arrived.

"You don't know?" William replied, staring down at the top of his son's bowed head. "I find that awfully difficult to believe. Awfully difficult indeed. I'm starting to think that you've turned your ears to listen to lies and false claims."

Reaching down, he took hold of the boy's chin and forced him to look up.

"I see weakness in your eyes, my child," he continued. "*Great* weakness, in fact. I always knew that there was some of that quality about you, but the sheer volume is an affront to everything I believe in. Why, does my own son believe me to be a lowly criminal? Have I failed so very badly that you, the boy I raised all alone with no help from any woman, have no faith in me whatsoever?"

"Of course not," Stanley whimpered, with tears in his eyes. "I'm sorry, Father. I -"

"Quiet!" William hissed, suddenly looking past him, watching the road along which they'd just travelled and swiftly spotting a trio of men racing away from the village on horseback. "I don't think I like the look of this," he murmured under his breath, before shoving the boy toward the side of the road. "Hide! The last thing I need right now is to have to talk to these ruffians!"

Ducking down, Stanley crawled into a thick, thorn-infested bush. He felt the sharp tips tearing at his flesh and clothes but he knew he had to keep his head down. A moment later, looking back out at the road, he was shocked to see his father running away toward a set of bushes opposite, only for the men on horses to swiftly gallop onto the scene. The ground shook beneath the beasts' mighty hooves and although they soon raced out of view, Stanley heard his father's startled cry in the distance – as if, indeed, somebody had done him a dreadful misfortune.

"Leave me alone!" he heard William shouting. "I have stolen nothing! Nothing at all! I am merely a travelling preacher, that's all. If you want somebody, take my son. He's practically worthless to me anyway, but I'm sure you could find work for him. Take him if you must, he's yours, but leave me alone to -"

In that moment Stanley heard a loud gasp, followed by another. Not daring to crawl out of the bush, he instead turned and looked the other way. After a few more seconds, hearing several harsh cries along with the distinctive sound of cracking bones, he squeezed his eyes tight shut and stuffed his fingers into his ears. He'd seen his father being beaten before, always for stealing, but he could tell that this was more than just another ambush. Already he could hear cries of "Thief!" and "Liar!" filling the air, but his father had fallen ominously silent.

Fully aware that there was nothing that he could do to help in the situation, he merely squeezed his eyes tighter shut and pushed his fingers harder into his ears and waited for all the misery to be over.

CHAPTER THIRTY-FOUR

WHEN HE FINALLY DARED to open his eyes and pull his fingers out from his ears, Stanley realised that he could hear only silence. He'd felt the thunder of horses' hooves again a few minutes earlier, and he'd taken that to mean that the men were gone, but he still wasn't entirely certain that he dared to leave his hiding place.

After a few more minutes, however, he began to turn around so that he could look along the road – and he felt an immediate thud of fear in his chest as he saw a crumpled human form on the ground. The sight seemed barely like a person at all, more like a dark smudge half pressed into the mud.

Staring, Stanley already knew on some deep hidden level that this was his father. A cold wind was blowing along the road, slightly ruffling the clothes on the figure's body, but that was the only movement. The dead bush into which he'd crawled was creaking occasionally as the wind blew through, and finally Stanley knew that he could hide no longer. Pulling himself free from the thorns, he stumbled to his feet and stepped out into the middle of the road, and then he looked both ways to make absolutely sure that the men on horses were gone.

Then he looked at his father, and he marked that the man had given no sign of life for quite some time now. Even the old man's clothes, which continued to flutter gently in the breeze, seemed almost to be mocking the stillness of his body.

"Father?" the young boy said cautiously, hoping to receive some kind of response.

He waited, but the whispering of the wind seemed almost to offer some rebuke to any sense of hope.

"F... Father?"

Although he was scared of what he might find, he began to make his way along the road. Approaching his father, he saw blood splattered across the dirt. The man's right arm was extended, and even a fool with no knowledge of anatomy whatsoever would have been able to immediately see that the thumb and all four fingers had been badly broken. There was no twitching of these damaged digits, no attempt to curl them, and as he stepped around to the other end of the body Stanley braced himself for the worst.

As soon as he saw his father's face, or what was left of it, he let out a shocked gasp and took a step back.

One entire side of William's head had been broken, perhaps by the heel of a boot, leaving plates of bone resting in pools of dark red blood; some slightly clearer patches had broken through between the pieces of shattered skull, perhaps hinting at chunks of brain matter that had become exposed. A foamy white substance had pooled around one part of the shattered bone.

The other side of the man's head was more intact, although the socket had been damaged and the remaining eyeball appeared to have somehow been forced partially into the top of the nasal cavity – where it had split open. Fresh blood was dribbling from a gap just beneath this eyeball, but after a few more seconds the man's broken jaw began to slip open slightly.

Staring at his father's sole remaining eyeball, Stanley saw that it was staring directly back at him. Had it merely been left in this position, he wondered, or had it somehow turned to look his way?

A moment later a faint whisper left the dying man's lips, and Stanley saw some change come into the eyeball. Years later, he would begin to fancy that he had seen the exact moment in which his father had expired, but on that cold morning such ideas did not yet occur to him. Instead he waited for his father to speak, and then – hearing nothing – he eased himself down and sat cross-legged next to the corpse. Although he knew that things looked bad, there was still some part of him clinging to the hope that eventually his father might stir.

All around, the bleak and cold countryside stood in silent vigil for the boy and his murdered thief of a father. Or for the boy, at least.

***

The sound of hooves broke through the night, stirring Stanley from a light daze. Opening his eyes, he saw that the sun had almost entirely set, and then he turned to see that a carriage was being pulled directly toward him.

Startled, he got to his feet just as the carriage thundered to one side and stopped, and he watched as a panel in the side slid open and a pale, painfully thin face peered out. This face – like the carriage itself – looked old and worn down, as if it might fall apart at any moment.

"What's this?" the man in the back barked. "What in God's name..."

The man stared for a moment, as the carriage's driver – who had so far been engaged in the task of reassuring the two horses – finally climbed down and made his way over. This man, in contrast to the passenger, was grotesquely fat and was almost spilling out from his too-tightly-buttoned uniform; his face was lined with thick creases and a huge bulge of extra fat was ballooning from the back of his neck, hanging like a gut over the rear of his jacket. Stubble decorated his face in uneven, asymmetrical clumps that contained several crumbs and stains from recent meals.

Using his boot, the driver nudged William's corpse until it rolled roughly onto its back. In doing so, he showed all the care and attention of a man idly examining a dead rat.

"An extinguished soul, yes?" he called back to the carriage's sole occupant. "As dead as they come. Looks like he's been this way for some hours, yes?."

He turned his gaze toward Stanley, who had so far resisted the urge to stumble away and retreat back into the bushes.

"And a young lad, no doubt linked in some manner to the remains, yes? Boy, tell me, who is this unfortunate fellow to you?"

"My... my father," Stanley replied.

"That's awkward," the man in the carriage opined.

"Where do you come from?" the driver continued. "We just passed a small village back there, yes? Is that your home?"

Stanley shook his head, while wondering why the man had to append the word "yes" with a question mark to the end of almost every pronouncement.

"Still, this whole mess must have something to do with the place, yes?" the driver went on, adding to the grammatical mystery. "Seems to me, young fellow, that you're fit to starve out here, yes? If you don't freeze to death first. Is that your plan? Are you just going to die away here by the side of the road?"

"I'm... waiting," Stanley explained.

"Waiting?" the man in the carriage barked. "Arthur, ask him what he's waiting *for*!"

"What are you waiting for?" the driver asked.

Stanley stared up at him for a moment before looking down at his father's ragged body.

"I see," the driver continued, with an edge of sadness in his voice as he slowly looked over at the man in the carriage. "When we stopped for refreshments just now, Father Lovelady, I heard some men in the public hostelry talking about a thief who'd recently been apprehended. They didn't sound too fond of him, no they didn't. In fact I got the distinct impression that they'd had to take care of the man, yes? Now I think I understand how they went about their task, yes?"

He looked down once more at the corpse.

"It's a different sort of care to the one I would have supposed."

"Dear oh dear," the man in the carriage – evidently known as Father Lovelady – said, shaking his head. "I heard that the Welsh provinces could be rather rough and wild, but I never expected to chance upon anything like this. What do you think will happen to the boy if we leave him out here?"

"He'll die, yes?" the driver muttered, looking Stanley up and down. "Might die anyway, regardless of whatever happens, yes? But out here, all alone... no chance."

"Do you really think so, Arthur?" the priest continued, sounding at least mildly alarmed by this prospect.

"I should think so, yes?" the driver – or Arthur as he shall be referred to from now on – replied. "Looks like he's got one foot in the proverbial grave already, yes? The other shan't be far behind – and then he'll be proper planted, no?"

"I don't know if we should just leave him out here," Father Lovelady replied, squinting a little as if a better view of Stanley might help him make up his mind. "He looks thin," he said finally. "And poor. And he's not very tall. Do we know his name?"

"What's your name, yes?" Arthur asked.

"S... Stanley," the boy replied uncertainly.

"His name's Stanley, yes?" Arthur called back in the general direction of the carriage, while keeping his eyes very much fixed on the child in question. "Not one of my favourite names, if I'm honest. I can think of twenty or thirty I'd choose for a boy before I settled on Stanley. Then again, it's at least a traditional name. I used to live near a Stanley Road, so he's got that going for him. Of course, old Stanley Road round my former digs wasn't very desirable, so that's a knock."

"Stanley," Father Lovelady said, before reaching out and tapping the carriage's door. "Come here at once."

Although he was reluctant, Stanley stepped around his father's corpse – and very carefully around the Arthur fellow – and approached the carriage, the door of which began to swing open. By the time he reached the foot of the vehicle, the boy could already smell the musty, dank interior.

"Stanley," Father Lovelady said in a stately tone, clearly trying to sound a little more formal, "I am on my way to Bristol, there to meet with several other members of the clergy. We have extremely necessary business to attend to, business that's more important than anything your little brain could imagine, and we might be in need of a boy to serve us from time to time. After that, I can guarantee you nothing, so it will be up to you to make a good impression and hope that somebody will take you on. I really can't say fairer than that, so what do you think?"

Stanley thought about the proposition for a moment, before hearing a rustling sound. Turning, he was shocked to see that Arthur was just about finished with the task of throwing his father's body into the bushes. Once he was done, Arthur – by now slightly breathless – brushed his hands clean and began to make his way back over to the coach. William's corpse, meanwhile, was arranged something like a scarecrow against the thorns.

"What's it to be, yes?" the driver asked. "Bristol or death?"

"I think an agreement has been reached," Father Lovelady said calmly. "Arthur, will you help young Stanley up?"

Before Stanley had a chance to respond, he was seized from behind and hoisted into the air, and from that vantage point he was then thrust into the carriage with such force that he stumbled and fell against the empty seat opposite Father Lovelady. Next he turned and wondered whether he might climb back out of the carriage, only for Arthur to swing the door shut and slide a bolt across.

"You won't regret your decision," Father Lovelady purred, watching Stanley with a curious expression that seemed almost hungry. "You'll be quite safe with us, quite safe indeed. And in Bristol you shall have the chance to show your true character so that you can perhaps go further in life. Nobody can say fairer than that, nobody in the whole world. Do you have any idea how lucky you've been today?"

As the priest continued to explain to Stanley just how much good fortune had rained down upon him like some kind of miracle, Arthur clambered up onto the front of the carriage and took hold of the reins before getting the horses going again.

"Keep it moving, yes?" he said to the beasts as they moved together along the now moonlit road. "No rest for the wicked. We want to get to Bristol nice and promptly, yes?"

The beetles in the hedgerow had already started work devouring William Neville's flesh.

CHAPTER THIRTY-FIVE

THIRTY YEARS LATER, IN a windowless room in a certain palace deep in the heart of one of London's most secretive buildings, Father Stanley Neville stood before a pair of gold doors and waited patiently to be greeted.

He had been in that particular spot for quite a while now, but he knew he had no other choice. He had his own particular place in the pecking order at the cathedral, and while he didn't particularly enjoy waiting around to be seen by his superiors, he took some pleasure from the times when he was the one causing others – more junior than him, of course – to wait. And as the years went past, he was slowly moving his way up the ranks.

He endured less waiting these days, and

enjoyed more *causing* of waiting.

Hearing the creaking of a set of hinges, he realised that this latest wait was over. He took a moment to correct his posture, and then he watched as Father Ambrose stepped through into the room.

"Father Sloane will see you now," Father Ambrose said archly. "He's terribly sorry for keeping you waiting."

"Not at all," Father Neville said as he began to make his way through. "I'm just so grateful that he's able to see me at all, especially at such short notice."

***

"St. Jude's is a rather... unusual problem for us," Father Sloane said as he sat behind his desk, studying the latest report. "It has stood empty and untouched for quite some time, but one cannot simply dispose of an old church. Can you imagine the outcry if we sent in a gaggle of dirty men with sledgehammers?"

"That is not what I am suggesting at all," Father Neville replied. "Indeed, it is precisely that sort of outcome that I am trying to prevent. There is clearly little prospect of St. Jude's ever being put back into service as a house of worship, but my understanding is that the doors were merely locked several years ago and nobody has been to the place since."

"That is correct," Father Ambrose told him.

"Closing a church is about more than merely shutting the doors," Father Neville pointed out, pleased that so far he was managing to steer the conversation in the direction he'd hoped. "There are certain things that need to be... wound down."

"Wound down?" Father Sloane asked. "Is there something in there that has at some point been wound *up*?"

"Loose ends must be dealt with," Father Neville went on. "For one thing, regrettable though it might be, we should be mindful that there *are* thieves in this world. What if somebody tried to break into St. Jude's in search of gold or silver?"

"Is there any gold or silver there?" Father Sloane replied.

"That's just the point," Father Neville continued. "We don't know. I would imagine so."

"You raise some pertinent issues," the older man murmured before turning to another page of the report. "One would like to believe that no-one out there would dare to break into a church, and that no-one would be so desperate, yet one does hear the occasional tale of woe."

"One certainly does," Father Neville added.

"Thieves can certainly be a problem," Father Ambrose said. "There are some truly wretched creatures in this world. Why, I'm aware of travelling preachers who back in the day used to hide behind religion so that they might more readily target the innocent and naïve."

Father Neville bit his tongue. He knew full well that Father Ambrose was hinting at his own father, whose story he had made no attempt to hide, but he had no desire in that moment to rise to this particular bait.

"Just a reminder," Father Ambrose continued as the faintest of smiles spread across his lips, "that we must all be on the lookout for such things."

He pursed those lips now, seemingly content that his nasty little point had been made.

"But there is another matter," Father Sloane said, setting the report down and leaning back in his chair. "St. Jude's was officially closed because it was barely being used, and because nobody could be found to take the place on. We all know, however, that there were other reasons. The late Father Wardell, before he died, prepared this very report and emphasised that St. Jude's should in no way be reopened. Not ever."

"With all due respect," Father Neville said, having anticipated this line of reasoning, "by the end of his life Father Wardell was not entirely... of sound mind."

"Are you saying that he was mad?" Father Ambrose mused.

"I am saying no such thing," Father Neville continued, watching Father Sloane carefully. "I merely mean to point out that Father Wardell's word on the subject should not be considered definitive."

"His skull was filled with more cancer than brain by the end," Father Ambrose pointed out. "The doctor said it had spread from his wrist, which was most unusual. But I believe he maintained some degree of clarity, even as the shadow of death approached."

"Father Wardell believed that something evil lurked at St. Jude's," Father Sloane said firmly. "These facts aren't known to the general public, but within the council we are sometimes forced to declare a place off limits. Father Wardell invoked such an order, and in this he was supported by several learned colleagues. The details of his concerns were sealed away but we can infer certain facts. He believed that something bad had been contained at St. Jude's and that it would be best to leave the place undisturbed. That has been done, has it not?"

"Most successfully," Father Ambrose suggested.

"I see no reason to change that arrangement now," Father Sloane continued. "I know some might argue that we're merely postponing a difficult decision, but Father Wardell was a good man and his opinion carried great weight." He paused for a moment, keeping his eyes fixed on Father Neville. "I'm not going to let you go to St. Jude's," he said finally. "St. Jude's is to remain out of bounds for the foreseeable future. Is that understood?"

"Perfectly," Father Neville said through gritted teeth. "I just thought I would raise the possibility, that's all. But I shall of course accept your judgement in full."

"I was there when Father Wardell died," Father Sloane explained. "Even as the cancer was eating him away, he told me that St. Jude's must be left untouched forever. I made a most solemn promise to him on that day, and I do not break my promises lightly. I looked into his eyes as the light faded, and I saw the terror. His wishes are to be respected."

"Indeed," Father Neville replied, bowing his head slightly. "One would never think of doing anything else."

***

"Idiots!" the same man snapped angrily as he stormed back into his room and slammed the door shut. "Small-minded, unthinking fools!"

Hurrying to the window, he looked outside and saw several monks in the courtyard. For a moment he wanted to scream, but he quickly reminded himself that he needed to get his emotions under control. He'd been playing the long game for several decades now, working slowly but surely toward his goal, and he knew that there was no need to hurry anything along in a panic now.

As he looked out at the dark London street, he thought of St. Jude's hundreds of miles away. The gloomy buildings opposite began to burn away as a vision of the church emerged from his mind's eye and filled his field of vision. Back when he was a young man visiting Laidlow with his pathetic thief of a father, he'd only seen the church briefly from a distance. He'd met the anchoress, however, and he'd seen the madness burning in her eyes. Ever since that awful day, he'd been trying to understand the words that had spewed from her mouth. Somehow, in the back of his mind, he felt sure that there had been some hidden wisdom in the woman's crazed utterings.

She had been the opposite of his own father. She had been pure, where William Neville had been filled with sin. And she had been truthful, at least in her own way, while William Neville had constantly lied.

The church faded from his eyes now and he found himself once more looking out at the street. Spotting movement down below, he saw Father Sloane emerging from the front of the building and heading into his waiting vehicle. He felt an immediate rush of pity for the foolish man, for he knew that Sloane and all the others were still sticking dogmatically to the old teachings.

"The anchoress saw something," he whispered now as he watched Father Sloane being driven away. "Something beyond our limited understanding. Is that why you want St. Jude's to remain sealed up? Do you want her knowledge – whatever it might be – locked away forever? And how long do you think your fear will protect you?"

He wanted to scream to the heavens and tell the world that something more vast awaited, but he reminded himself once again that he had to wait. His own father had once claimed to bring new teachings to the world, and while such promises had been shrouded in ill intent, he told himself that he was going to be a better man. He'd researched the anchoress of St. Jude's extensively and he knew as much as possible about the life of Margaret Crake. All that was left was for him to journey there himself – and to find out whether, as he suspected, she might yet linger.

"Leave that place alone," he remembered Father Wardell gasping shortly before his death. "Promise me."

"I promise you," he whispered now. "I promise that I shall find a way to contact the anchoress of St. Jude's. And when I do, I shall learn all the secrets she uncovered."

CHAPTER THIRTY-SIX

January 1940...

"SO YOU FINALLY ADMIT it," John said, staring with contempt at Father Neville as the elderly man remained perched on a chair in the Red Lion's smaller guest room. "It *was* you all those years ago. I knew I recognised you."

"I cannot say the same for you," Father Neville replied, and he too was making no attempt to disguise a sense of genuine disgust. "Even now, I barely remember our little squabble in the yard."

"This man's father was a liar and a thief," John continued, turning to Harry and Barbara. "He claimed to be a teacher or a... preacher of some kind, but he was run out of town for thievery. He liked to knock on doors to ascertain whether or not anybody was home, and then he'd sneak around to the back and help himself to whatever he could find. Or sometimes he'd seduce an elderly widow for an hour or two and take whatever he could find in her bedroom. By all accounts he was known across several counties, and wanted by the authorities in most of them."

"And then he was beaten to death," Father Neville added.

"Some men from the village followed him when he was expelled," John admitted. "What happened after that, I cannot say."

"He was beaten and left in the road," Father Neville explained. "I might have died right next to him if I had not been picked up by a passing carriage. From there I was taken to London, and by a complicated route I found myself joining the priesthood. I always remembered my encounter with the anchoress Margaret Crake here in this village, and I swore that one day I would find my way back."

"So the scheme to find metal was just a ploy?" Harry asked.

"Father Sloane once warned against any attempt to come here," the older priest replied. "As I expected, however, the years wore down his opposition. I could not simply come here alone, I knew I had to do it with the full backing of the church. Eventually Father Sloane even forgot the promises he made to the dying Father Wardell. When I proposed coming to St. Jude's this time, I met with almost no opposition at all. The one stipulation was that I must not come without company, so I resolved to select the stupidest and most easily manipulated assistant I could find."

"I see," Harry said softly.

"You're lucky I haven't already heaved you out through the window," John snarled. "I'm not a monster, but as soon as you're well enough, you'll be wanting to get on your way. Your sort really isn't welcome here."

"And what is *my sort*?" Father Neville asked. "Someone who seeks the truth? Someone who believes that there might be more than the church acknowledges?"

John opened his mouth to reply, but in that moment Harry turned and hurried out of the room. Barbara looked around briefly before rushing after him, leaving John and Father Neville alone.

"My own man always told me," John muttered finally, "that the apple never falls far from the tree. It takes several generations for sin to wash from a family line. You're really not very different to old William Neville after all, are you?"

With that, he too turned and stormed out.

"I never said I was very different to my father," the old priest said, before looking down at the bandages on his wrists. "Only smarter. And braver."

***

"Are you alright?" Barbara asked as she stepped out into the yard behind the pub and saw that Harry had finally stopped to get some air. "That can't have been easy to hear. You mustn't put too much stock in that old fool's words, though. I feel bad saying this about a priest, but... he's clearly not a good man."

"One tires sometimes of being treated as a fool," Harry replied, turning to her. "Even if deep down one knows that there might be some truth to the claim. Or rather a lot of truth, in this case."

"You are no fool," she countered.

"I am always treated as the junior member of any party," Harry continued. "As the one least equipped to deal with the realities of the world. I have told myself for many years that eventually I shall become more respected, but if anything the reverse seems to be happening. Sometimes I fear..."

His voice trailed off, and after a moment he shook his head.

"This whole expedition has been a farce," he added finally, before pulling the notebook from his pocket. "While I have been dutifully cataloguing every metal bar and rivet at St. Jude's, Father Neville has been searching for this anchoress who he believes is still there."

"She *is* still there," Barbara told him.

"Not you too," he said with a sigh.

"How can you doubt it now?" she asked, making her way over to him. "Alright, so Father Neville went out there to find her. Did you not see the state he was in when he returned? He nearly died!"

"That doesn't mean that he found anything."

"Do you seriously believe that he didn't?" she continued. "I have half a mind to go up there right now and ask him directly. That's assuming my uncle hasn't already cast him out by his ear."

She waited for Harry to say something, but she could tell that he was already lost in his own thoughts again. More than anything she wanted to rush over and tell him not to worry, and to remind him that he shouldn't take Father Neville's words to heart, yet she wasn't sure whether it would be appropriate to even touch a man of the cloth. In truth she had become very fond of Harry Stone during his short stay at the Red Lion so far and she felt there was nothing she wouldn't do to try to help him.

"There's nothing there," he said suddenly.

"Where?"

"At St. Jude's," he continued, turning to her. "Yes, I heard a few noises that I can't explain, but otherwise there was no hint of any... ghostly presence."

She sighed.

"Wouldn't I have felt it?" he asked. "I am a priest, just as Father Neville is a priest. If he is so... in tune with such monstrosities, then what would it say about me if I was oblivious?"

"I never said that you -"

"Or do you think that I am just some blundering idiot who doesn't notice evil – pure evil – when it's right under his nose?"

"I never said that either."

"But you're thinking it," he went on. "Father Neville is aware of it, *you're* aware of it, the whole village of Laidlow apparently senses this thing yet I am apparently the only one who has noticed nothing of note at all! Either you are all wrong or I... I am blind!"

She tried to think of some way to answer him, but she could see the desperation in his eyes and she worried that she might only make everything worse.

"What would that say about me?" he asked, and now he seemed close to tears. "Perhaps everyone is right about me, perhaps I am uniquely ill-equipped to deal with the real world. Perhaps I should indeed be confined to some desk somewhere, pushing around paperwork and occasionally getting wheeled out as a useful idiot to help men like Father Neville with their schemes."

"Nobody has ever suggested such a thing," she told him, before making her way over and putting her hands on the sides of his arms. "Do you know what I feel when I look at you?" she asked, ignoring an urge to pull away. "I see a good, honest man with a proper heart. I see someone who looks for the best in the world around him, and who is absolutely dedicated to duty. I see someone I would trust with my life."

"I fear I would let you down," he murmured.

"I *know* you would not," she said confidently, before hesitating for a moment to look up into his eyes. "As for Father Neville, he is clearly a twisted and bitter man, and you would do well to remove yourself from his company. Why, just from the things he said upstairs today, I am quite sure he deserves to be defrocked. Please, do not judge yourself by his standard. You are a far, far better man than he could ever even imagine."

She waited for him to reply, but after a few seconds she began to worry that her outburst had been a little too forward. Pulling back, she worried that she might have shocked him, or that she might have broken any number of rules about how a young woman should talk to a priest when they were alone.

"I must decide what to do next," Harry told her cautiously. "Before I call Father Sloane's office,

I must determine the best course of action." He looked up at the higher windows in the building, and in that moment he saw Father Neville withdrawing from one of those windows – as if the entire conversation had been observed. "One thing is certain," he added. "From this moment on, I shall be nobody's fool."

CHAPTER THIRTY-SEVEN

"HE IS IN SUCH pain," Barbara said a short while later, standing in the Red Lion's kitchen and watching as her uncle continued to search through the cupboards. "Spiritual pain, I mean. Or emotional. I'm not sure of the difference. Do you think there is anything I can do to help him?"

"He's a priest," John muttered, sounding as if he was keen to end the conversation as swiftly as possible. "I rather think he should be able to come to the correct conclusion on his own. If anything, he's the one who should be helping other people – or he's not much of a priest at all."

"But if he can't even -"

"If he can't, then perhaps he has no business *being* a priest," he added. "You have to admit, he doesn't *look* much like one."

"And what is a priest *supposed* to look like?" she asked.

"Wiser," he said as he finally pulled out the correct pan. "Older, maybe. A dash of confidence would help."

"More like Father Neville, then?" she replied. "More like the lying son of a thief who sits upstairs right now with his wrists bandaged? I mean, *he* certainly looks the part, does he not? He looks like a priest, he acts like a priest, he talks like a priest... but do you trust him?"

She saw her uncle roll his eyes as he made his way toward the door.

"What do you think is really out there?" she called after him.

He pulled the door open as if he fully intended to ignore that question, but at the last second some inner concern perhaps held him back. Once he finally turned to his niece, there was fear in his eyes.

"Do you think the... malevolent spirit of some long-dead anchoress is really lurking in St. Jude's?" she asked. "Do you think that's what drove Tilly out of her mind? And almost Father Neville too? Or do you think it's just a load of gossip perpetuated by idle minds? I really want you to be honest, Uncle John. You know I've always trusted your opinion on any matter."

She waited, but she was already starting to

think that perhaps he wasn't going to speak.

"All those years ago," he said after a few more seconds, "when you and Tilly went out there and got into all that trouble, I thought your father was overreacting. I thought you were just two foolish girls who were playing games, and that what happened to Tilly was little more than some terrible misfortune. But over time, Barbara, I started to realise that you might have been *very* lucky to escape unscathed."

"Me?"

"We all know what happened to Tilly," he went on. "The fact that you managed to get her back to the village at all, and without any injuries yourself, is as much of a miracle as I've ever personally witnessed in my life. And while your own parents saw fit to disown you, I always viewed you as something of an inspiration. You have to understand, Barbara, that you're the only person from this village who has ever been caught up in anything at that church and lived to tell the tale. As far as I'm aware, at least."

"When you put it like that," she replied, as a shiver ran through her bones, "I realise that I must count myself very lucky indeed."

"That's why I don't like you getting involved with these priests now," he added. "I hate the idea of that *thing* in the church getting a second chance to strike at you. I don't think it'd miss this time."

"I'll be careful," she told him.

"I hope so," he said firmly. "Whatever happens to those two priests, remember that they're capable of making their own decisions. You have no duty whatsoever to rescue them from any consequences that might follow. They're men of the church. It's their *job* to handle this situation."

***

As she headed into her bedroom, Barbara told herself that she was just going to be a few minutes and that then she'd head back down to help her uncle prepare for opening. Grabbing a hairbrush, she made her way to the mirror in the corner and sat down, and then she froze as she saw a nail resting on the dresser.

Staring at the nail, which was black and slightly twisted, she quickly realised that it must be from the shed in the yard downstairs. Its origin was no mystery; the mystery was how it had made its way upstairs, and how it had ended up on her dresser when she knew full well that it hadn't been there earlier.

She looked at her own reflection in the cracked mirror, and then she began to search the rest of the image for any trace of a figure in the darkness.

"Tilly?" she said out loud, as a trace of

dread whispered its way up her spine and into her voice. "I know you're around sometimes, even if you don't actually talk to me. But are you here now?"

She swallowed hard as she waited, and after a few seconds she heard the faintest, softest touch of something pushing down against one of the room's looser floorboards.

"Tilly," she continued, "I don't know what to do. I don't trust anyone to leave that place alone. After you died... after that awful night, someone should have burned that church to the ground. It's know it's sacrilege, but I should have done it myself."

She waited, hoping that perhaps her old friend might appear and offer some wise advice, but instead she now heard only silence.

"Tilly," she went on, "I worry that even if Father Stone and Father Neville leave, someone else will be along eventually. People *forget*, Tilly. No matter how awful something might be, no matter how shocked people might feel, over time they always forget. Think of the war, so many people were horrified by the war twenty-odd years ago, yet now another has broken out. Horror always fades."

She felt a terrible sense of realisation as those words left her lips, for she knew deep down that they were completely and utterly true. She was right, too: horror *does* fade, sometimes within a generation and sometimes from one to the next. Things that seem unrepeatable *are* eventually repeated, given enough time. Having come to this realisation, however, Barbara now felt completely powerless to stop it.

"You should be the last victim of that place, Tilly," she said softly. "Of the anchoress. There should be no -"

Stopping suddenly, she thought back to that awful day, to the minutes before her friend's mind had been irreparably destroyed.

"It's really spooky," Tilly had insisted while peering into the church. "Oh Barbara, you simply *must* come up and look. If you don't, then on Monday morning I'll tell everyone at school that you're the most dreadfully cowardly little thing."

"Why did you have to do that?" Barbara whispered now, close to tears. "Why didn't I find a way to stop you?"

"There's somebody in there!" Tilly had exclaimed suddenly. "I'm not lying! There's somebody inside the church! It's a woman, I think! It must be the same old woman that Joseph's sister's friend saw!"

And then, almost immediately, she'd fallen. Barbara still remembered the horrifying sight, and the sound of Tilly's body hitting the ground, and she still wondered why she hadn't been able to catch her. A moment later the window panes nearby rattled in the wind, and somehow that sound transported Barbara back to the awful moment years earlier when – in the same room – Tilly had taken her own life.

"I can only hope to shatter her," Tilly had whispered, "so that she might finally let me rest."

Moments later she'd driven the nails into her own eyes, and Barbara could still hear the horrific squelching cracks that had erupted as the nails' tips had broken through the backs of the sockets. She turned and looked over toward the spot where the awful deed had occurred, and she found herself wondering how many other people would have to die before the horror of St. Jude's and its evil anchoress might end.

"I should have saved you," she said under her breath, wondering whether Tilly could hear her. "I know I failed you that day. You were the one who wanted to go to the church, but I should have found some way to stop you."

She waited, hoping desperately that Tilly might respond.

Getting to her feet, she looked all around the room.

"Tilly, if you're here and you can hear me," she continued as tears filled her eyes, "*please* tell me that you understand. And that you forgive me. Because I can't forgive myself, Tilly. Not for something like this. I need you to do it for me."

Again she waited, yet she wondered now whether she might in fact be all alone. She wanted nothing more than for Tilly to appear and make everything alright again, even if she knew deep down that this was unlikely.

"I get it," she said finally as the first tears rolled down her cheeks. "You can't appear and forgive me, because you *don't* forgive me. You know I should have done better. And these nails are your way to keep reminding me of the fact that I let you down. I just wish there might be some way to make it up to you, Tilly. Please, if there's anything, anything at all... can't you tell me?"

"Barbara!" John's voice called out suddenly, from the bottom of the stairs at the other end of the landing. "It's time to open up! Are you coming or not?"

CHAPTER THIRTY-EIGHT

HEARING VOICES SHOUTING LOUDLY at one another as the evening's drinking got underway, Father Stanley Neville stood in his room upstairs at the Red Lion and felt a shiver of revulsion run through his body.

"Despicable reprobates," he sneered under his breath. "Do you have nothing better to do with your lives than drink them away? Does all that beer drown out your fear of the truth?"

The voices continued unabated, only serving to make the old man's fury calcify in his heart. He wanted to storm downstairs and demand silence, to tell the men that they should mend their ways, but at the last second he reminded himself that it wasn't his job to deliver such fools from evil.

Not now.

Making his way across the room, he took his coat from the hook and began to slip his arms into the sleeves. He was still stiff and in pain, so the process took longer than it should. As he finished, he spotted movement out of the corner of his eye. He turned, half expecting to find that there was someone behind him, but he saw nobody at all. For some reason, however, in the back of his mind he felt as if a woman had almost appeared.

Or a girl.

"Hello?" he barked. "If there's someone lurking in here, you'd do well to identify yourself immediately. This might be a rented room but I still have every right to be left alone."

Again he waited, although the silence he heard told him that perhaps he had been mistaken all along. He knew that his mind was not quite in its proper state and that there was a risk he might be a little jumpy. The sun had set outside and he worried that he might not be up to the journey out to St. Jude's, but he knew that there was no time to waste and that – besides – the anchoress was for her own reasons much more active at night.

Looking down at the bandages on his wrists, he felt a flicker of irritation. He'd panicked when he'd seen her a few nights earlier and he'd almost paid for that panic with his life. After years and years of preparation he'd made mistake after mistake, yet he told himself now that he must have survived for a reason.

"To bring knowledge to the world," he whispered, supposing that this was the only reason that made sense. "To shatter the old falsehoods and reveal a new truth to the masses. A truth uncovered by the anchoress Margaret Crake."

For a moment he thought back to the first time he'd encountered her, in the village street all those years earlier. He'd been so terrified at first, and his mind had recoiled from her garbled pronouncements; but he'd also been *horrified* by her sagging old body and by her foul breath. As he'd grown up, he'd never been able to look at women – any women – as anything other than disgusting creatures of filth, and even the prettiest of them all had been filled with the potential to eventually look as foul and as putrid as Margaret Crake. The woman's words, meanwhile, had found a place to live in the back of his mind and had twisted there, eventually becoming something more ordered and more organised until one day he'd been struck by a singular thought.

"My father's methods might have been reprehensible," he'd whispered out loud, "but the basic idea... the idea of finding some new truth and teaching it to the masses..."

He'd never quite completed that thought, but the idea was good enough to stand on its own – albeit uncertain and half-finished. Margaret Crake possessed a truth that he needed to hear, a truth that he in turn was going to deliver to the world. He just needed to get to that truth first, and he knew now that he had waited long enough.

He stepped toward the door, and already he had the basic form of a plan in his mind. He was going to steal out to the church under cover of night, and this time his mind was going to be ready. He'd under-estimated the effect of Margaret Crake, and the impact of coming face-to-face with her; he'd ended up running from her, after almost being destroyed by her when she'd attacked him in the pulpit. Hell, he'd damn near hollowed out his own wrists, but this time he was going to face her down and make her reveal her truths.

And then, as he began to open the door, he felt a sudden sense of discomfort at the back of his throat. He expected this sense to disperse after a second of two, but instead it became stronger. Stepping back, he took a deep breath and told himself that there was no need to be concerned, but a fraction of a second later he began to splutter and gasp as he felt something moving against the very deepest part of his tongue.

Barely able to breathe now, he lowered himself to his knees and reached out. With his left hand he supported himself against the side of the bed and with his right hand he leaned against the dresser, but finally he began to bend forward.

Retching, he felt as if he was about to vomit, yet something hard was scraping against the back of his throat. Finally he took his right hand – which was doing less to support him than his left – and reached into his mouth, and to his shock he felt something thin and hard emerging from his gullet.

He took hold of the object with two fingers and pulled it forward. Another part of the metal scraped against his tongue, but by slowly turning the object he was able to get it free. Finally he pulled it out, and he was horrified to find that he had produced – from deep within his own body – a slimy, saliva- covered black nail with a twisted four or five inch length topped by a partially flattened head. Staring in utter dismay at the nail, he couldn't even begin to understand how it had found its way into his throat, but finally he cast it aside before stumbling to his feet and hurrying to the door.

Once he was out on the landing, he made the mistake of glancing over his shoulder. In that instant he saw a young girl standing in the room, where previously there had been no young girl at all, and he saw too that her eyes were entirely gone. He felt a strange sense of peace radiating from her, as if she wanted him to stay with her so that everything would be alright, but he quickly realised that she was a fool like all the rest.

Slowly she reached a hand out toward him, extending an offer for him to remain.

After pulling the door shut, he began to make his way silently to the top of the stairs.

***

"And *I* am telling *you*," Harry said as he stood in the back room, with the telephone's receiver once again pressed against the side of his face, "that I must speak to Father Sloane immediately. I'm sorry, but an intermediary won't do. What I have to tell him..."

His voice trailed off for a moment as he realised that he risked coming across as a madman. At the same time, he also knew that he couldn't hide anything, and that he had to report the truth to the authorities.

"I might never be taken seriously again," he added, "but I must tell him nonetheless."

He waited, convinced that as always he was going to be fobbed off and told that Father Sloane was busy, that he had gone to dinner or that he was in a meeting or that he was otherwise engaged. After a moment, however, he realised that something seemed very different, and that he could hear other muffled voices in the very background of the call.

"Hello?" he continued.

"Father Sloane... cannot come and speak to you," the voice on the other end of the line said uncertainly, almost trembling with fear. "Father Sloane is unavailable because -"

"I don't want to hear it!" Harry snapped, before quickly pulling himself together again. "I must speak with him!"

"Father Sloane is dead," the voice replied.

At this news, Harry hesitated for a moment.

"Dead?" was all he could say, finally, in return.

"A most regrettable turn of events has occurred," the voice continued, as others began to shout at one another in the background. "He asked me last night about your progress. Yours and Father Neville's, at least. I told him everything I had heard from either of you. He listened in silence and bade me leave. This morning, I arrived to open up his office as usual and I found..."

Harry waited for the man to continue.

"Oh, it was too horrible," the voice added finally, and the trembling state of his tone indicated that this was no word of a lie. "What he had done to himself... I have never seen so much blood in all my life. He had taken a letter-opener to his wrists and cut them open to such an extent that one hand was barely hanging on at all. It was as if he'd tried to turn his arms inside out. I could see that the bone itself had been partially carved away."

"Father Sloane killed himself?" Harry whispered "After learning of our work here? Are you sure that is the reason?"

He hesitated. A moment later he heard a shuffling sound, as if someone had reached the bottom of the stairs. He looked through and saw no sign of anyone, so – assuming that he had been mistaken – he turned to face the window again.

"I must go," the voice on the other end of the line stammered. "Call back tomorrow, I might have more to offer you but... I can't tell you how awful things are here right now. Last night, as I left Father Sloane, I swear I saw a look in his eyes as if... as if he was contemplating the end of the world itself."

CHAPTER THIRTY-NINE

STEPPING OUT THROUGH THE Red Lion's back door, having easily slipped past the room where he might have been spotted by Harry, Father Neville stopped for a moment to take a deep breath in the cold night air. He knew that he faced a long journey out to the church, but he also knew that he had no choice. As roars filled the air, blasting out from the drunkards in the pub, he stepped forward and began to make his way across the yard.

"Going somewhere?"

Startled, he turned to see that John was in the process of rolling a barrel through from a small shed on the yard's far side.

"You're up and about," John continued. "That's good, I suppose. It means there'll be no reason for you not to leave first thing in the morning."

Father Neville hesitated before turning to simply walk away. Arriving at the gate, he reached out for the latch, ready to pull it open. As much as he wanted to argue with the landlord and put him in his place, he told himself that he needed to be the bigger man and simply walk away. Besides, he was too busy to waste any time on such simpletons.

"Now that I remember you," John sneered, "I can't believe that I forgot you at all. You and your pathetic thief of a father were among the most miserable wretches to ever pass through this village."

After resting his hand on the latch for a few seconds, the priest turned to look over his shoulder. At that moment cheers and roars rose up from inside the pub; the useful idiots in the bar area, he noticed, were making a good amount of noise. Indeed, he felt that there was enough noise to cover up almost anything that happened outside the building.

And while he was certainly pressed for time, he began to reason that he had a couple of minutes to spare.

"I've never been particularly trusting of men like you," John explained as he manoeuvred the barrel into position and then stepped back. "Priests, I mean. Men who dress themselves up in fancy clothing and act like they're better than everyone else. Of course *some* priests are wise and learned men, but many are just liars and charlatans. At least your father lacked the costume, though. William Neville looked like a thief from the moment I first set eyes on him."

"He *was* a thief," Father Neville replied solemnly.

"So you admit it?"

"I could not do otherwise," the priest said, spotting a chisel that had been left on a nearby bench, and slowly starting to make his way over so that he could slip it into his right hand. "My father was everything you make him out to be and more. You don't even know the half of it. His supposed revelations were mere fantasies he'd thought up for the express purpose of deceiving the weak and desperate. He didn't believe a word of that nonsense, but he was rather good at making *other people* believe it. He had an almost supernatural ability to bend the wills of the weak and feeble-minded."

"You sound almost proud."

"I'm not proud in the slightest," Father Neville continued. "He got what was coming to him. He deserved to die exactly as he did. I don't even know what happened to his body after Father Josiah Lovelady plucked me up from the street and took me away, but I can't bring myself to care too much. His bones are perhaps out there still, abandoned in some hedgerow where they belong. I can only hope that at least his flesh provided a hearty meal for some passing vermin."

"I'm surprised by your attitude," John said, turning away so that he could reach down for the barrel once more. "And to think... all those years ago I beat you in a fight here in this very same yard."

"Beat me?" Father Neville replied, raising an amused eyebrow. "You didn't *beat* me at anything. We merely took... an extended pause before returning to finish things."

"And what -"

In that moment the priest rushed at John and wrapped an arm around the man's throat. He knew that John was bigger and stronger than him in almost every regard, so he made haste to raise up his right hand and drive the chisel straight through the side of his opponent's neck. Indeed, he used such force that the sharpened end crunched through the man's trachea and twisted out on the other side. Then, worried that John might call for help, Father Neville turned the handle around and forced the metal out through the front of his lifelong foe's throat.

He heard a loud splattering sound in the darkness. For a moment he had no idea where this might be coming from, until he realised that blood was positively spraying from the wound as John let out a series of pained gasps.

Seeing that his work was done, Father Neville waited a moment longer until he felt the man's legs buckling. Holding him up, he dragged him around to the side of the shed; finally too weak to support him for even a moment longer, he lowered John to the ground. By the time he set the man down he could tell that he was dead, so he stepped back and took a few seconds to remind himself that he had to avoid any further diversions – no matter how pleasurable they might be.

After secreting the chisel in a flowerpot, the priest slipped out through the back gate. Voices were still laughing and cheering inside the Red Lion as he hurried around to the front and set off on the long trek out to St. Jude's. And then, at the very last moment, he spotted a figure riding a bicycle to a halt and dismounting near the front of the pub.

***

"Come off it," one of the many drunks in the Red Lion roared as he set his pint glass down, "I'll bet *all* of you that this war'll be over by Christmas! By now Adolf realises what a mistake he made. We just have to offer him a way to climb down without him losing face, and he'll shake our outstretched hands so fast and so hard that he'll damn near yank them off!"

"Excuse me," Harry said, squeezing through the crowd and feeling utterly out of his element. "I'm sorry, has anyone seen -"

"You've never been more wrong about anything in your life, Jim," another voice called out. "This is going to be a long war, mark my words. Longer than the last one, that's for sure. It's gonna spread, too. Soon the whole world'll be caught up in it."

"Not the Yanks," a third voice suggested.

"Oh, them too," another man – perhaps the second, perhaps a new entry into the discussion – retorted. "They'll be dragged in kicking and screaming, whether they like it or not. The only question is whose side they'll be on!"

"Ours, of course!"

"Excuse me," Harry continued, turning the other way so that he could slip between two men, finally allowing him to reach the bar – where he saw no sign of anyone actually working. "I'm sorry to bother you," he murmured, turning to one of the revellers, "but do you know where -"

"It's old Joe Stalin I've got my eye on," another man muttered, and now all the voices seemed to be merging into one as Harry desperately looked around for some sign of John – or preferably Barbara. "He'll have his finger on the scale before too long."

This suggestion prompted a barrage of

predictions, ranging from the rational to the utterly ridiculous, and soon Harry was unable to separate out one argument from another. The men of the Red Lion – and fifty at least had crowded into the room for what had turned into an impromptu debate – were all keen to air their thoughts, and they were clearly all determined to shout over one another rather than taking turns to speak. The result was a terrible din that was now taking on a life entirely of its own, and Harry – a man more accustomed to the quiet libraries of the church's offices in London – felt as if he was rapidly losing all sense of place and time.

"Right," he said finally, feeling as if he needed to get out of the crowd so that he might at least hear himself think. "If you'll excuse me..."

Now he was trying to get to the front door, and indeed he couldn't shake the fear that he might be on the verge of passing out due to sheer lack of oxygen. So many opinions were being shouted all around him that he wondered whether any air was left in the room at all, and by the time he somewhat miraculously reached the door and pulled it open he genuinely worried that he might have been about to suffocate. Just as he was making his way outside, however, he had the misfortune to encounter an extremely angry man who was in the process of marching in the other direction – as if, in some moment of utter madness, this man thought it a good idea to *join* the airless throng of voices inside the Red Lion.

"Sorry, Father," the man said, at least recognizing the sin of almost flattening a priest. "I didn't see you there."

"It's quite alright," Harry replied. "I was only -"

"Some bugger's stolen my bike, that's all," the man continued angrily. "I only leaned it against the wall five minutes ago and now someone's been off with it. Can you imagine that?"

"Indeed, I cannot," Harry said, shocked that anyone in such a close-knit community would steal a bicycle – before suddenly realising that perhaps it wasn't someone from the local community who was responsible for the theft at all. "Wait," he stammered, looking up at the higher windows and seeing that there was no light in the room supposedly occupied by Father Neville. "Did you see which way the miscreant went?"

CHAPTER FORTY

THE BIKE RATTLED AND shuddered as it was shoved crudely against the stone wall, and then again as it tipped over and landed in the long grass.

By this point, a rather breathless Father Stanley Neville was already marching past the gravestones and heading toward the front of St. Jude's. On this moonlit night he could see well enough, and the church was picked out in an ethereal blue glow that made it seem almost as if it existed in another world. Reaching the door, Father Neville found that it was locked, but this time he was in no mood to wait.

Stepping back, he told himself that the task of breaking the door down shouldn't be beyond him, so he turned his shoulder and stormed forward. He felt the door shudder, as if it might yield, but in truth he hadn't expected to break it down so easily. Filled with a sense of righteous determination, he set about striking the door again and again, and after just half a dozen attempts he was able to break the lock and crack the door open, finally stumbling into the church's interior.

"You were right to lock it up securely, Father Stone," he muttered under his breath. "So pathetically, obediently... *right*."

A ripple of irritation ran through his bones.

"Fat lot of good it'll do you, of course. Typical arrogant priest."

He froze, immediately remembering his panicked flight from this very spot just a few nights earlier. For a moment he felt the same fear starting to flood into his soul, but he immediately forced himself to stay strong. Yes, he'd almost died in the pulpit when Margaret Crake had sought his soul, and even the hastily-assembled crude crucifix had only bought him a matter of a few minutes' respite. He *had* escaped, however, and he very quickly reminded himself that this miracle must have occurred for a reason.

"I have been chosen," he whispered.

As he looked across the church, however, he saw no sign of the anchoress. He knew that young Father Stone had been out to the place during the day and had seemingly survived unmolested, so he could only assume that the anchoress had retreated.

She would surely return for him, however, now that the entire church was filled with nothing but moonlight and shadows.

Indeed, he felt sure that she must already have sensed his return.

"I am here," he said softly, slowly starting to make his way along the aisle, reaching out and touching the sides of the pews as he passed them. The wood was so very cold, each pew a little colder than the one before. "This time I am prepared. I ask only that you tell me what you learned during all your years in isolation as an anchoress. And then I, in turn, shall find the best way to reveal this new truth to the world. You cannot keep it all to yourself forever, you know."

The only sound he heard, as he reached the chancel, came from his own shoes patting against the floor. Finally he stopped so that he could listen better, yet even now the silence of the church seemed to be answering him with its own defiance. He looked around, watching the shadows to see if any of them might move, before finally he looked toward the sacristy and saw the bare wall that hid the chamber of the anchoress.

"There is one difference between today and my last visit," he said out loud. "This time I know precisely where to find you. You are not hidden from me, as you are hidden from other men."

He began to make his way slowly and

calmly toward that wall, and with each step he felt now as if his confidence was increasing.

"I come to you as a friend," he added, stopping at the wall and reaching out to touch its smooth whiteness. "As a fellow believer in the importance of the truth." He hesitated, before looking up at the ledge above the wall. "This time I am going to prove to you, from the start, that I am on your side. And that I can understand the truth without losing my mind."

***

"Gone?" Barbara said, puzzled as she hurried behind the bar and began to deal with the backlog of requests for beer. "Gone where? I'm sorry, I'm confused. First, where's my uncle?"

"Haven't seen him for a while now," Martin Green muttered, sliding his empty glass toward her. "We've all been yelling for service but he hasn't been back since he went to sort out one of the barrels."

"Alright, give me a moment and I'll find him," she said as she began to pour two pints at once. "And what did you say about Father Stone again?"

"Only that he went out the front and I haven't seen him since," Martin went on as the debate raged all around him. "To be honest, he looked a little peaky. I'm not sure that a man like him really feels too at home in a place like this."

"That much I can well believe," she said with a sigh, as she glanced over her shoulder but saw that there was still no sign of John. "It's so utterly chaotic in here."

"We considered serving ourselves," Martin admitted, "but then some of us remembered how John reacted last time that happened and... well, I wouldn't put it past him to bar a few of us for a week, just to prove a point."

"You were right not to do that," Barbara told him as she slid the first beers across the bar and immediately began to pour two more. She still couldn't help glancing around, convinced that her uncle had to reappear at any moment. "He rules this pub with an iron fist. Sometimes I'm even amazed that *I'm* allowed to pull pints."

"John dotes on you," Martin reminded her. "He sees you as the child he and Bea never had. I mean it. Beneath that gruff exterior, he's a decent fellow."

"Here you go," she said, setting the next two pints down before wiping her hands on a tea towel. "I'll be back in a moment," she added as she headed through into the kitchen. "I just want to find out where he's gone."

Once she was away from the others, she began to check various rooms at the rear of the pub.

Her uncle hadn't mentioned plans to go anywhere and she couldn't remember the last time she'd lost track of him; he certainly wasn't the type to go wandering off and she couldn't shake the slightest niggling sense of concern at the back of her mind. Even as she stepped out into the moonlit yard and took a look around, she was trying hard to convince herself that everything was fine, but after a moment she spotted a barrel that had seemingly been left out in the cold.

"What the..."

She made her way over and took a look at the barrel, and then she once again glanced around the moonlit yard. No matter how hard she tried to tell herself now that there was no need to be concerned, she felt as if some hidden extra sense had begun to tug at the extremes of her consciousness.

She looked around again, then again, each time convinced that eventually she was going to notice something that so far she'd missed.

"Uncle John?" she said cautiously, convinced that he must be nearby. "Is everything alright? I thought you were out here but..."

She hesitated, telling herself that he was clearly gone, yet she felt sure that some aspect of his soul was nearby, almost as if she could sense his lifeblood itself. Stepping past the barrel, she made her way toward the far wall, as if drawn by some hidden essence that she still couldn't quite detect. After a moment she tripped and stumbled slightly; she reached out and supported herself against the wall, before pulling her hand away and turning to look back across the yard.

"Uncle John?" she said again. "Are you -"

Before she could finish that next question, she realised that her hand was wet. She looked down and saw that her palm was discoloured. Holding her hand up, she realised that it was coated in something dark, and when she moved it closer to her face she picked up the faintest hint of blood.

"Uncle John?" she called out, sounding far more frantic this time as she hurried past the shed. "What -"

In that moment she saw him. Her uncle's crumpled body had been left partially hidden behind some boxes near the shed's door. Even as she hurried over, she sensed somehow that he was dead. When she moved the boxes aside, she let out a shocked gasp as she saw the confirmation: his throat had been cut open and she could now see a pool of blood that had gathered at the base of the wall.

She opened her mouth to scream, but at the last second the sound caught in the back of her throat. Instead she let out a brief gasp, as if the effort of holding the scream in was too much, before stepping back and bumping against the side of the shed. As much as she wanted to cry out, she knew already that attracting more and more attention would only add to the horror and confusion.

Instead her sense of shock was already being diverted into the need to do something, into the need to avenge her uncle's death and to make sure that nothing like it could ever happen again. After a moment she looked up at the windows above, but she already knew that Father Neville wouldn't be there. Certain that the elderly priest must have killed her uncle, she told herself that there was only one place he could possibly be now.

CHAPTER FORTY-ONE

HAVING BORROWED A BICYCLE from a man at the Red Lion – and having promised to get it back in one piece before morning – Harry finally reached the moonlit graveyard in front of St. Jude's and dismounted. He carefully leaned the bike against the wall, and in that moment he saw a second bike a little further on.

"I knew it," he said under his breath, before starting to pick his way through the long, dark grass. "Why couldn't you just stay away?"

As he approached the church's front door, which he already saw had been broken open, he realised that he had absolutely no plan whatsoever; indeed, he didn't even have the faintest outline of the concept of a plan. At the same time he felt sure that he would be able to talk Father Neville out of whatever crazy action was about to take place, or that he would be able to subdue the man if necessary, and that somehow the Lord would watch over them and make sure that nothing went too wrong. Convinced that his superior must have lost his mind, he stepped through the doorway and stopped to look across the church, and he was shocked to realise that there was no sign of anyone at all.

"Father Neville?" he called out, certain that he couldn't possibly be alone. "I know you're here. You *have* to be here. Father Neville, I need you to make yourself known to me immediately."

He heard nothing in response, but this did little to calm his fears. Making his way along the aisle, still looking all around, he felt his heart pounding as he realised that Father Neville was perhaps hiding somewhere nearby, in which case he was quite clearly out of his mind. Thinking back to the awful state of the man upon his return from the church, he began to worry that something quite terrible was about to happen and that Father Neville might indeed be hell bent on finishing the job he'd already started.

"Father Neville, you must speak to me at once," he continued, trying to hide a sense of panic. "Father Neville, where are you? I know you're here somewhere, I saw the bicycle outside."

Reaching the chancel, he looked around and

tried to work out what had changed. *Something* was different, of that he felt certain, yet he couldn't put his finger on the precise nature of the change until finally he saw what appeared to be some tools that had been left near the door to the sacristy. He hurried over and spotted what appeared to be a few chunks of stone, but he still couldn't quite work out exactly what Father Neville had been doing.

"Father," he went on, trying to hide a sense of irritation now, "I really must insist that you reveal yourself. This sort of behaviour is entirely out of character and I have grounds to worry greatly about your state of mind. If you are here then -"

Suddenly he heard a scrabbling sound, as if somebody had kicked a loose piece of stone. He turned, half expecting to find Father Neville directly behind him, but once again there was nobody around.

"I don't know what you think you'll gain from these games," he said, "but this conduct is highly unbecoming of... of a man of your status. Why, what do you think Father Sloane would say if he knew about all this?"

As those words left his lips, he realised that Father Neville likely hadn't even heard the awful news from London. He considered holding the information back, but after a moment he began to wonder whether this might be just the revelation to jolt the older man back to reality.

"I am sorry to inform you," he said cautiously, "that I telephoned Father Sloane's office before I came out here and I received the most dreadful news. Father Sloane is dead by his own hand. I'm sure I don't have to explain the implications of this fact or -"

Before he could get another word out, he heard someone laughing nearby. He turned and looked over his shoulder, and after a moment he spotted a figure stepping out from the shadows.

"Father Neville?" he said cautiously. "Perhaps you didn't hear me correctly, but I just explained that Father Sloane is dead. I don't know exactly what's going on here but I think we should withdraw from the church and await further instructions."

"Dead," Father Neville laughed, grinning from ear to ear as if he was genuinely amused. "Finally. That stupid old fool, I knew he was weak but I thought it might take a little more to finish him off. Still, I suppose one less priest in the world is a good thing."

"I don't think you're showing the proper level of respect," Harry replied.

"Oh, forget about that," Father Neville chuckled, stepping behind him and heading toward the sacristy door, before taking a ladder that had been left propped against one wall and moving it to another. "You only met Father Sloane a few times, I believe. I knew the old idiot for years, and let me promise you that nobody will mourn his death. Not really. That man wouldn't have known the truth if it walked up to him and slapped him in the face."

He took a moment to check that the ladder was secure.

"Father Neville," Harry said cautiously, "I don't know what you're doing out here, but I must insist that we go back to Laidlow. And then, tomorrow, we must secure passage to London at the earliest opportunity."

He waited for a reply, but after a few seconds Father Neville began to climb the ladder.

"What are you doing?" Harry called after him.

"Come and see! Forget about Father Sloane, he's yesterday's news. No-one actually cares about that man at all. Give it six months and he'll be entirely forgotten. He'll just be rotting in some grave somewhere."

"Where are you going?" Harry asked as he watched Father Neville stepping onto a narrow ledge at the top of the wall.

"Come and see!" Father Neville said again, before leaning down and lighting a candle that had already been placed on a plate nearby. The candle's flickering light immediately cast a range of dancing shadows across his features. "It's no good standing down there and gawping up at me like some kind of fool, Father Stone. I know you can be a rather reluctant adventurer, but the time has come to grasp this opportunity. We're on the same side, you and I, so come on up."

"I would rather that *you* came *down*," Harry said with a sigh.

This time, as he waited, he realised that his plea had fallen on deaf ears. Father Neville was clearly far more interested in whatever he had found at top of the ladder; even now he was muttering to himself as he stepped around the candle and looked down at something, and Harry was starting to understand that he was never going to get a sensible answer from the man's lips.

Finally, very much against his better judgement, he walked over to the ladder. He gave it a cursory check of his own, to make sure that it was really secure, and then he began to climb. Deep down he felt sure that he was making a mistake, but as he reached the top he saw that he was at the edge of a narrow platform atop one of the walls. From below he hadn't noticed this space, yet now he found that there was room for him to step out onto the rocky surface, while he saw that Father Neville was at the edge of a small gap that had been revealed when a stone had – at some point previously – been pushed aside.

"It's ingenious, really," Father Neville muttered as the candle continued to flicker. "It took me quite a while to work it out. Once I identified the most likely resting place of the anchoress, my first thought was that I would have to break through the wall. I must admit that I was relieved when I noticed this ledge up here, and then again when I found the stone and realised that it could be moved aside..."

His voice trailed off as he continued to stare down into the hole, and then he turned and gestured for Harry to join him.

"Come, come," he added. "We stand at the threshold of something extraordinary. And please, wipe that gormless look from your face."

"Gormless look?" Harry replied, bemused by that suggestion.

"Get over here, young fellow," Father Neville continued. "I won't bite! I've been dreaming of this moment for so very long. There's really no need to be scared."

As much as he wanted to climb down the ladder and insist upon an immediate return to the village, Harry understood that he had to play along, at least for now. The ledge was only about a meter wide, and he felt somewhat unsteady as he began to inch his way along to join Father Neville. While he'd never considered himself to be scared of heights, he couldn't help but imagine the injuries that one might sustain by falling from such a position, and he was rather perturbed to realise that the one metre clearance was narrowing slightly as he reached the other priest.

"You're perfectly safe," Father Neville said, picking up the plate and the candle. "You'll be fine. Now, what do you think this hole is, eh?"

"Father -"

"You must have guessed. Come along, don't act the fool, Father Stone. You might be a somewhat naïve young fellow, but even that has its limits."

Harry still hesitated, convinced that there had to be some other way to talk Father Neville down from the ledge. Finally, however, he began to make his way over, until he looked down at the hole and saw nothing but darkness below.

"You *know* what this is, do you not?" Father Neville whispered, still holding the candle. "You must be able to sense it. When I moved the stone, I found that I had uncovered a way into the chamber of the anchoress Margaret Crake. This is where she has been hiding all these years."

"She has hardly been hiding," Harry replied cautiously, still staring into the darkness but seeing nothing down there. "She has been dead."

"It was very kind of Father Wardell to leave this route into her chamber," Father Neville continued. "In truth, I imagine that was simply an oversight left behind when the chamber was constructed. Or perhaps whoever built the damn thing couldn't bring himself to truly seal the woman inside, so he left an easy way to break it open if necessary. We'll never know for sure." He paused, before handing the candle to Harry. "Kneel and look, young man," he added. "You must see her."

"I do not need -"

"Kneel and look," Father Neville said firmly. "Then perhaps you will understand. If you do not, we can talk about leaving this place immediately."

Although he was reluctant to comply, Harry had already taken the candle and he supposed that there was no harm in at least looking into the so-called chamber. He wasn't even sure that there would be anything to see, yet slowly and very carefully he dropped down onto his knees before peering into the gap. Still, however, he saw nothing below.

"You must hold the candle down," Father Neville told him. "Reach through."

"I'm not sure that -"

"You're quite safe. You don't fear that she might suddenly lunge up and grab you, do you?"

"Of course not," Harry replied, before telling himself that he was going to have to prove his lack of fear.

He hesitated again, before steadying himself with one hand against the side of the opening and then leaning down until he'd managed to reach his other hand – holding the candle – into the admittedly cold and slightly damp space beneath the gap. He wanted to point out that he could still see nothing, but he knew this wouldn't be enough so instead he simply turned the candle a little while leaning further, hoping to -

In that moment he froze as he saw a dark, domed shape just a couple of feet further down. Already, even without looking more closely, he could tell that this was the top of a person's head, and that the person in question was wearing what appeared to be a black veil.

"It's her," Father Neville said softly, perhaps to Harry or perhaps merely to himself.

"I..."

Swallowing hard, Harry moved his hand a little further away from the top of the head. His heart was racing even though he knew there was no need to panic, but he was finally starting to understand the sight before him. There was indeed a figure – a woman, he could tell – sitting on a wooden chair inside the chamber. Although her body was covered in a dark shroud with a veil that hid her features, there was something about the woman's upright posture that immediately told Harry this was indeed the anchoress about whom he'd heard so much. She was entirely still, and he realised after a few seconds that her corpse had clearly been propped up in the chair and left in this manner.

The rest of the chamber, such as it was, seemed hardly large enough for somebody to walk around the chair. The candle's flickering light caught the bare stone walls, although after a few seconds Harry began to notice what appeared to be various scratch marks all across the surfaces.

"Isn't she magnificent?" Father Neville whispered.

"This is most certainly an arresting sight," Harry replied, struggling to resist the urge to pull away. "I confess that I can scarcely believe she was left in such a way."

"You consider it sacrilegious?"

"I consider it... unusual. Should she not have been taken out from this place and buried in hallowed ground?"

"Old Father Wardell must have had his reasons," Father Neville murmured. "Besides, it's also possible that the anchoress herself *truly* requested this fate. Not everything has to be a lie."

"And she has been sitting here ever since," Harry mused, genuinely shocked by the idea. "Are we to leave her like this? Surely that would be wrong, would it not?"

"By my count she has been like this for fifty-four years," Father Neville pointed out. "That is how much time has elapsed since her death. Before that she spent sixty-one years almost entirely within the confines of this chamber. That makes -"

"One hundred and fifteen years," Harry said, finishing the older man's sentence for him as he felt a sense of awe starting to fill his chest.

"Do you struggle to comprehend such a momentous length of time?"

"I consider myself to be a man of God," Harry replied, "yet the idea of hiding myself away like this from the world, and for so long, is almost impossible to imagine. I commend her soul highly and I can only assume that she must have been one of the most devout people who ever lived."

"She had the courage to face the truth," Father Neville said darkly. "She sought answers. When those answers turned out to be not what she wanted to hear, she did not bury her head in the sand. She didn't fall back on old lies. Instead she continued to listen, and she began to understand a grander truth that we all might yet learn. I met her once, many years ago, and I got only the slightest taste of her knowledge. Now I want it all."

Reaching up, he pulled his collar away.

"It must be done, however," he continued, "on her own terms. I fear she no longer tolerates those of us who wear such vestments. And she wants a token of respect."

"What do you mean?" Harry asked, looking over at him. "Father Neville, she is dead."

"I come to her as a man ready to learn," Father Neville continued, tilting his head slightly as he continued to look down at the anchoress. "Last time she became furious at the sight of me, but I know now that this was because I was wearing the dress of those she came to hate. She attacked me and almost killed me, almost drove me insane. This time will be different, for now I understand how she sees the world."

"She is *dead*," Harry pointed out once more. "Her soul is with the Lord now."

"I freed her once from this chamber," Father Neville said under his breath. "She returned to it once I was gone. Now I shall call for her to rise again, and I am certain that she will recognize me as a true disciple of her cause. First, though, I fear I must make an offering to her. A sacrifice, if you will."

"What kind of sacrifice?" Harry asked, before silently admonishing himself for entertaining such madness. "Father Neville, I do not think we should be doing this. We need to arrange for her to be buried properly so that her soul can truly rest in peace."

He waited for a reply, but Father Neville was now merely staring at the top of the dead woman's head.

"Such greatness awaits," the old man whispered finally. "To be the first, the very first, to hear the words of Margaret Crake and to spread those words to an unsuspecting public... I can only express my profound gratitude for the fact that I have been placed in this position. But first, let me show the anchoress that I understand what she needs."

He bowed his head a little more.

"Anchoress," he added, speaking so softly now that his voice barely rose above a whisper. "I give you my offering."

"This is foolishness," Harry told him. "I must protest about -"

Suddenly Father Neville lunged at him, knocking him over and sending him crashing down through the gap. The candle fell also, snuffing out as it hit the wall. Missing the woman in the chair, Harry slammed down against the stone floor and let out a pained gasp as he rolled onto one side, but already he could hear a grinding sound and as he looked up he saw in the moonlight that Father Neville was pushing the stone slab back into place.

"Wait!" Harry shouted, trying to get to his feet – only to feel a sharp jolt of agony in his right foot. "What are you doing?"

"Forgive me," Father Neville said breathlessly as he finished sliding the slab across the gap, cutting off all the light and plunging both Harry and the anchoress back into darkness. "I have no choice! I must give her an offering before she shows me the truth! I must feed her a priest!"

CHAPTER FORTY-TWO

STANDING IN PITCH DARKNESS, unable to see so much as the nose in front of his own face, Harry took a moment to try to better understand his situation. He'd just about managed to stand now, despite the pain in his right foot, and his back was brushing against the rough stone wall of the chamber. The air all around him was cold, almost like ice, but in his mind's eye he could still somehow see the anchoress in her chair.

She was in front of him, he knew that much. He was trapped with her now in a chamber measuring no more than ten or so feet in any direction.

"Father Neville?" he called out finally, looking up toward the slab that he knew must still be there above him in the darkness. "Father Neville,

I don't know if this is some kind of trick or joke or... or test, but I must... I must demand that you let me out immediately!"

As he waited, he realised that he could hear only silence. He knew that the other priest couldn't possibly have hurried away so quickly, but after a few seconds he heard a scrabbling sound accompanied by the metal clang of a ladder.

"Father Neville, come back!" he shouted, turning and banging a fist against the wall – a move that he instantly realised was foolish. "Father Neville, I demand that you release me at once. Do you hear me? I will not... I will not -"

As those words caught in the back of his throat, he realised that Father Neville must have entirely lost his mind. There seemed to be no possibility of reasoning with the man, of appealing to his sanity. Indeed, he could only imagine that Father Neville was even at that moment lost in a sense of rampant expectation, filled with delusions about some great truth he believed he was about to learn.

"Father Neville, you must see that this is so very wrong," Harry said, even as unwanted thoughts of the anchoress began to leech into his mind, and as he began to worry that he might suffocate in such a small and enclosed space. "Father Neville, you..."

His voice trailed off.

"You must understand that this is..."

He hesitated, and then slowly he turned and looked into the darkness.

Although he could see nothing – absolutely nothing, not even so much as the tiniest glimmer of light – Harry knew full well that the anchoress must be seated on her wooden chair no more than a foot or two away from him. He'd lost track of his bearings during the fall so he couldn't be sure which way the corpse was facing, but he knew she was close. As much as he told himself that there was nothing to fear, and that the anchoress had been dead for many decades, he couldn't help picturing her in his mind's eye as he tried to focus on the need to stay calm.

His mouth was poised to open, but he fought the urge to speak.

Instead, determined to work out exactly which way he was facing, he held up his right hand. As much as he hated the idea of reaching out and touching the corpse, he supposed that this would be the logical first step in any attempt to escape from the chamber – after all, he needed to know which way was which, and she was his only compass. The air seemed colder already, as if it had chilled in a matter of minutes, as he slowly reached his hand out and waited for his outstretched fingers to touch *something* in the darkness.

"I apologise," he said out loud. "I mean no

disrespect, only -"

In that moment he flinched as his fingers brushed against loose fabric. He slowly pulled back, before forcing himself to moved his hand forward again. This time when he touched the fabric, he forced himself to feel a little more carefully, and after a few more seconds he began to pick out the top of the dead woman's head. He could just about feel hair pressed flat beneath the veil, but he still wasn't entirely certain which way she was facing. Hoping desperately to avoid touching her face, he moved his hand down until – to his immense relief – he realised that he was in fact feeling the back of her head.

Letting out a sigh of relief, he knew now that he was standing directly behind the woman. To confirm that point, he moved his hand down and – indeed – felt the back of the wooden chair. This meant that as he looked up, he knew that the slab had moved aside in one particular direction, although he was by no means certain that he could get it out of the way himself.

Taking care to avoid touching the dead woman again, he limped around the chair until he reached the other side of the chamber. Next he tried to find something that he could use to get a purchase, and to climb up toward the ceiling, but the walls of the chamber were mostly flat. Holding his hands up, he stood on tiptoes and was just about able to touch the ceiling, although he knew that this would not allow him to exert sufficient pressure.

For a moment he stood in the darkness and tried to come up with a better plan, but at the back of his mind he was already starting to realise that there was one very obvious solution.

The chair.

"No," he whispered under his breath, shaking his head slightly in the darkness. "Absolutely not."

He imagined himself gently lifting the dead woman off the chair and setting her on the floor, an act that he felt went against almost everything that he believed in. He tried to think of some other solution, yet deep down he knew that there was no other way to get up to the ceiling. Desperate to avoid any action of disrespect, he stared into darkness and waited for some other idea to strike him, but as the seconds passed he was feeling increasingly hopeless.

"I can't," he said out loud, before – filled with another sudden burst of frustration – he banged his fists against the wall.

"Father Neville!" he yelled at the top of his voice, once again feeling – or *imagining* that he was feeling – rather breathless. "Let me out of here at once! If you don't, I shall find my own way out and then... and then I shall not be responsible for my actions!"

He waited, hoping that the other priest might come to his senses, yet still he heard nothing.

"You must have lost your mind entirely," he said finally. "I should have recognized this fact much earlier, and then perhaps I would have been able to do something. I should have set my concerns down in writing so that they would be more difficult to -"

Suddenly he heard a brief, abrupt splitting sound coming from directly over his shoulder. He froze, and the sound had already ended, yet he already knew that it had been close.

Very close.

Mere inches away.

"I shall," he continued, trying in vain to ignore his growing sense of fear, "write a very strongly worded... letter... just as soon as I am..."

Staring straight ahead, toward a wall that he couldn't see in the darkness, he felt the hairs standing up on the back of his neck.

"...out of here."

As much as he tried to think of some other explanation, he couldn't ignore the possibility that the corpse on the chair had moved. He imagined the old, withered limbs surrounded by dried and bloodless flesh, and he wondered whether periodic changes in the air might indeed cause the corpse to in some way shift its weight slightly.

After a moment he reminded himself that he

had actually *touched* the corpse's head briefly, and he wondered too whether this action might have caused a slight shift.

Convinced that he had solved the mystery, he opened his mouth to call out to Father Neville again – before hesitating once more as he realised that there was no point. Indeed, he wondered now whether shouting and hollering might in fact please Father Neville, in which case wasn't it a better idea to remain silent? He tried to think of something he could say that might convince the other priest to let him out, but he couldn't help imagining him lurking on the other side of the wall, perhaps listening out for any hint of panic.

Perhaps *enjoying* everything that was happening.

"Clearly I must find some other way out of here," he said under his breath, speaking out loud precisely because he hoped that he might better organise his thoughts. "I only know that -"

In that moment he heard the splitting sound again. He flinched, but the sound continued for a couple of seconds this time and seemed almost to be twisting and tearing in the darkness. Finally the sound fell away once more, yet this time Harry was unable to quite convince himself that it had been caused by the corpse somehow 'settling' on the chair.

This time it had sounded as if something

was actually moving, something that perhaps had not moved for some time – or something that should not move at all.

"Calm yourself," he said out loud, keeping his voice low in the hope that at least Father Neville wouldn't hear him. "You can breathe. Do not let foolishness into your thoughts."

Convinced that somehow Father Neville was orchestrating this entire debacle, Harry nevertheless turned around. Looking into the darkness, he still couldn't see anything at all, but he knew that the dead woman was still on the chair. He was worried now that at any moment he might descend into panic, that *any* mind would be disturbed by the crude noises emanating from some spot so close, so he took a deep breath and tried to focus on the fact that eventually he *was* going to find a way out of the chamber.

If nothing else, Barbara at the Red Lion was bound to notice that he was missing, even if he would have to wait until morning to be rescued.

"Lord give me strength," he whispered under his breath as he once again contemplated the possibility of somehow – very respectfully – removing the dead woman from the chair so that he might be able to climb up and push the slab away from the ceiling.

"And guidance," he added after a moment. "Would it be so terribly wrong if I..."

Falling silent, he worried that he already knew the answer, yet he felt that panic wasn't far from his heart. As much as he hated the idea of disturbing the dead woman, he supposed that in the long run he would be able to give her a proper burial, and that he might very well be able to make amends. Finally, in the absence of any other possibility, he resolved to get the matter completed as quickly as possible.

"I am sorry for what I am about to do," he said, raising his voice slightly. "Deeply and profoundly sorry. I mean no disrespect or harm, and I assure you that I will preside over the service myself when you are finally found a proper grave. I can do no more than that, and I hope... I hope that you will forgive me."

He waited, listening to the silence, but he knew that he just had to get on with things.

After taking a deep breath, he began to reach out with both hands, hoping to take hold of the dead woman by her shoulders and gently tilt her out of position, after which he was going to oh-so-carefully lower her onto the floor so that he could borrow the chair.

And then, just as that idea was taking shape properly in his mind, the fingers of his right hand touched something in the darkness. He flinched, and already he could tell that this 'something' was not a head, but a few more seconds passed before he finally realised what he'd found.

A hand.

Pulling back slowly, he stared into the darkness as he tried to calm his racing mind. He was sure that the woman had simply been sitting with her hands resting on her knees, yet now he had felt one of those hands not only raised up but also seemingly reaching out toward him. He told himself that this was completely impossible and that he was at risk of going as crazy as Father Neville, and finally he zeroed in on the possibility that he had been mistaken.

Yes, that was it.

He hadn't felt a hand.

How *could* he have felt a hand? The raised hand of a dead woman?

The idea was utterly ludicrous.

Yet... as he continued to look into the darkness, he could think of no other explanation. And a few seconds later, with his mind still drawing a blank, he began to hear the splitting sound again. He pulled back against the wall and waited for the sound to stop, but this time it seemed to be continuing indefinitely - and it was also doing something even more concerning.

It was getting closer.

"No," he said out loud, convinced that his senses had to be deceiving him. "I shall *not* fall for this. I have a strong mind and I am not the type to conjure up... foolish notions of impossible things."

Yet even as those words left his lips, the sound was slowly moving toward him through the darkness. He held his ground for a few more seconds, until finally a sense of fear overcame him and he stepped to one side. As he did so, his feet brushed against the floor and his shoulder scuffed against the wall, and the splitting sound once again came to a halt.

Taking a few more steps out of the way, Harry told himself that he now had to be more or less directly behind the chair.

"Lord, give me the strength to overcome my fears," he said, a little louder this time, "and the courage to do what is right. Let me ignore the fears that even now are filling in mind, and guide me to the right path so that I might do your bidding and -"

Suddenly he heard the twisting, splitting sound again, this time for just a couple of seconds before it stopped again.

Standing in silence, Harry told himself that he was in danger of letting his fears run out of control. Convinced that he'd indulged those fears for too long now, he took a series of deep breaths and felt himself starting to calm down; he continued to breathe deeply for several more seconds before coming to the understanding that he needed to prove that nothing unusual had happened. As much as he was terrified of touching the dead woman again, he knew that he had no choice, so he slowly reached out with both hands and promised himself that this time he was going to prove that nothing untoward had occurred.

His hands moved through the cold air for several seconds as he waited to feel the top of the dead woman's head. Finally, after a little longer than he'd expected, his fingertips touched something else entirely. He felt the chair's wooden back and briefly wondered whether he had somehow turned around in the confined space, but a moment later he reached down and felt the seat, and in that instant he felt a shiver run through his bones as he realised that something had indeed changed.

The chair was now empty.

CHAPTER FORTY-THREE

"FATHER NEVILLE! FATHER NEVILLE, I must insist that you let me out of here at once! Father Neville, please, help me!"

As he stood near the altar in the moonlit church, Father Neville realised that at last young Father Stone's pleas had taken on a much more panicked – perhaps even terrified – tone. He'd been listening for a while now to these cries and he was satisfied that they were ramping up nicely. Perhaps Margaret Crake had taken longer than anticipated to react to the arrival of a guest in her chamber, but Father Neville told himself that she must now recognize that an offering had been provided.

Not just *any* offering, either.

A priest.

As far as he could tell, Margaret Crake

hated priests, and in truth he couldn't really blame her. Priests had been responsible for her final fate in the chamber, and had ignored her very real claims to have uncovered great truths. He understood now that he'd made a dreadful mistake by presenting himself as a priest when he'd first found her resting place, but he knew that this was easily fixed. First, however, he was going to let her do as she pleased with the naïve young man who even now was desperately banging on the walls and trying to secure an escape.

"Father Neville, help me!" Father Stone screamed. "Please, I'm begging you, get me out of here! I fear that something truly ungodly is about to happen!"

"I'm counting on that," Father Neville said softly, under his breath, and now he couldn't help but smile as he imagined the young priest's horrified realisation that the anchoress was indeed capable of gaining revenge from beyond the grave.

What form that revenge would take, he couldn't possibly imagine, but he supposed that by the end she would be grateful to have been given the chance. And that, the old man told himself, was when he would strike and persuade her to tell him everything. He was willing to let her do anything to Father Harry Stone, just so long as she would then be prepared to cooperate. Young Harry would simply have to be sacrificed.

Suddenly feeling something brushing against his right hand, he turned. He saw no sign of anyone, but he felt sure that for a fraction of a second a set of invisible fingers had touched him.

And then, before he had a chance to react, he spotted a light in the distance. Looking toward the open doorway at the front of the church, he furrowed his brow as the light approached, and after a few more seconds he realised that he could also hear the distant hum of an engine.

***

As soon as she'd slammed her foot on the brake pedal and had switched the engine off, Barbara climbed out of her uncle's van and looked toward the church. Her heart was racing and she wasn't even sure what she was going to do now that she'd made the journey, but after a moment she spotted two bicycles nearby and she realised that her worst fears had been confirmed.

A moment later a figure emerged from the church. For a fraction of a second Barbara hoped that this might be Harry, but she quickly realised that in fact Father Neville was on his way to meet her – and the sight of the old man filled her with an immediate sense of pure hatred.

"You!" she snarled, rushing toward him.

"Go away!" Father Neville shouted at her,

waving his arms frantically. "This is nothing to do with you! Leave this place at once!"

"You're a murderer!" she shouted angrily.

"You're interfering in something you can't possibly understand!" he protested as she reached him. "I must insist, upon the authority of the church itself, that you -"

Before he could get another word out, she grabbed him by the collar and shoved him back, slamming him against the side of the church with such force that she brought a shocked gasp from his lips.

"You killed my uncle!" she sneered.

"I did nothing of the sort!" he snapped, pushing her aside and then taking a moment to fix his collar. "He was the aggressor! I merely defended myself, that's all!"

"You murdered him!"

"You're such a tiresome little thing," he said darkly, hoping to manipulate her fury. "Your uncle was a simple bully. He tried to start a fight with me many years ago and finally I got around to making him pay. And so far, from your rather unladylike behaviour tonight, it would seem that you have inherited many of his less desirable traits. Why, I wonder if -"

"You're a liar!" she shouted, rushing at him again.

This time he was ready for her. Having

successfully riled her up, he had no trouble wrapping an arm around her throat and pushing a foot between her legs to trip her. As he shoved her down against the ground, he gave her a kick in the head for good measure, and then he grabbed the back of her collar and began to haul her up with surprising strength.

"I think you'd better listen to me," he said firmly. "You and your uncle don't matter to me at all. Do you understand that? In the grand scheme of things, you don't matter to anyone. I've got much bigger things to deal with here, and frankly you're nothing more than a distraction."

He adjusted his grip on her collar while wrapping an arm around her neck again, this time with the intention of twisting it hard.

"I have to get back inside," he continued, "but rest assured that your little attempted intervention will amount to absolutely nothing. In fact, in about ten minutes from now, I'm fairly sure that I will have permanently forgotten that you, your uncle and even that wretched pub ever existed."

He began to twist her head, intending to break her neck, although she was at least able to fight back. Pushing against him, she tried to force him aside, only to find that they were both locked in a struggle that neither seemed poised to win. Letting out a series of gasps, she tried to slam the old man against the wall, but he was just about strong enough to stand firm.

A moment later, as she was about to cry out for Harry's help, Barbara looked past some nearby gravestones and saw Tilly standing in the moonlight. For a few seconds, too shocked by the sight to know how to react, she could only stare with a growing sense of shock, before suddenly she felt a sharp pain in both her hands.

Looking down, she saw a sharp, dark tip starting to burst through from the bases of her palms. She could feel something twisting deep inside her wrists, and finally she watched with a growing sense of horror as a single slightly bent black nail emerged from each of her hands. At the last second she managed to grab the nails, holding them tight just before they could fall down onto the grass. She turned them around and tried to work out exactly how best to use them, before simply thrusting them directly upward.

She immediately heard a cry of pain from Father Neville, and as he loosened his grip on her neck she managed to stumble away and turn to him.

Still holding the nails, she saw that she'd managed to stab the priest's cheek. He immediately rushed toward her, and this time she aimed at his shoulder, driving the nails into his flesh before letting go and ducking under his outstretched arm. Stumbling, she tripped and fell down hard against the ground, and already she could hear the old man letting out a series of pained cries.

Realising that she was running out of time, she somehow found the strength to haul herself up.

"Harry?" she called out, frantically worried that the ghost in the church might have got to him already. "Harry, where are you?"

She limped toward the open doorway, and then she froze as she looked through into the moonlit church. Glancing down, she saw that she'd almost crossed the threshold, that she'd so nearly entered the building, and now she could feel a great force holding her back. She'd spent so many years warning others that they must never set foot inside St. Jude's, and now she felt as if there was absolutely no way that she could go against that same advice.

"Harry?" she whimpered, hoping desperately to spot him somewhere inside the church. "Can you hear me? Harry, are you here?"

She waited, and after a moment she heard his anguished but muffled cry ringing out from somewhere deep inside the building. Although she immediately began to step forward, she once again held back as she realised that under no circumstances could she possibly *ever* set foot inside St. Jude's, even if somebody's life was on the line.

"Harry, just come out," she sobbed, feeling

utterly useless and humiliated now. "I'm begging you. Harry, you know I can't come to you. Harry, please, just -"

Suddenly a roar of anger filled the air as Father Neville lunged at her from behind. Having pulled the two metal nails from his own shoulder, he cried out with fury as he slammed Barbara down against the ground and drove the nails directly into the back of her neck.

CHAPTER FORTY-FOUR

"LORD, GIVE ME THE strength to resist this evil," Harry whispered, pressing his back against the wall of the chamber as he waited for any further hint of movement in the darkness ahead. "Give me the strength to... to... to maintain a strong mind and..."

As his voice trailed off, he realised that he was running out of prayers. No matter how hard he tried to convince himself that he was wrong, he couldn't help but imagine the withered form of Margaret Crake having oh-so-slowly risen from the chair. He'd heard several more twisting and creaking sounds, and in his terrified mind these sounds had seemed to be caused by old bones moving long after death had dried them out; he'd also heard what he believed to be a series of rattling gasps, and he couldn't quite shake the fear that these gasps had emerged from the dead woman's lips.

Yet deep down, in his heart of hearts, he still clung to the hope that the Lord was watching over him and that something so monstrously evil could not possibly occur

"I know that you will keep me safe," he continued, trying in vain to hide the fear that even now was filling his voice. "I *know* that you are watching over me and that -"

Before he could finish, he heard a brief cracking sound – the cracking of a bone, perhaps, or the splitting of some long-dead piece of flesh.

"- and that you will keep me safe," he went on, desperate to believe the words that even now trembled as they left his lips.

He waited, and as silence settled in the darkness he began to hope that perhaps he had been given a reprieve. He'd lost all track of time, he had no idea how long he'd spent in the chamber now but he felt sure that he must have been trapped for several minutes at least; he'd also lost any sense of space and no longer knew which wall separated him from the rest of the church and which separated him from the graveyard outside. Even his original plan – to use the chair and climb up – was in tatters.

He opened his mouth to issue another prayer, but part of him was terrified that by speaking he might only end up inciting the dead woman to move again.

Instead he stood in complete silence and barely even dared to breathe. In his mind's eye he imagined the dead, veiled figure standing just a few feet in front of him, but after a few seconds he began to convince himself that he had to be wrong. What if, in a state of absolute terror, he had simply imagined the whole thing? As the worst of his fears started to fade, he imagined the corpse still sitting in the chair and he wondered whether everything else had simply been the product of his feverish imagination. Or had she simply fallen aside?

Finally, determined to prove to himself that there was no reason to be fearful, he held up his right hand and tried to bring his raging mind back under full control.

Reaching out, he fully expected to find that the dead woman was somehow still sitting on the chair after all, and that all his earlier impressions – including the idea that she had moved – would be blown away. He moved his trembling hand forward so very slowly, and he worried that his whole body was shaking now, but he told himself that at any moment his fingertips were going to touch a -

Suddenly a loud scraping sound rang out. Looking up, Harry saw that the slab high above was being pushed aside, and a moment later he was shocked to see Barbara leaning into view and looking down at him.

"Harry!" she shouted, reaching a hand down

toward him. "Hurry!"

Turning to look at the veiled anchoress again, he was shocked to see in the moonlight that she was indeed standing up and that one of her hands was moving slowly toward him. For a fraction of a second he remained frozen in place, not daring to move, before he heard Barbara's voice again.

"Harry!" she screamed. "Get out of there!"

Reaching up, he grabbed her hand and allowed her to start pulling him to safety. He quickly took hold of the top of the wall and hauled himself up, although at the last second he felt a hand grabbing his left ankle from below and trying to pull him back down.

"She has me!" he gasped.

"Pull!"

With Barbara's help, he managed to haul himself further up – and finally the hand lost its grip on his ankle, albeit while digging sharp fingernails into his flesh. Throwing himself over the top of the wall, Harry almost toppled down the other side, only for Barbara to grab hold of him at the very last second.

"We have to get down!" she hissed. "Now!"

They crawled toward the top of the ladder, and Barbara climbed down first while Harry waited and then began to follow. The ladder rattled under their combined weight but finally they both reached the bottom and took a step back, listening as a low growl rose from the top of the opened chamber.

Staring up at the ledge, Harry opened his mouth to reassure Barbara, to tell her that there was no need to worry, yet he couldn't quite get the words out of his mouth. No matter how hard he tried to rationalise everything that had happened to him in the chamber, he couldn't get past the fact that the dead woman *had* risen from her seat.

"We have to go," Barbara said, sounding as if she was close to tears. "Right now!"

"You came into the church," he replied, turning to her.

"Only to fetch you," she pointed out, taking one last look toward the top of the wall before grabbing his hand and starting to lead him toward the aisle. "I couldn't exactly leave you to fend for yourself. And believe me, I'm not staying."

Reaching up, she touched a bloodied spot on the back of her neck.

"Your Father Neville tried to stop me," she continued, "but I managed to fight him off. He was surprisingly -"

Before she could finish, they both saw Father Neville struggling to his feet in the church's doorway. Slowing her pace but not stopping, Barbara began to clench her right fist as she prepared to fight her way past him one more time, and she quickly saw the anger in his eyes.

"You shouldn't have interfered," he snarled.

"Harry," she replied, stopping for a moment, "this man killed my uncle."

"That's quite impossible," Harry said, although his voice betrayed a hint of uncertainty. "He might have made some mistakes but -"

"That idiot deserved to die!" Father Neville hissed. "I remember being irritated by him when we were both young boys. It's just a shame that it took me this long to come back and finish him off. My only excuse is that I quite forgot that he even existed until now."

"You bastard!" Barbara snapped, stepping toward him – only for Harry to squeeze her hand and hold her back.

"If this happened as you say," he told her, "and I'm certainly not saying that it did, but *if* it did then... then it's a matter for the police."

"Forget the police!" Father Neville shouted, before stepping aside and indicating the doorway. "Fine, you might as well leave. You're clearly not ready to learn the truth. Leave me to converse with the anchoress alone."

"The anchoress is dead," Harry said firmly.

"Yet she has truths to tell us all," the older priest replied. "Come now, Father Stone, I heard your panicked voice calling out for help. You were begging me to let you out. Those were not the words of a man devoid of fear. You can try to lie to yourself, but we both know that you have seen the proof."

"The anchoress -"

Stopping himself at the last moment, Harry thought back to the sight of the dead woman sitting in her chamber – and then to the sight of her standing as he was hauled to safety. He was still trying desperately to think of some explanation for everything that had happened, yet he was unable to come up with an easy solution.

"You killed my uncle," Barbara sobbed, with tears running down her face as she continued to stare at Father Neville. "You'll pay for this. I'll make sure that you rot in jail."

"Spare me the petty threats," he replied, stepping toward her. "Do you think I care one jot about the old order? The anchoress Margaret Crake is about to convey to me the truth about our world. I stand on the verge of a new chapter."

"You can't possibly mean that," Harry told him. "You perhaps need a little... spiritual help."

"You don't believe me?" Father Neville said, before looking past them both as a sense of great anticipation began to fill his eyes. "Then turn to see her. Witness the anchoress in all her glory."

"The anchoress is dead!" Harry said again.

"The anchoress is here," Father Neville replied, as Barbara turned to follow his gaze. "I have proved myself to her and now I am sure she will share the truth with me. She almost did that when I was but a young boy. Fools got in the way, but only temporarily." He stepped between the pair of them and began to make his way along the aisle. "I have always been destined to reach this moment."

Turning to watch him, Harry was about to call after the older man when he spotted a figure standing at the other end of the aisle. He felt a shiver pass through his chest, but already he knew that he could no longer deny the evidence before his own eyes.

The dead woman from the chamber – the anchoress, the woman once known as Margaret Crake – had left her final resting place and was now waiting as Father Neville made his way toward her.

CHAPTER FORTY-FIVE

"WE HAVE MET BEFORE," Father Neville said, with tension in his voice as he stepped closer and closer toward the veiled figure. "Twice, in fact. I am hoping very much that the third time will have a more positive outcome."

With each step he felt the air becoming colder all around him, and finally he stopped just a few feet short of the undead woman.

"I no longer consider myself to be a priest," he continued, pulling the remains of his collar aside and tossing it onto the floor. "Not in the conventional sense. Not of the old church. I stand before you as a man transformed, as a man awaiting news of a greater calling. If you want to think of me as a disciple, so be it. I prefer to see myself as a vessel through which your great knowledge shall finally be transmitted into this vain and desperate world. I merely await your instructions."

"He's insane," Harry whispered.

"We need to go!" Barbara hissed, pulling on his arm, trying to force him to the front door. "Harry, we *can't* be here!"

"We can't leave him."

"We have to!" she snapped.

At the other end of the aisle, wearing a black robe and with a black veil covering her face, Margaret Crake merely stood in silence. She showed no sign that she had even heard Father Neville, no sign that she was considering his request, no sign that she had any interest in the world around her. Yet she had left her chamber once more and as she stood bathed in moonlight she appeared to be looking more or less directly at Father Neville himself.

"Please," the old man continued, taking a shuffling half step toward her before dropping to his knees. "What more do you want? How else can I prove myself to you? Just tell me what you want and I'll give it to you!"

He waited, and after a moment the anchoress tilted her head slightly to one side as if she was finally listening to him. At the same time a creaking, splitting sound emerged from beneath the veil.

"My name is Stanley Neville," he went on.

"You remember me, don't you? More than half a century has passed since I was but a young boy in the streets of Laidlow. I was dragged away from you, just as I began to believe that I might learn your knowledge, but that was not my choice. I have waited so long to get another chance with you. I have searched for you, I never gave up. Now I *beg* you to tell me what you know."

Watching her veil, he began to hold his breath.

"I admit that I struggled," he continued. "I vacillated. But when this war broke out, I finally knew for certain that I could wait no longer. The world is on fire. The old teachings are leading us to death and disaster. We can only survive if we embrace this new knowledge!"

After a moment, the anchoress slowly took one more step forward. The bones in her body creaked and complained, clearly unused to moving after so many years without blood, but now she was looking down at Father Neville and after a moment she leaned forward slightly and moved her face to one of his ears.

"What is it?" he asked. "Tell me."

"We have to go, Harry!" Barbara sobbed, pulling on his hand again. "Hurry!"

"*You* go," he replied, standing his ground as he watched the anchoress still leaning close to Father Neville. "I have to see this."

"No, you don't!" she whimpered, tugging at his hand now. "No-one does! If that murderous old fool wants to throw his life away, then so be it... but I've seen what the anchoress does to people! I saw what she did to Tilly!"

"If -"

"Tilly must have looked through the tiniest crack that day," she continued, still trying to make sense of everything that had happened. "She was so unlucky. She looked directly into the chamber, and the truth of what she saw drove her out of her mind!"

"Speak to me," Father Neville whispered, staring straight ahead as he heard a faint rattling sound coming from the dead woman's throat. Tears were filling his eyes now as he realised that he was close to the fulfilment of a lifetime's journey. "I am ready."

The anchoress hesitated, before leaning a little closer. This time, reaching up, she slowly moved the veil aside slightly, exposing a withered mouth with patches of skin clinging tight to the bone. And then, tilting her head a little more and moving even closer to Father Neville's ear, she began to whisper to him more clearly.

"She's speaking," Harry said, unable to make out what the dead woman was saying. "She's dead, that much is clear, but... she's actually speaking to him."

"Harry, please," Barbara cried, still trying to lead him to the door. "This is wrong!"

"What is she saying?" Harry continued, instead taking a step forward while Barbara tried to pull him in the opposite direction. "I must know."

"No, you must *not*!" Barbara snarled.

"Go if you must!" he snapped, pulling his hand free. "I won't judge you, but *I* must know what is happening here! This is a message from beyond life itself!"

"Please don't do this," she cried, and now tears were streaming down her face. As much as she wanted to run after him and pull him away, she couldn't bring herself to go any closer to the deathly figure at the far end of the aisle. "Harry, stop!"

Ignoring her pleas, Harry made his way up behind Father Neville. He could still hear the anchoress whispering into the elderly priest's ear, yet he was unable to make out any of her words even though he could tell that she was speaking very fast.

"Father Neville," he said cautiously, "I think you should come away from here."

He looked at the back of the man's head, but he saw no sign of any reaction at all.

"Father Neville, please, if -"

"Harry, run!" Barbara screamed, clinging to one of the pews as she fought the desperate urge to leave him behind. "Harry, please, you mustn't go near her!"

Still unable to discern any actual words coming from the mouth of the anchoress, Harry began to step around Father Neville. As he did so, he saw that the man's mouth was hanging open and that his eyes were even wider; seemingly lost in a daze, Father Neville appeared to be unable to react as the anchoress continued to whisper into his ear, until finally the dead woman fell silent and pulled back.

"What – what did she say?" Harry asked cautiously.

He waited, but Father Neville showed no sign that he'd even heard the question.

"What did she say?" Harry asked again, trying to stay calm. "Father Neville, you must come with me right now." He looked at the veiled figure and felt a shiver run through his bones. A moment later he reached out a hand, hoping desperately that the older priest would finally react. "Father Neville, we must leave immediately!"

"Leave him!" Barbara yelled frantically. "Let him die here if he wants but *we* must go!"

"Father Neville?" Harry replied, perturbed now by the lack of a response. "What -"

Suddenly Father Neville stood, as if filled with some sudden urge to react. At the same time, the anchoress slowly stepped aside, and a moment later the elderly man began to make his way toward the altar. He walked with the stunted, shuffling gait of a prisoner condemned to the gallows.

"Father Neville?" Harry called out again, while taking care to keep away from the anchoress. He knew he should run, yet curiosity compelled him to remain. "What did she say to you? What did you hear?"

Again he waited for a response, but Father Neville merely walked to the altar before stopping and dropping once more to his knees.

Unwilling to go any closer to the anchoress, Harry could only watch as his colleague stared at the altar.

"Harry, please!" Barbara shouted, somehow sounding even more desperate than before. "This isn't something we can put right! He's lost to her now but we still have a chance if we just get out of here!"

"She told him something," Harry replied. "She -"

"I know the truth now," Father Neville gasped suddenly. "I heard it all from her. My eyes have been opened and I am filled with a truth that I could never previously comprehend. It is at once both impossible to imagine yet so very simple. And now that my mind has been opened, I can only..."

His voice trailed off for a moment.

"I can only..."

A solitary tear ran from his left eye.

"There is only one possible reaction to this awful truth..."

He stared up toward the ceiling for a moment before looking at the altar. And then, with no further warning, he pulled back slightly before lunging forward, smashing his forehead against the altar's hard stone edge with such force that the front of his skull immediately cracked.

"No!" Harry shouted, stepping forward, only for Barbara – who had finally found the courage to get closer – to grab him from behind and drag him back. "Father Neville!"

With blood already pouring from the wound on his forehead and running down his face, Father Neville hesitated for a moment before dashing his head against the edge of the altar again, then a third time, and now his forehead had begun to collapse in on itself. Reaching out, he slowly and uncertainly got to his feet, and then he leaned down and smashed his face against the altar's flat top so hard that blood immediately splattered out to either side.

"Get it out!" he gasped. "I don't want to know! Take it back! Return me to my ignorance!"

"Stop!" Harry yelled as Barbara continued to hold him back. "Let go of me! I must stop him!"

As those words left his lips, however, Father Neville had begun to smash his face again and again against the altar. He'd already obliterated most of his features and had cracked open his forehead, and he began to strike the altar harder and faster as if determined to end his life as swiftly as possible. Finally his knees buckled and he dropped down, but he still tried to break his forehead wide open against the altar's edge until finally fragments of bone began to fall down accompanied by chunks of brain matter. Blood was flowing freely from several wounds on his face. And somewhere in all the mess, as he broke his own head apart and the crown of his skull slopped off in a river of blood, he was laughing.

CHAPTER FORTY-SIX

AFTER A COUPLE MORE seconds Father Neville's body fell still. On its knees in front of the altar, with its head mostly smashed apart, the body remained upright for a few more seconds before accepting the inevitable, tilting back and falling down the steps, finally landing with a sickening squelching thud next to the first row of pews.

Blood was slowly oozing from broken gaps on the man's face, but otherwise he was entirely still.

"Father... Father Neville..." Harry stammered. "What -"

"Move!"

Grabbing his hand and this time refusing to take no for an answer, Barbara began to lead him back along the aisle. She could see the broken doorway hanging from its hinges up ahead, and she told herself that everything was going to be alright just as soon as they could both get outside into the night air. She knew Harry was going to want to understand what had happened, that he was probably going to suffer from some crisis of faith, but she figured that could all wait until they were safely away from the church and he could ask his millions of questions without -

Suddenly the broken door slammed shut with such force that it shuddered in the frame. Reaching the end of the aisle just a moment too late, Barbara grabbed the handle and tried to force the door open, only to find that it was somehow wedged into the opening.

"Damn thing!" she gasped, trying a couple more times before stepping back. "Harry, you must be stronger than me. Hurry!"

Seemingly in something of a daze, Harry tried frantically to get the door open, but he too quickly found that it wouldn't budge.

After watching him for a moment, Barbara turned and looked back along the aisle, and in the moonlight she was just about able to make out the dark sight of the anchoress slowly making her way closer.

"She's coming!" she shouted, turning and grabbing another part of the door, hoping to help Harry in his attempt to force it open. "Hurry!"

They tried for a few more seconds before Barbara looked over her shoulder. She could see that the anchoress was getting closer and closer, and after a moment she began to look all around.

"Harry, how do we get out? You're a priest, you must know the layout of these places. There has to be another way!"

She waited for him to reply, before turning and pulling him away from the door. In the corner of her eye she could see the anchoress still advancing steadily but she told herself that they still had a few seconds before she was too close.

"Harry, listen to me," she said breathlessly. "We need to find another way out of here. Can we do that? Harry, there's no time for trial and error so can you please tell me which way we can go?"

He stared at her for a moment, open-mouthed and clearly in shock, before slowly turning to look at the approaching black-veiled figure.

"Don't look at her, look at me!" Barbara hissed, grabbing his face and turning it so that he was staring into her eyes again. "Harry, say something! We can't just stand here!"

"Why did he do that?" Harry stammered. "What did she say to him to make him dash his head open in such a way? He said he wanted to be ignorant again. What kind of truth could possibly have done that to his mind?"

"Oh, you're no help at all," she muttered,

pulling back against the wall as she saw that the anchoress was edging ever closer. "I've been round the side of the place and I don't remember seeing another door. Then again, I was so young, I'm not sure that I remember properly. But there must -"

"Halt!" Harry shouted, suddenly stepping past her and standing in the aisle as if he meant to block the anchoress. "In the name of the Lord, I command you to stop!"

Barbara opened her mouth to ask him if he was insane, but at the last second she froze as she saw that somehow his order had actually worked: the anchoress had indeed stopped, albeit just a few feet short of the spot where Harry was now standing. As she stared at the veil, however, Barbara couldn't help but wonder about the face beneath, and how that face had – many years earlier – driven her friend Tilly out of her mind.

"The power of Christ compels you to obey me," Harry said with uncharacteristic determination, as if he refused to acknowledge the possibility that his authority might be ignored. "Whatever you are, do not try to cross me, for the Lord sees us now and He will step in to deal with your... your evil."

Again Barbara opened her mouth to ask Harry what he was thinking, but she couldn't deny that he had indeed managed to get the anchoress to stop – so far, at least. And although she was shaking with fear, as she stepped back against the wall she began to feel as if perhaps the dead woman could be reasoned with after all. Looking past her, she saw the bloodied corpse of Father Neville at the other end of the aisle, but she told herself that his mistake had been hubris and that a calmer approach might yet work.

Harry, meanwhile, was staring at the veil as he began to realise that he could just about make out the pale, deathly features beneath. He could see two dark eyes glaring at him, although most of the details were lost in darkness.

"I know your name," he said finally, still trying to take charge of the situation. "I... I know who you are. You are Margaret Crake and you were the anchoress here at St. Jude's for many years. For decades. And you... you sought some greater connection to God. Some deeper understanding."

He waited, as if he expected her to somehow respond.

Barbara, meanwhile, was still looking around in the hope that she might spot some other way out of the church. After a moment she saw the two black nails on the floor, where Father Neville must have thrown them after pulling them from his body.

"Margaret Crake," Harry continued, "you are still a humble servant of the Lord. Whatever you *think* you have learned, it does not make you better than the rest of us. And as a man of the cloth, as a priest I -"

Before he could finish, he heard a faint sighing sound coming from beneath the veil, as if the mere mention of that word 'priest' had in some way aroused the dead woman's anger.

"I command you to remember your place," he went on, even though his voice now betrayed more fear than before. "You gave an oath when you became an anchoress, did you not? I'm sure you must have done. What has happened here tonight, what has happened to Father Neville, is wrong. Despite his faults, Father Neville was a good man who was only seeking enlightenment."

"He was a murderer," Barbara sneered under her breath.

"Only the Lord can judge him," Harry continued, keeping his eyes fixed on the anchoress as the sigh continued for longer than any sigh should. "The Lord will judge all of us, in the end. And what do you think He will think of these events here tonight? What will He say when he sees one of his most devoted servants over there with his head cracked open? What truth could you *possibly* have delivered to Father Neville that would have made him do what he did? He was a good priest and -"

In that moment the anchoress began to snarl, and this time Harry was unable to help himself – fear took over and he instinctively took a step back.

After a few seconds, the anchoress stepped forward.

"No!" Barbara gasped, before picking up the nails and forming them into a cross, then holding them up for the anchoress to see. "Stay back!"

"They are not bound," Harry whispered to her.

"What?"

"They are not bound together," he continued. "They have no power if you just hold them. Even if -"

"Do you have something we can use?" she asked, interrupting him.

"No, but -"

"Fine!" Reaching up, she grabbed a length of her own hair and pulled as hard as she could manage, letting out a gasp of pain as she ripped the strands from her scalp. She quickly wrapped them around the intersection of the two nails before holding them up again. "How about this?"

Letting out another gasp, the anchoress took a step back and finally fell silent.

"It's working!" Barbara said, clearly in shock.

"Can she have strayed so far from the Lord," Harry replied, "that now one of His symbols becomes poisonous to her?"

"You really don't talk like a normal person," Barbara muttered darkly. "You know that, right?"

Harry waited, but now the anchoress was merely standing motionless. As he stared at the dark veil, he imagined a pair of dead eyes watching him, yet he began to believe that he might finally have managed to get through to her.

"This is ungodly," he continued. "I scarcely believe that it is possible, yet -"

Before he could finish, he spotted movement at the far end of the aisle. Looking past the anchoress, he was shocked to see that somehow Father Neville was slowly getting to his feet. He knew full well that there was no way the man could still be alive – indeed, even now he could see much blood splattered all across the altar – yet the dead priest was indeed standing and a moment later his animated corpse began to turn around until Harry saw what remained of his mangled and battered head.

"No," he whispered, making the shape of the cross against his own chest. "This cannot be. This *evil* cannot exist in a house of the Lord. Whatever else she might be, I refuse to believe that this anchoress is filled with pure evil!"

Once it was fully on his feet, Father Neville's battered body began to slowly rise up into the air, making its way above the altar and moving toward the church's high arched ceiling. At the same time, a new sound emerged from beneath the veil of the anchoress, a sound that was very different to the earlier growl: a sound that was twisted and bitter, and which took a few more seconds to become recognizable.

"Laughter," Barbara whispered. "She's laughing."

"No," Harry said through gritted teeth.

"She is!" Barbara insisted. "Can't you tell?"

"I don't know what she thinks she learned during her time here as anchoress of St. Jude's," Harry said as he saw Father Neville's corpse reaching the ceiling, "but whatever it is, it has clearly driven her – and anyone else who hears it – completely out of their -"

In that instant Father Neville's body slammed down with such force that it hit the stone floor in a fraction of a second, exploding as it did so into a shower of blood and bone.

"Harry, the door!" Barbara gasped, stepping behind him and pulling on the door – which had indeed begun to come loose. "Hurry!"

Grabbing him by the arm, she pulled him through the gap, which was already narrowing. As the anchoress continued to laugh, the pair of them spilled out and tripped, landing on the ground outside just as the door once again slammed shut.

AMY CROSS

CHAPTER FORTY-SEVEN

"THIS WAY!" BARBARA SAID, holding Harry up as the pair of them limped across the dark graveyard, heading toward the van she'd parked at the side of the road. "Hurry!"

Slipping, Harry dropped to his knees. He reached out and steadied himself against one of the stones, but a couple of seconds passed before he was able to get to his feet. Even then, his injured right foot was throbbing with such pain that he wondered whether he could take so much as another single step forward.

"She destroyed him," he stammered as he and Barbara set off once more, although after a moment he glanced over his shoulder and looked back toward the church. "She was enjoying herself. She didn't just kill him, she tortured him and then she... she mocked him. And she humiliated his corpse!"

"Why did you have to go in there?" she gasped angrily, struggling to help him as they reached the stone wall. "Harry, I warned you! Why didn't you listen? Why couldn't you both have stayed away?"

"Father Neville thought he was going to learn some great -"

"Yes, I know that!" she said, helping him across the wall before opening the door on the passenger side of the van and easing him onto the seat. "I'm no fool! Are you alright?"

"I'm not hurt at all," he replied, although he took a moment to get his breath back. "Apart from my foot. I think I'm just in shock."

"You're not the only one," she told him.

"Whatever she told Father Neville," he continued, looking toward the church once more, "it was enough to break his mind. Not just *break* it, but destroy it completely. And it destroyed *her* mind as well. What realisation could possibly do that to someone? Father Neville begged to learn her secret, and then he begged to *unlearn* it. What realisation could make a person lose all touch with reality and become something so awful?"

"I don't know," she whispered, staring along the side of the van as if she was lost in thought.

"I know you won't believe me," he went on,

"but I swear to you, Father Neville was a good man. Once, at least. But he must have become corrupted by the thought of whatever truth the anchoress possessed. All his piety was subsumed beneath the urge for her knowledge, and when he received it... he couldn't keep it in his mind. He couldn't retain his sanity. As much as you think I must be losing my own senses, please... you have to believe me."

"I do," she said softly, still looking toward the rear of the van. "That's not the problem."

"I don't know what evil festers in that church," he added, "but clearly it should be left untouched by any of us. You were right all along, we should never have opened that door and disturbed whatever's in there. I don't know the name of whoever tried to seal that thing up in the church, but I fear they had the right idea all along."

"Perhaps," Barbara said, before pausing for a moment. "Or perhaps not."

"Father Sloane knew," he continued. "He must have done, or at least he suspected. That's why he was so reluctant for us to come here, but eventually he must have been persuaded to relent. And then when he began to hear what was happening, he understood that his worse fears were coming true and he... he..."

For a moment, he could barely contemplate the awful truth.

"What force could have driven two priests

to take their own lives? What supposed truth did the anchoress Margaret Crake uncover during her years in that chamber? Where could it have come from?"

"Be careful," Barbara said, pushing him a little further onto the seat before swinging the door shut. "This can't go on. The pattern can't be allowed to repeat."

Hurrying to the rear of the van, she pulled the back open and clambered onboard. Stepping past old beer barrels that were waiting to be returned to the brewery, she searched for a moment in the darkness before finally finding what she wanted. Climbing back down with a spare cannister of petrol in her right hand, she made her way toward the front of the vehicle.

"She can't be left in there," she told Harry as she looked once more toward the church. "I always thought that eventually people would understand the need to leave this place well alone, but I couldn't have been more wrong. People will forget everything that has happened here. I suppose that's human nature, in a way. One generation's horror is the next generation's scary story, and then just a joke for whoever comes after."

"I'll speak to some people," he replied.

"Speak to some people?" she said, clearly shocked by his response. "To *who*, Harry? Isn't it obvious that people already knew about this church all along? *Your* people knew! Priests!"

"Yes, but -"

"I'm not going to let this happen again," she continued, still holding the petrol cannister as she took a step back, while tears began to fill her eyes. "I'm going to stop her."

"What are you talking about?" he asked. "Barbara, you're acting irrationally."

"I -"

"You can't go in there and burn the church down!" he continued. "Think about it for one moment! Think about the utter foolishness of this idea!"

She opened her mouth to argue with him, but already she was faltering; in the back of her mind she was starting to think that he might be right, that she couldn't take the law into her own hands in quite such a massive way.

"I grant that tonight has been traumatic," Harry said firmly, "but petrol and flames are not the solution. You're not the kind of person who goes around committing arson, Barbara. Please, listen to reason!"

She hesitated, before turning to look at the church. For a fraction of a second she found herself agreeing with him, and losing the will to take action, but at the last moment she spotted a figure standing in the church's open doorway.

"Tilly," she whispered, seeing her friend staring back at her – and waiting.

"Get the van started," Harry continued, sounding exhausted now. "Once we're back at the Red Lion, I shall make a list of people to telephone in the morning. There'll be someone back in London who'll know what to do."

"There's someone *here* who knows what to do," she replied, turning to him.

"I beg your -"

"Stay in the van!" she snapped.

"No!" he replied, grabbing her by the arm and starting to climb down. "Barbara -"

"Let go of me, Harry."

"I refuse to let you go back in there!" he hissed. "You're not -"

Before he could finish, she kicked him hard in the right ankle, aiming for the spot where he was already injured. He immediately winced and pulled back, letting go of her arm in the process.

By the time he was able to overcome the pain, he saw that she was already hurrying away toward the church.

"Barbara!" he yelled, trying to follow her, only to let out a gasp of pain as soon as he put pressure on his injured foot. "Come back! I can't let you do this!"

***

As soon as she reached the church's front door and

looked through into the moonlit interior, Barbara came to a halt. She saw no sign of Tilly now, yet she knew that the girl had been present just a minute or two earlier. Still hearing Harry shouting at her from the van, she once again considered turning around – before reminding herself of the horror that St. Jude's had caused over so many years.

How many people had set out to stop the anchoress, only to falter at the last moment, only to convince themselves that there was no need?

Stepping into the church, she began to douse the pews in petrol, taking care to splatter as much as she could as she slowly made her way along the aisle. She knew that if she stopped to think, she might weaken as so many others had weakened before her.

"I won't let this happen again, Tilly," she muttered, while glancing around to make sure that there was no further sign of the anchoress. "I won't let her sit here waiting for the next fool to come along."

Reaching the end of the aisle, she looked down for a moment at Father Neville's battered and burst body. She felt nothing but contempt for the man as she made sure to pour some of the petrol directly onto him, and then she looked toward the wall that hid the anchoress and her chamber.

"You've gone back in there, have you?" she sneered, stepping over the dead priest and leaving a trail of petrol in her wake as she headed to the wall. "You think you can hide again, do you?"

In the distance, Harry was still yelling at her, begging her to stop.

Grabbing the ladder, she leaned it against the wall and immediately began to climb up. Once she was on the ledge she looked down into the chamber, ready to pour petrol onto the anchoress herself, only to see to her shock that there was nobody sitting on the wooden chair at all.

"What -"

Suddenly a hand grabbed her foot from behind and pulled, bringing her crashing down from the ledge until she slammed against the church's stone floor. Losing her grip on the cannister, she watched the rest of its contents spilling out before she looked up and saw the horrific sight of the anchoress towering above her.

Before she could react, the dead woman reached up and lifted her veil aside, revealing a pale dead face. Flesh was still clinging to the skull in places, while a few bare patches revealed the bone beneath; the eyes, meanwhile, were shrivelled and had shrunk into their sockets, while strands of thin hair hung down on either side to frame the horrific visage.

"I won't let you do it!" Barbara sobbed as the anchoress leaned down. "Don't tell me anything! I'm not like that priest! I don't want to know your secrets!"

She tried to get up, but she immediately felt a sharp pain in her hips. Trying to push past that pain, she began to realise that she must have seriously injured herself in the fall. She clenched her teeth and prepared to try again, but a moment later she heard a scratched, gravelly voice emerging from the depths of the dead woman's throat. The anchoress was leaning directly toward her ear now and had begun to impart the same knowledge that had driven so many others out of their minds.

"I don't want to know!" Barbara screamed, trying to block the voice out.

Reaching into her pocket, she fumbled for a moment before pulling out the box of matches she'd brought from the van. Some of the petrol had spilled against her own shirt now, soaking one side of her body, but she knew she couldn't back down. With the anchoress still whispering, and determined to not hear any of the words, Barbara let out an angry cry as she took a match from the box and struck its head against the side.

In that moment she saw Tilly standing directly behind the anchoress.

"This is for you," Barbara said through gritted teeth as the anchoress continued to whisper directly into her ear. "And for Uncle John."

In that moment she dropped the match into the pool of petrol.

***

"Barbara!" Harry shouted, having only made it as far as the stone wall before stopping once more to support himself. The pain in his injured foot was immense and he had no idea how he was going to get to the church, but he knew he couldn't hold back. "You have to stop and think about -"

Suddenly he saw flames erupting inside the building, accompanied by an agonized scream.

"Barbara!" he called out, stumbling forward but immediately dropping down onto his knees as the pain in his foot proved to be too much.

He tried to get up, leaning against a gravestone now, but he could barely stand. Ahead, St. Jude's was ablaze with flames not only filling the doorway but also roaring on the other side of the stained glass windows, illuminating the panels in a burst of constantly changing light. Barbara's cry was still ringing out into the night air, but only for a few more seconds before finally petering away to nothing.

For a moment Harry wondered whether he could hear a second scream beyond the sound of roaring flames, but – if it had been real at all – this second scream quickly faded away to nothing.

"Barbara!" he shouted, still on his knees as he watched part of the church's roof already starting to collapse. "This isn't the answer! You have to get out of there! Barbara!"

CHAPTER FORTY-EIGHT

BY THE TIME THE sun rose the following morning, the full scale of the devastation was clear.

Although the stone walls of St. Jude's had mostly withstood the inferno, the entire ceiling had collapsed and ominous creaking sounds indicated that the very foundations might no longer be safe. Alerted by the sight of something burning on the horizon, several dozen men from Laidlow had hurried out to see what was happening; unable to do much to stop the flames, they'd held back and waited until – shortly before sunrise – the worst of the fire had burned itself out.

Now the remains of the church stood silhouetted against the reds and oranges of the morning sky. Nobody dared to go into the smoking ruins and search for survivors, but in truth nobody *needed* to get that close. There was simply no chance that anyone could possibly have survived such a conflagration.

"Easy there," Doctor Harold Connor said as he continued to examine Harry's injured foot. "I'm pretty sure you've broken something in here. We'll have to get it checked out properly to be sure."

Sitting in the van's forward passenger seat, Harry had never felt more useless. Although he was aware of the doctor examining his injuries, he was unable to stop staring at the ruined church. He was replaying Barbara's final screams over and over, and wondering whether there might have been anything more he could have done to stop her. Despite the pain in his foot, he felt that he should have found some way to push through the agony and catch up to her, or that he should have anticipated her plan sooner. Deep down, however, he'd never understood the depth of her hatred for the anchoress of St. Jude's.

Until now.

"Father Stone," Frank Welling from the village said, making his way over and then stopping to lean against the van's open door. "I'm sorry to ask you this again, but... are you sure Barbara was in there?"

Still staring at the church, Harry offered only a faint nod in response.

"But she might have made it out, mightn't

she?" Frank continued, with the tone of a man still clinging to some desperate scrap of hope. "And then... I don't know, isn't it possible that she went back to the village?"

"No," Harry murmured, barely raising his voice above a whisper. "I'm afraid that is not at all possible."

Letting out a sigh, Frank turned and looked at the church again.

"It'll be some time before anyone's able to get in there," he explained. "It's just not safe. There'll be no repairing it, either. Eventually the whole thing's gonna have to be torn down."

"Can you move your foot at all?" Doctor Connor asked, looking up at Harry. "Come on, let's stick to practical matters for a moment. Try to wiggle some of your toes."

"Nothing can possibly have survived in there," Harry continued, still unable to avert his gaze from the sight of the church. "Not even that... thing. At least Barbara will have achieved what she set out to do. I only wish that -"

Suddenly cries rang out and all the men near the church began to run. A rumbling sound could be heard, and a moment later one of the exterior walls collapsed, falling into what remained of the church with a devastating thud that even shook the ground as far away as the van.

"There's nothing else for it," Doctor Connor

said finally, standing up and taking a moment to light a cigarette. "Can someone drive us to the nearest hospital? I need to get this man's foot looked at properly!"

***

"Old John'd be having chickens if he could see this," Alf Scrace said as he stepped behind the bar of the Red Lion and poured himself another pint. "If we carry on like this, I won't be surprised if his ghost comes back and haunts us all."

"Then there's the question of who's gonna take over," Ken Symes replied, studying the surface of his own pint for a moment before taking a sip. "There's no family left to run the place. I suppose someone's gonna have to appeal to the brewery to do something, but I don't even know if *they'll* be up for it. We can't let the place shut down, though. Without a pub, Laidlow wouldn't even be a village, not any more. It'd just be a few roads criss-crossing each other in the middle of nowhere."

"No church and no pub," Alf added as he stood behind the bar and sampled his latest beer. "What's the world coming to?"

"I know which one *I'd* rather have back," another voice murmured. "If I had to choose, that is."

"We've not had a church for a good long

while," Leonard Stapleton chimed in. "Not really. I know there was them what wanted to open St. Jude's up again, but I don't think anyone took them that serious-like. It was just gonna stand there empty. The only shame's that now it can't even be picked apart for scrap."

"It was still a house of worship," Alf pointed out. "Don't let my Marjorie hear you talking about it like it was just any old place, because some people still felt that it deserved respect."

He thought for a moment.

"I'm not saying that's *my* opinion on the matter," he added, "just that there's plenty around that saw it that way. And if that anchoress was still in there after all these years, who's to say that she was dangerous? We've only got the word of children and women on that point."

"True enough," Ken said, before supping at his pint. "True enough."

"It's done now," Leonard reminded them, just as more men made their way into the pub after a long morning spent attending to the ruined church. "It don't matter what the likes of us might say as we stand around in here nattering. Our opinions, I'd remind you, aren't worth as much as the manure out at my cousin Matthew's farm. No-one cares what any of us in here believe. The thing about opinions is you can't even use them to feed the pigs."

"That's true," Dave Sanders said as he

stopped at the bar. "Right, who's serving? I don't know about the rest of you, but I don't remember the last time I was so badly in need of a drink."

***

"Hit it!"

Kicking the ball with all the welly he could muster, Joey kicked the football against the side of the house and then raced over to try to get it on the rebound. At the last second, however, Matty Webster slid past him and sent the ball bouncing over to some of the other boys.

"You just got lucky!" Joey gasped, already hauling himself up despite some grazing on his palms.

"That's what you always say," Matty said with a grin as he too got to his feet. "Blimey, who's that?"

Turning, Joey looked toward the Red Lion. For a moment he had no idea what his friend was talking about, until he looked up at one of the upstairs windows and saw a woman staring back down at him. Something about the woman immediately struck him as being rather peculiar, although he couldn't quite put his finger on the reason why. He saw the sadness in her eyes, and he felt as if he shouldn't be the first one to look away. Instead he kept watching her, even as his friends yelled at him to get back into the game, yet the woman seemed content to merely stand and look back at him.

Finally he offered a smile. When this didn't achieve anything, he followed it up with a tentative wave.

"Look!"

Hearing Matty's excited cry, accompanied by the roar of engines, Joey turned just in time to see half a dozen planes roaring across the mid-morning sky. Something about the planes filled him with a sense of hope, and he joined the others in using a hand to shield his eyes from the sun and turning to watch as the planes shot off toward the coast.

"They'll be off to bomb the Germans," one of the other boys said excitedly. "I bet they'll bomb 'em good and blow up all their bases! Then they won't be able to come over here and invade!"

The rest of the boys let out cheers and raised their fists in defiance. Joey did the same, although after a moment he remembered the sad woman at the pub's window. He turned to look back at her, only to find that she was gone now. He waited in case she might reappear, but somehow deep down he knew that she was gone forever – and that perhaps she hadn't really been there at all, at least not for a while.

And then, looking down at the ground, he

was surprised to see that someone had left a long and slightly twisted black nail next to his left foot.

***

"Alright, let's try lifting this section," a man said, as he and several others picked their way through the rubble of St. Jude's. "We've got to start somewhere."

Over the next couple of minutes, the half dozen men took up their positions around a large section of the wall that had collapsed at some point during the fire. Each man braced himself to lift, and a few murmured instructions were passed around, before finally Burt at the far end gave the order to heave. Straining slightly, the men struggled at first before finally managing to haul the broken wall up, moving it aside to reveal the smouldering dirt beneath.

At the last second, however, one of the men let out a shocked gasp and pulled back.

"What is it?" Burt asked, scrambling across the debris to take a look. "What did you -"

In that moment he froze as he saw the horrific sight. Beneath the damaged wall, two charred human figures had been uncovered. One was Barbara – or what remained of her – while the other was a more skeletal corpse that had its hands held out, holding the sides of Barbara's head as if even in death she was still trying to scratch the flesh away. Barbara's head, meanwhile, was tilted back and her mouth was open, and her dead eyes were staring up at the grey sky as she remained locked in a dying scream.

AMY CROSS

EPILOGUE

One month later...

FOOTSTEPS ECHOED IN THE long corridor, finally reaching the doorway. As soon as Father Everett reached his desk, however, he saw the solitary figure sitting on a nearby chair.

"Can I... help you?" he said cautiously.

"I certainly hope so," Father Harry Stone said, getting to his feet. "I recognize your voice. As it happens, I believe you and I have conversed a number of times on the telephone. You used to work as a permanent secretary for the late Father Sloane and I believe that you now perform the same role for his successor Father Thompson."

"That is correct," the man said cautiously. "And you are..."

"Father Stone," Harry replied, limping forward and holding out a hand, which the man reluctantly shook. "I was down at Laidlow with Father Neville a while ago and I had cause to telephone this office on a number of occasions."

"Indeed," the man said, clearly feeling highly suspicious as he pulled his hand back. "Well, I -"

"I need to speak to Father Thompson," Harry said firmly. "I'm afraid I have been in hospital for a few weeks, but now I'm back in London and I must talk to Father Thompson immediately. I have left a number of messages for him but I haven't heard anything in return. In fact, I believe I left a message with *you* just a few days ago."

"Did you?" the man replied airily. "I really don't recall..."

"I need to talk to him about what happened at Laidlow," Harry continued. "This isn't a matter that can be forgotten or ignored or covered up. I'm quite sure that Father Sloane had some inkling of the truth. Whether or not that contributed to his demise, I'm not sure, but it is quite clear to me that the situation at St. Jude's near Laidlow was not a complete surprise to people in the hierarchy here. It wasn't an isolated incident, either. I believe others, perhaps not many but a few, have experienced something similar. I have attempted on several occasions to submit a report of my experiences there, but as far as I can tell nobody is taking any notice."

"I believe your report has been filed," the man said archly.

"Yes, that's what I'm afraid of," Harry told him. "I think it's best now if I speak to Father Thompson face-to-face. That way I can make sure that he understands the urgency of the situation."

"Father Thompson is... rather busy."

"But he is here today, is he not?"

"He is," the man continued, clearly trying to pick his words with great care, "but he remains..."

"Busy?" Harry replied, raising an eyebrow.

"Exceedingly."

"What happened at Laidlow must be confronted," Harry said firmly. "The anchoress Margaret Crake discovered something, something true, and the church can no longer pretend otherwise. If we try to ignore this situation, things will get worse. If we confront things head on, on the other hand, I firmly believe that we can overcome anything that is thrown at us. The alternative, any attempt to ignore or appease this evil, simply will not work in the long run."

"If -"

"I conducted some research during my forced rest," Harry went on. "I believe that hints of this dark new knowledge have been scattered throughout history for hundreds – if not thousands –

of years. The events at Laidlow were merely the latest in a series of occurrences over the years that hint at something much bigger." He paused for a moment as he struggled to hold back tears. "People died there," he added. "Good people. I refuse to let their deaths go in vain. The sacrifice made by Barbara Dewhurst..."

He paused again, as if on the verge of being overcome by emotion.

"These sacrifices must be honoured," he added. "I refuse to let them be forgotten."

"Father Thompson really is *very* busy," the man suggested. "Would you perhaps like to leave a message?"

"One that can be ignored again?"

The man opened his mouth to reply, but he hesitated as if he understood that this time the young Father Stone would not be so easily dismissed.

"He is busy," Harry said finally. "He has many responsibilities and I'm sure there are many people each and every day who wish to speak to him. I can very well understand that. But the thing is, when I became a priest I thought my job was to bring truth and knowledge to the world. Not to hide the truth behind a wall of comforting lies."

Stepping back, he sat down in the same chair he had been occupying for quite some time now. As he did so, he briefly winced as he put more pressure on his injured right foot.

"It's fine," he continued, looking toward the double doors that he knew Father Thompson must use whenever he finally left his office for the day. "I'll wait."

Also by Amy Cross

The Haunting of Hadlow House: The Complete Series

Beth Cooper is far from happy when her parents announce that they're moving to the countryside. Hadlow House stands just beyond the edge of a small village, and as far as Beth's concerned her life might as well be over. She has no idea, however, that this particular house is home to a number of terrifying ghosts – some of which have been around for more than three hundred years.

Back in 1689, Richard Hadlow was determined to restore his family's name, but a series of tragedies destroyed his plans. Ever since, Hadlow House has been plagued by the ghosts of the lost souls that have died within its walls. Several families have tried to call the house their home, only to fall victim to the horrors that still haunt the property. And every time disaster strikes, another ghost is created.

But why has Hadlow House seemingly been cursed for all these years? Does one ghost lurk further back in the shadows than most, orchestrating everything?

AMY CROSS

THE ANCHORESS

Also by Amy Cross

**The Horrors of Sobolton:
The Complete Series**

When he takes on a new job as sheriff of a remote town, John Tench has no idea that his life is about to be changed forever. At first Sobolton seems like a nice, quiet place – until the body of a young girl is found trapped beneath a frozen lake. Meanwhile wolves have been heard howling in the forest, but everyone knows that there are no wolves near Sobolton.

As John investigates the case, he starts to peel back more layers of this strange town. The disappearance of local veterinarian Lisa Sondnes seems to be the key to everything, yet wherever he turns John finds that the locals are closing ranks. Something dark and sinister is waiting in the forest, something that has been kept at bay for many years by an uneasy truce. Is that truce about to shatter with devastating consequences?

Covering hundreds of years of the town's history, *The Horrors of Sobolton* is an epic paranormal horror story taking in the modern world, the wild west, Vikings, ancient prophecies, warring wolves and a battle for the heart of an American town.

AMY CROSS

THE ANCHORESS

For more information, visit:

www.amycross.com

AMY CROSS

Printed in Great Britain
by Amazon